Charlotte Mary Yonge

Aunt Charlotte's stories of American history

Charlotte Mary Yonge

Aunt Charlotte's stories of American history

ISBN/EAN: 9783744749183

Printed in Europe, USA, Canada, Australia, Japan

Cover: Foto ©Andreas Hilbeck / pixelio.de

More available books at **www.hansebooks.com**

Charlotte Mary Yonge

Aunt Charlotte's stories of American history

ISBN/EAN: 9783744749183

Printed in Europe, USA, Canada, Australia, Japan

Cover: Foto ©Andreas Hilbeck / pixelio.de

More available books at **www.hansebooks.com**

SHERIDAN'S RIDE. [p. 386.

AUNT CHARLOTTE'S

STORIES OF

AMERICAN HISTORY

BY
CHARLOTTE M. YONGE
AND
H. HASTINGS WELD, D.D.

London:
MARCUS WARD & CO., LIMITED, CHANDOS STREET
AND AT BELFAST AND NEW YORK
M.DCCC.LXXXIII.

CONTENTS.

Contents.

LIST OF ILLUSTRATIONS.

STORIES OF AMERICAN HISTORY.

CHAP. I.—THE NATIVES OF AMERICA.

ALL the time that Palestine was being taught by the messengers of Heaven, that Greece was finding out all that the mind of man could accomplish, and Rome was conquering all the lands she knew of; yes, and long after the True Light had been known in Palestine, and had shone over the world, and the Roman Empire had been broken up into the kingdoms of Europe, no one in these historic nations knew anything of the lands that lay on the other side of the world.

Indeed, the world was at first thought to be a flat circle, where nothing but clouds and mist lay beyond the Atlantic Ocean, though the Greeks had some notions, taken perhaps from Phœnician sailors, that there was a great country in the far West, which they called Atlantis. The Carthaginians were also said to have found a great island which lay beyond the western seas. This island figures, in tradition, down to the time of Columbus as Antilla; and it was this that it was supposed Columbus had re-discovered. But while the use of the compass was not known, it was impossible to sail far out of sight of land; and whatever may have been learned by one generation was soon forgotten by another. Even when it came to be believed that the world was a globe, it was supposed that the Atlantic Ocean reached all round from Ireland and Spain to India, with only a few scattered islands in it; and these islands, some people said, were the tops of the mountains in the old continent of Atlantis, which had sunk beneath the sea.

Nevertheless there was not only a great continent, but it was full of inhabitants, as we know from the remains they have left. Along the banks of the river Mississippi and Ohio are curious mounds, containing rude pottery, stone arrow-heads, and tools. These must be very ancient, for the trees which stand upon the tops of the mounds are the growth of centuries. In Central America there are wonderful remains of large buildings, of which the history is not known. In the territory now called New Mexico, belonging to the United States, there are remains of walled and

AZTEC MOUNDS NEAR MARIETTA, OHIO.

fortified villages on the hills, with no gateways. The only entrance is by flights of stone steps on the outside.

There was a great empire in the south of the Northern Continent, in Mexico, the dominant tribe in which was the Aztecs ; and another of like dense population and advanced organization in Peru. But the main body of the two American continents, when first they became known to Europeans, was inhabited by large tribes of men, living a wild and roving life. They had copper-coloured skins, high cheek bones, small eyes, and straight black hair. The Northern Continent had two leading tribes—the Iroquois, or Six Nations, and the Algonquins. There were, besides, an immense number of smaller families or tribes, who spoke languages that were constantly becoming more different from each other, as they dropped old words and formed new, and generally very long ones.

Mostly they lived by hunting. The men, as " braves," thought nothing manly but war and the chase. They would show great patience in bearing pain without a murmur. Their great glory was to bring home the scalps of their enemies. If they made a prisoner, they put him to the worst tortures they could devise ; and he would think his honour saved if he could bear all, even to death, without a sigh or a groan. The wives, or "squaws," had to do all the work—digging the ground to grow maize, beans, pumpkins, tobacco, and sunflowers for the sake of the oil. To the squaws fell the preparing of the skins, of which garments were made; carrying burdens, and setting up the houses whenever the tribe moved; removal taking place whenever game became scarce, or the resources of a region were exhausted. Their houses, called "wigwams" (an English adaptation of two or three similar Indian words), consisted, in many tribes, of large sheets of bark fastened upon stakes. Indeed, birch bark was one of their most valuable materials. Of it they made canoes, snow-shoes, and baskets, and also cases in which their infants were packed up, and suspended, either from the mother's back or from the branch of a tree.

The tribes had chiefs, and matters of peace or war were conducted by councils with great ceremony and deliberation. Some tribes were much more warlike than others; some lived entirely by hunting, some cultivated the ground more than others, some fished; but, in general character and appearance, they were all much alike. They had very little religion, but there was a common belief in a Great Spirit; and in every tribe there was at least one Medicine Man, who dressed himself up strangely, and used wonderful incantations to discover what was to be done at any difficult moment. Some of the South American natives lived in strange abodes, raised on stages high among the branches of the mangrove trees that fringe the coast. These were a very gentle and amiable people, with much less endurance and activity than their northern brethren. In a region where fruits are so abundant by Nature, they made no attempt at cultivating the soil.

In the far South were the Patagonians, a rougher and a duller race, men of very large stature, and very wild and savage in their ways. Whence these races came, and how they settled in the great Western Continent, no one knows. Some may have come by the North, where the Eastern and Western Continents nearly meet. Others may have made their way by the chain of Islands in the Pacific. Or there may be some truth in the story of the lost continent of Atlantis; and there may have been traffic with Europe before the date of history. At any rate, many of these people, in especial the Aztecs, had a tradition that teachers and conquerors should come from the East.

CHAP. II.—THE BEGINNING OF DISCOVERY.

968—1430.

ALL who have read the history of England remember how the Northmen and Danes used to trouble our coasts. These people were great sailors. They settled in Iceland, and, going on farther to the West, they came, somewhere before the year 900, to a country which they first saw in the summer, when there was plenty of grass. It was named Greenland by one Eric the Red, who hoped to persuade people to follow him thither when he settled there. They set up their homes, in spite of the cold and fogs, to which they were well used in Iceland and Norway. In the year 986, a young man named Biorn, whose father had settled in Greenland, sailed to follow him, but lost his way, and found himself on the coast of a country of small hills, covered with wood. He knew that Greenland was mountainous, and had no wood at all;

so he did not stay there, but in about a week's time set sail for his father's settlement in Greenland. Some time later, about the year 1000, the son of Eric the Red, Lief the Lucky, set out from Greenland, with thirty-five men, among whom was a German, to find the country that Biorn had described. Going to the south-west, they saw first some great icy mountains, with a plain covered with flat slaty stones, between the mountains and the sea. Not liking this, they coasted along till they saw a level and wooded country ; and still further on, after two days, they found a place where a river, which came through a lake, fell into the sea. They determined to winter there, cut down trees, and build themselves log huts. One day the German was lost. They went out to look for him, and met him, rolling his eyes, and talking to himself in his own language, which they could not understand. At last, however, he came to himself, and they found he was almost wild with joy, having been reminded of his own land by coming upon a spot full of vines bearing clusters of grapes. They called the place Vineland, or Vinland, and loaded their ships with the timber, so scarce in Iceland and Greenland, where no trees grew.

Two years later, Lief's brother, Thorwald, came in search of more wood, and the place pleased him so

well he said he should like to stay there.   He returned
the next year ; but this time the party saw three
mounds on the beach, and, going up to them, found
that what had been taken for mounds were three
canoes, with three natives hidden under each.   Like
fierce Northmen, as they were, they killed eight of
them.   One escaped in his canoe, and brought, on a
night soon after, the whole tribe against the Northmen.
A fleet of the savages attacked the ship on which the
Northmen were, and poured upon them a shower of
arrows.   The natives were repulsed, but Thorwald
was mortally wounded.   At his dying request, he was
buried on the spot he had liked so well, and the next
year the party returned to Greenland.   Thorstein, his
brother, sailed from Greenland, with his wife Gudrida,
and his whole family, with the intention of bringing
home the body of Thorwald.   But Thorstein did not
even reach Vineland.   Driven by a storm upon an
uninhabited shore of Greenland, he was compelled to
winter there.   Want and fatigue proved fatal to him,
and to several of his crew.   In the spring, Gudrida
returned home with the dead body of her husband.

However, the accounts of Vineland induced a large
party of Icelanders to try to make a home there.
Thorfinn Karlsefne, a wealthy Icelander, married
Gudrida, and set sail with her for Vineland.   The

expedition was embarked in three ships, carrying one hundred and sixty men (some with wives), and was furnished with tools, furniture, and cattle. They settled at a place which they called Hop. Vineland is considered by antiquaries to have been in or near the limits of the present State of Rhode Island ; and the Hop of Thorfinn is claimed to be the present Mount Hope. The Indian name of the eminence was Montaup, and it can only be connected with the Hop of Thorfinn by supposing that both Northmen and the later English settlers, with an interval of centuries between them, adapted the native name. The spot was fruitful in native products, and answered generously to cultivation. Here the Northmen built log houses, and let their cattle feed upon the grass. The natives came about them, and brought grey furs to exchange for cloth and milk-soup. But they were dreadfully frightened at the first hearing of the lowing of the cattle, and all ran off. After a while they took courage, and ventured upon another attack, such as they had made upon Thorwald. They were beaten off, chiefly by the courage and readiness of Gudrida. The Northmen remained two years at Hop. Gudrida had there a son born—the first white child born in the Western Hemisphere—whom she named Snorro. The repeated attacks of the natives tired the Northmen out, and they returned home, enriched with the valuable furs and woods which they had obtained. Though the precise point where Thorfinn landed cannot be positively determined, there can be no doubt of the general truth of the story. Snorro, born in Vineland, became the head of an illustrious race of Icelandic chiefs, and to his grandson, Bishop Thorlak Runolfson, we are probably indebted for the preservation of what we know about these early voyages. Gudrida, after her return from Vineland, lived with Thorfinn in princely state. After her husband's death, she made a pilgrimage to Rome, and returned to pass the evening of her eventful life in a religious retreat which her western-born son, Snorro, had founded.

In the year 1167, when Owen Gwynned, King of North Wales, died, there was a dispute among his children who was to succeed him. One of his sons, named Madoc, sailed away to the West with his followers, and after some years came back, declaring that he had found a beautiful mountainous country across the sea. Inviting men to follow him, he embarked with a large party. No more was heard of him. Indeed, after the North-men gave up their long voyages, no one knew or cared much about the Atlantic, or what might be beyond it. In the time of that awful sickness, the Black Death, all the Danish seamen died who knew how to reach the coast of West Greenland. The settlement there, said to have been large enough for a bishop and several churches, was thought to have perished. But recent discoverers think that the West of Greenland never was settled.

The romance of adventure places Robert Macham, an Englishman who lived in the time of Edward III., among the first of what may be called modern discoverers, though his claim rests upon accident, not intention. He ran away with a young lady of noble birth, named Anne Dorset. They sailed from Bristol, meaning to go to France; but a great storm arose, and their vessel was driven before it—Anne in utter dismay at the punishment that had followed her sin. At last they came to a lovely island, full of fine trees and beautiful scenery. They landed, to refresh themselves; and, another storm coming on, the ship broke from her moorings, and was driven out to sea again. The poor lady, in horror and grief, died three days later, and Macham five days after, broken-hearted. The crew buried them under a great cross, with an inscription, begging any good Christian who should find the spot to build a church over their remains.

The crew left the island in the ship's boat, were cast upon the coast of Africa, and were made galley slaves in Morocco. There they met with Juan de Morales,

a Spanish pilot, to whom they told their sad story.
Whether they were ever released from slavery does
not appear, but Morales was. When quite an old
man, he entered the service of Don Enrique, known
in history as Henry the Navigator. Don Enrique
was the son of João I., King of Portugal, and Philippa,
daughter of John of Gaunt. He was the first man of
modern times who had a real thirst for discovery, and
he listened eagerly to Morales. Enrique is said to
have been the first to apply the compass to the purposes of navigation. He sent out vessels on voyages
of discovery from time to time, and on one of these
voyages, in 1419, Madeira was discovered, and Porto
Santo, an island near Madeira. The tradition is that
the bay where the lovers died was called Macho, after
Macham. The isle was named Madeira, from the
Portuguese name for wood. The Canary and Azore
Isles were found about the year 1450, and all were
held by the King of Portugal. But what Enrique
cared for most was to trace round the coast of Africa,
an undertaking accomplished afterward by his countrymen. So no more discoveries to the westward were
at that time made.

CHAP. III.—COLUMBUS.

1492—1506.

AMONG the brave mariners of the Italian city of Genoa was a family named Colombo. Several of them became famous captains, and fought against the pirates in the Mediterranean. One of the family, named Domenico, though himself a woolcomber, had three sons, whose names are connected with one of the most important events in the history of the world. Cristofero, the eldest, took early to the sea. Bartolomeo became so able a mathematician, that he was appointed a map-maker at the Court of Portugal, which was under the influence of Don Enrique (Henry the Navigator), the great centre of maritime enterprise. Diego, as well as Bartolomeo, shared in afterlife in the honours and toils of their brother, whose Latinised name is Christopher Columbus. Christopher soon reached the command of a vessel in a squadron fitted out by the Colombo family. In a naval engagement his vessel took fire, and he saved his life by jumping overboard, and, with the aid of a plank, swimming ashore.   After this escape, Columbus repaired to Lisbon, where he joined his brother Bartolomeo (Bartholomew) in his work as a map-maker.   By-and-by he married Felipa, the only daughter of a navigator who had shared, in the service of Don Enrique, in the discovery of Porto Santo and Madeira.   His bride's father had left what proved to Columbus a rich inheritance in nautical instruments, besides a grant of Porto Santo, conferred by Don Enrique.   The bridegroom and bride sailed to take possession of their islet, hoping to do great things with it ; but behold, they found it altogether overrun with rabbits, which ate up all that they planted, and were so numerous that it proved of no use to try to kill them down.   So after about a year, during which a son, named after his uncle, Diego, was born, they left Porto Santo to the rabbits, and came back to Lisbon, where the young wife soon after died.

That disappointment about his island was the beginning of greater things.   Columbus had seen branches of trees cast up by the sea, carved bits of wood, and bodies of birds, all plainly coming from the West.   He thought that they must be from India.   As the Portuguese were striving to make their way round the coast

COLUMBUS BEFORE THE COUNCIL AT SALAMANCA.

of Africa, and get to India by the East, he believed
that he could find a much shorter way by the West,
if only he had ships and men. It was the hope of his
heart to use the wealth of India to attack the
Mahometan power, make a new crusade, and deliver
the Holy Land. He carried his plans first to the
chiefs of his native city, Genoa; but they thought him
only a dreamer. Then he went to Portugal, but the
King, to whom he gave a detail of his plans, secretly
sent an expedition, which returned to report them as
vain fancies. He next tried Spain, but a great war
was going on, and no one was inclined to listen to
him. Travelling on foot with his son Diego, to seek
his brother-in-law, who resided at a small town in
Andalusia, Columbus stopped at the gate of a Franciscan monastery to ask food and drink for his son.
Fray Juan Perez, the Prior of the monastery, was
attracted by the appearance of the stranger. When
the heart is full the speech is ready, and Columbus
poured his story into the ears of one who could
appreciate his pious hopes. Fray Perez detained the
wayfarer as his guest. He procured interviews for
him with the navigators of the neighbouring port of
Palos. And better than all, Fray Perez brought
influences to bear which, after seventeen years of
waiting, secured to Columbus a friend in the great and

good Isabella, Queen of Castile in her own right, and wife of Fernando, King of Arragon. She aided him with means, and commissioned him to fit out three vessels for the voyage of western discovery. With these, on the 3rd of August, 1492, Christopher Columbus set sail from the port of Palos, and the Franciscan brothers could witness, and speed with their prayers, the wayfarer whom they had entertained, now sailing forth as High Admiral and Viceroy of all the lands he might discover. Columbus had sent his brother Bartholomew to England; and King Henry invited Columbus thither. But Bartholomew was detained by pirates, and meanwhile Queen Isabella gave the aid required.

It would require too long to tell of all the troubles of Columbus with his crews, who were full of fright at the strange currents they met, and, when they came to the many acres of floating sea-weed brought by the Gulf Stream, thought they were come to the verge of the world, and would perish there. If Columbus had not been one of the most patient as well as the most daring men in the world, he would have turned back long before. On the night of the 10th of October, a light was seen; and in the morning a lovely island appeared, with a white beach, luxuriant palm trees, green sward, and a lake glittering in their midst. Columbus, full of thanksgiving, landed, and dedicated it to the Christian faith, by planting a great cross, and naming it San Salvador. It was one of the Bahama Isles, the northern ones that close in the Gulf of Mexico. The natives came down to see the strange people, who they thought had come from Heaven in their white-winged ships. They were gentle, brown-skinned people, and Columbus was much drawn to them, and hoped to make them Christians. But his crew—rough, greedy sailors, whom he picked up as he could—only thought of the bits of gold they wore, and asked, by signs, where they came from. They were understood to answer that there was a great chief in Cubanacan, who was served in cups and plates of gold. They meant the interior of the great island of Cuba, but the sound of the word made the discoverers think they intended the Khan of Tartary, of whom all Europe had heard, through the Venetians. So, making sure that this place was a little isle to the extreme East of India, where East had become West, the Spaniards called these islands the West Indies, a name they have ever since kept. The term Indian has been applied to all the natives of the whole hemisphere, except those of the extreme South.

Columbus sailed from one lovely island to another, and making the discovery of the island of Cuba, coasted along its shores. Sailing from Cuba, he found the island of Haiti, which he called Hispaniola, or little Spain, where he made great friends with a good and gentle chief, a cacique named Guacanagari. It was impossible, however, to keep the Spanish sailors in order. They cared only for greed and pleasure, and, the moment his eye was off, disobeyed the Italian stranger. The fleetest of his ships was commanded by Martin Pinzon, and was sailing a few miles in advance of Columbus, when, having determined to change his course, he signalled to Pinzon to follow. Pinzon paid no heed. Night came on, and in the morning Pinzon was no more to be seen. This was on the 19th of December, 1492. On the morning of the 25th, Columbus having charged the officers and pilot of his vessel to keep strict watch, retired to take rest, and was awakened by the striking of his vessel on a shoal. The wreck, which was on the coast of Hispaniola, was complete, and Columbus had only one of his three vessels left, and that the smallest. With the assistance of Guacanagari, Columbus built a fort of material saved from the timbers of the wreck, and called it La Navidad (the Nativity), in honour of the day of his escape ; and he determined to return to Spain, and defeat the treachery of which he suspected Pinzon. The design of the runaway, Columbus thought, was to reach Spain before his commander, and defraud him of his honours and rewards. He left thirty-four men in the fort, with such munitions as could be spared, charging them so to live, till his return, that the natives might still think they had come from Heaven. Alas! so far were the garrison from heeding him, that all except their captain so misused the natives that they rose on them, and killed them every man. Meantime, Columbus, and his runaway Pinzon, both sailed into Palos on the same day, the 15th of March, 1493. Columbus had found Pinzon just after leaving Navidad. They had stormy passages, sometimes in company, and sometimes separated; and Columbus never quite overcame his distrust, while Pinzon feared arrest for disobedience. At the very last they were separated by a storm. Columbus entered Palos at noon. Pinzon, unaware of his arrival, came in at evening. All Spain welcomed Columbus. When he came to the court, the King and Queen rose to receive him, and honours of all kinds were heaped upon him. A coat of arms was assigned him, to which was annexed the motto: "To Castile and Leon, Columbus gave a new world."

A new expedition was fitted out, with clergy, to convert the natives, and preparations to build a city and found an empire in the New World. Unfortunately, few good or honourable men joined in these schemes.

Even the head of the mission priests, Bernalo Boyle, or Boli, was a hard-hearted and greedy man, who had none of the zeal of Columbus to win souls for the Church and deliver the Holy Land. The second expedition set sail from Cadiz, on the 25th of September, 1493, with seventeen vessels, three large ships, and fourteen of lesser tonnage. Touching at the Canaries, they proceeded West, till on Sunday, the 2nd of November, they discovered the central island of the group known as the Caribees. It was called by Columbus, Dominica. Several other islands in the group were visited, and suspicious signs were found that the natives were man-eaters. The word cannibal is supposed to be a corruption of Caribee, or Caribal. The natives of the Caribee group were found to be far fiercer than those of San Salvador and Hispaniola. From the Caribee islands the fleet sailed to the bay of Navidad, Hispaniola, trusting to be welcomed by their friends in the garrison, but finding only the ruins and ashes of the dismantled fort. Not a man was left to give the Spanish version of the disaster.

A city was founded in Hispaniola, named Isabella, after the Queen. Explorations by land and sea were made, in one of which the island of Jamaica was discovered. Mines were opened ; but with the development of enterprise came also the growth of

RECEPTION OF COLUMBUS BY FERDINAND AND ISABELLA.

faction and enmity toward Columbus. There was a disposition among the Spaniards to treat the Genoese as a foreigner. Evil reports against him were sent to Spain, and among the authors of these was Father Boli. Columbus remained, as long and as far as he could, the protector of the Indians. He strove to think charitably of Guacanagari, who claimed, and with good show of evidence, that the destruction of Navidad was the work of another tribe. The preponderance of testimony seems to be in his favour, as he died in poverty, and in the contempt of his own people. The more Columbus tried to protect the Indians, the more the Spaniards hated him. The result of their representations was that Don Juan Aguado was sent from Spain, as commissioner, to examine and report upon the condition of things. Aguado was selected as a friend of Columbus ; but proceeded in a spirit so arrogant and unfriendly, that Columbus decided to return with him, and defend himself. This he did, leaving his brother Bartholomew in command of Hispaniola, with his other brother, Diego, to succeed him in case of his death. On the 11th of June, 1496, Columbus landed, with Aguado, at Cadiz. His reception by Ferdinand and Isabella was, contrary to his fears, highly favourable. He was loaded with honours, and his heirs were entitled to bear his coat of arms, with its honourable motto. For all this, so persistent were his enemies, that it was not till May, 1498, that he sailed from Spain on his third voyage of discovery.

On this third voyage Columbus discovered the large island near the mouth of the Orinoco, which still retains the name which he gave it, Trinidad. It was the first time the continent was reached ; but though Columbus saw the mainland in the distance, he fancied it to be an island. He inferred, rather than knew, the existence of the great river Orinoco, and followed the coast of Trinidad through the fearful straits, to which he gave the names of the Dragon's Mouth and the Serpent's Mouth. The great difficulty in passing them was caused by strong currents. From the freshness of the water, which poured from the mouths of the Orinoco, Columbus judged that only a continent could supply such streams. Columbus was disposed to think that he was near the object of his search, the Indies, and that he should reach that country if he went along the coast, to the north-west. Indeed, he persuaded himself that this was the Indian Ophir, from which Solomon obtained the gold of the Temple. But the great Admiral was growing old, and was ill with the gout, and he was forced to make for the settlement in Hispaniola. He

found Hispaniola in a sad state. The Spaniards had
provoked wars with the natives, and were at discord
among themselves. The ground was untilled, and the
whites found it impossible to work in the tropical
climate. Columbus then decided that the Indian
prisoners had better be put in charge of the Spanish
settlers, to do their work, and learn Christianity
and civilized ways. This was so reported to Queen
Isabella, that she thought he was making slaves of
her subjects the natives. A commissioner, Francisco
de Bobadilla, was sent from Spain, who exceeded
his authority, and at the instance of the enemies of
Columbus, sent him and his brothers, Bartholomew
and Diego, home in chains. No sooner, however, was
he able to explain matters to the Queen, than she
understood how cruelly he had been wronged, burst
into tears, and besought his pardon. It was at the
end of the year 1500 that Columbus returned to
Spain. Old as he was, he longed to pursue the track
he thought he had found. After over a year's delay,
he prevailed to be sent out a fourth time, though the
King forbade him to set foot on Hispaniola. In this
last voyage, Columbus sailed along the coast of
Veragua, vainly seeking the outlet to India, which he
had expected to find. The glimpses of the continent
which he had seen were supposed to indicate islands.

At length, after a storm of eighty-eight days, with his
vessels shattered, and disease and discontent among
his crews, he was forced to change his course and
return.   He reached Jamaica, upon the shore of which
island he stranded his unseaworthy vessels, and, with
his crews, lived on the wrecks.   In two canoes, bought
of the Indians, and strengthened, the perilous voyage
was made to Hispaniola by messengers begging for
relief.   For seven months Columbus did not know
whether his messengers had reached Hispaniola.   It
was a year before the vessels arrived to his relief,
in which he sailed to Hispaniola.   Thence, after a
month's stay, he sailed for Spain, reaching Seville,
after a tempestuous passage, in November, 1504.   Ill
and worn out, the first tidings that met him were that
the good Queen Isabella was dying.   All his hope was
over now.   He knew he should never lead his Indian
crusade to free the Holy Sepulchre, and that his plans
of making Christian men of the Indians had brought
misery and slavery on them.   A few more months
passed of weary striving for his rights.   His health
entirely broke, and he died at Valladolid, on the 20th
of May, Ascension Day, 1506, being about seventy
years of age.   His two sons kept the motto and coat
of arms which had been assigned to him.

CHAP. IV.—THE ADVENTURES OF ALONZO DE OJEDA.

1499.

IT was an Italian who found the great Western Continent, and it was another Italian whose name it bears. In 1499, a Florentine merchant, named Amerigo Vespucci, set forth on an expedition, commanded by a brave and daring Spanish gentleman, Alonzo de Ojeda, who had been with Columbus on his second voyage. Hearing of the great Admiral's third voyage along the Gulf of Paria, Ojeda persuaded the rich merchants of Seville to fit out four ships, with which he hoped to bring them home more gold than the islands had yet produced. Ojeda was a very small man, but wonderfully brave, daring, and spirited. He was withal very devout, and carried about with him a little picture of the Blessed Virgin, which he thought shielded him from all hurt. Amerigo Vespucci wrote an account of this expedition, and therefore it was that

his name came to be given to the lands he beheld.
After passing the Isle of Trinidad and the Dragon's
Mouth, the ships came to a bay filled with tranquil
water.   In this bay were bell-shaped houses, built
upon piles driven into the sand, communicating with
the shore by drawbridges, and by canoes, which were
drawn up around the houses.   This place, the Indian
name of which was Coquibacoa, the discoverers called
Venezuela, or little Venice.   The Indians were very
fine, handsome people, armed with bows and arrows.
They fought with the strangers, but were worsted.
Ojeda did not gain much by his voyage.   He returned
to Spain, and, through his personal friends, obtained
the appointment of Governor of Coquibacoa.   His
second voyage ended in his arrest by his partners, and
a lawsuit, by which, though successful, he was left
penniless.   It had now, despite the misfortunes of
discoverers, become the fashion for every one who was
adventurous to set out on a westward voyage to seek
the land of gold.   El Dorado, the place of gold, was
thought to be somewhere in the West.   Ship after
ship was fitted out in quest of it, and each surveyed a
bit more of the coast of South America, and generally
taught the Indians more and more hatred of the white
man.   Of a third voyage which Ojeda is said to have
made there are no records.   For several years he

remained in obscurity. But, in 1509, King Ferdinand of Spain was induced to send out four ships, with three hundred men, to found a settlement in the place where Columbus thought he had discovered the gold of Ophir. The settlement was to be called Carthagena, or New Carthage. Ojeda joined the expedition at Hispaniola, commissioned as governor of a province to be called New Andalusia. Among the men engaged in this expedition were two of whom we shall hear much later — Fernando Cortes and Francisco Pizarro. The former, however, had to be left at Hispaniola, because of an inflammation in his knee. Juan de la Cosa, a most accomplished pilot, familiar with the coasts and seas to be explored, and who had visited Spain to forward the enterprise, came out with the ships to join in the voyage. Under the guidance of the veteran pilot, the ships anchored, in the autumn of 1509, in the bay of Carthagena. Cosa, who had touched at the place on a former voyage, warned Ojeda that the natives were Caribs, and very fierce, using great palm-wood swords, osier shields, and poisoned arrows, and the women fighting as well as the men. He advised going on to the Gulf of Uraba, where, he thought, the natives were less ferocious, and did not poison their weapons; but Ojeda would not heed advice, and advanced into the country. A body

of Indians met him, whereupon he charged a priest to
read a paper taking possession of the country, and
then held up presents, and tried to make friends. The
Indians would not listen, blew war notes on their
conch-shells, and drew their bows. After a sharp
fight, the Spaniards gained the victory; but, against
old Cosa's advice, pursued the flying enemy too far
inland. Other Indians joined the foe in great numbers. Ojeda was cut off, and, with a few men, obliged
to defend himself in a hut, where he would have been
overpowered, if faithful Cosa had not come to the
rescue. Cosa defended the door, while Ojeda sprang
forth on the enemy, cut his way through them, and
dashed out of sight. Then Cosa and one other man
attempted to regain the ships, but Cosa, who had been
pierced by several poisoned arrows, sank down on the
way, and died. His companion was the only man, of
seventy, who reached the ships. There the crews
waited, watched and searched the shores for the
others, till, after many days, they came to a great
wood of mangroves, curious trees which grow in the
water, but with roots rising far above the surface,
before the trunk begins, so that there is a great matted
thicket half under the sea. There they thought they
saw a man in Spanish clothing, and found Ojeda,
lying speechless with hunger and fatigue on the matted

roots; his sword in his hand, and his shield on his
arm, without a wound, though there were the marks
of three hundred arrows on his shield. On his recovery, he followed the advice which Cosa had given,
sailed to the bay of Uraba, and founded there a city,
which he named St. Sebastian, but he did not find the
country much more favourable. The vegetation was
beautiful, but the forests were full of wild beasts and
venomous serpents, and the rivers were full of alli-
gators, so large that they could kill a horse. Ojeda
built here a fortress, and surrounded his settlement with
a stockade. The Indians swarmed around it, and shot
down the Spaniards who came out in search of food,
and the poisoned arrows caused death in terrible
agony. Ojeda had never yet been struck. He
thought himself under the special care of the Blessed
Virgin, and the Indians thought he was protected by
some spell. They told off their four best archers to
watch and hit him. Three of their arrows glanced
from his shield, but the fourth arrow pierced his thigh.
Even then, his dauntless spirit was not broken. He
caused two plates of iron to be heated red-hot, and
placed on each side of the wound, and endured the
horrible agony without a groan, and without being
held. Afterward he lay in sheets steeped in vinegar,
to allay the heat that raged through his whole body;

and this strange treatment cured him. While he was
disabled, a runaway party arrived from Hispaniola,
fancying he was getting rich. But when they saw
the misery of the colonists, they had no wish to stay
there, and Ojeda resolved to go back in their ship, and
obtain the supplies so much needed at St. Sebastian.
The crew were a set of wretches who put him in irons.
As soon as a storm rose, they were forced to let him
loose again, as he was the only man on board who
could manage a ship in danger. All that even he
could do was to run the shattered wreck aground on
the island of Cuba. Here was no Spanish settlement,
but the natives had heard enough of the white men to
hate them, and drive them away. They had to toil
through swamps, which were frightfully deep ; the
route furnished nothing to eat or to drink, for these
marshes were salt. All day long they struggled
through water up to their waists, and at night climbed
into mangrove trees to sleep. Every day some were
drowned or smothered in the mud, and the food
brought from the ship was scarcely eatable. Still at
each pause Ojeda knelt and prayed, and he made a
vow that, if he were saved this time, he would build
a chapel, and set up his picture of Our Lady among
the heathen. After thirty days of misery in the
swamps, Ojeda, with a very few, survived, and found

a path which led them to a village of friendly natives, who sheltered and nursed them, nay, treated them like angels. And here Ojeda raised a little hut, where he hung his picture, and bade the Indians take care of it, till he should come back to found a church. Then he and the others made their way to Jamaica in canoes. Thence he returned to Hispaniola, but he never could obtain means of going back to St. Sebastian, or of building his church. He was a ruined man ; and it is said that he ended by taking the vows of the Brothers of St. Francis, and died as one of that order. Though proud and passionate, he was one of the best of the Spanish adventurers.

CHAP. V.—PRINCESS ANACAONA.

THE mountains of Cibao, in the midst of the island of Hispaniola, and the rivers flowing from them, were found to contain gold. Columbus explored this region in 1494. A settlement was formed by him for working the mines, and a fort, called San Thomas, built for the protection of the miners. The city and bishopric of San Domingo were founded four years later, and the name has spread to the whole island.

The difficulties of government were great. Crowds of needy Spaniards came out, wanting gold first and land next, and when they had land they wanted people to till it. At home Queen Isabella had been most anxious for the good of the poor Indians. So was the council who governed Castile, after the death of Isabella, in behalf of poor mad Juana, daughter of Ferdinand and Isabella. Bishops, priests, and brethren of the preaching orders of St. Francis and St. Dominic were sent out to convert the natives. But nothing good could be done in the presence of the Spanish settlers. They would attack and offend the Indians by their pride and greed of gold, which, indeed, some of the natives thought was the white man's god. Then the Indians were stirred up, and even in the time of Columbus it was necessary to take the field against them, as they were reported to be forming a league against the Spaniards. There were murders and fightings, and when the white men gained the advantage, as with their fire-arms and horses they were sure to do, they took many prisoners, and received the submission of tribes. Then, considering the great need of workmen, Columbus had thought it fair to make these captives work; portioning off a chief and his family on what was called a *repartimiento* to a Spanish settler. The settler was, in return for their labour, to teach them the Christian faith and habits. But this arrangement generally ended in the Spaniards teaching them nothing but hard work in the mines, of which they died.

In Spain orders and orders were given for the protection of the poor Indians ; and governors were chosen in the hope that they would restrain the greedy settlers. But these governors no sooner touched the western soil than they seemed to catch the same infection of cruelty. Nicolas de Ovando, who came out as governor of Hispaniola in 1502, was one of the worst and most cruel of these men. The first news that met Ovando on landing was that an enormous nugget of gold, worth £416, had been raked out by accident, at the mines, by an Indian woman ; and that there was a rising of the Indians, so that there would be plenty of slaves. Almost every one who had come out with Ovando rushed off to the mines. There they could get no wholesome food, fell sick, and died in large numbers. Sensible people soon perceived that the men who sought for gold were only wretched and miserable, while those who cultivated the ground soon grew rich on that very gold. But farmers and gold-diggers were equally savage to the poor Indians ; and when the beaten, over-worked wretches ran away, they were hunted down with great Spanish bloodhounds, which often tore them to pieces in a most horrible way. Of all the piteous stories of savage things done in that island of Hispaniola, perhaps the most grievous is that of the Princess Anacaona.

It will be remembered that the friendly cacique, Guacanagari, represented to Columbus that the destruction of the fortress Navidad was the work of another but unfriendly cacique. The name of this cacique was Caonabo. He remained to the last the foe of the Spaniards, fomenting plots and instigating

wars against them. He is said to have been of Carib
birth, a race more fierce and warlike than the Indians
of Hispaniola, over whom he appears to have exerted
great influence. He was deceived, made captive by a
stratagem, and placed on board a vessel to be sent to
Spain, but died on the passage. The wife of Caonabo
was Anacaona, a princess celebrated for beauty and
accomplishments. Her brother, Behechio, was cacique
of Xaragua, a large district at the western extremity of
the island, and with him Anacaona retired after the
defeat of Caonabo and his confederate caciques.

Anacaona is said to have been sensible that her husband had provoked the enmity of the Spaniards, and
to have retained the admiration for them with which
the Indians first saw them. She was, moreover, wise
enough to perceive that resistance against them was
hopeless. She had great influence over her brother,
was beloved by his subjects, and when Behechio died,
succeeded him in the government ; always restraining
her people from intercourse with the Spaniards. It
was believed or pretended that she was planning a
revolt. Thereupon Ovando set out for Xaragua with
three hundred foot-soldiers and seventy horsemen fully
armed, under the pretext that he was coming to make
a friendly visit. Anacaona received him after the hos-
pitable custom of her tribe ; coming out to meet him

at the head of all her chief kindred, the maidens dan-
cing and waving palms before him, and greeting him
with songs.   Perhaps these songs of welcome were of
her own composing ; for it is said of her that she was,
in her native fashion, a poet.   She lodged him in the
largest house in her beautiful village, among the
palms and bananas, and entertained him day after day
with feasts, songs, and dances, as she had always treated
her white visitors.

It is to be hoped that it was really true that Ovando
fancied she meant to betray him.   But even if that
were true, he acted with frightful cruelty and treachery ;
for she had not done a single unfriendly act when he
arranged his plot.   He offered to show off the Spanish
sports ; and on Sunday, after dinner, in the central
place in the village, his horsemen tilted against each
other with long reeds, in the Moorish fashion, and one
of them made his horse curvet and dance to the music
of a viol.   Suddenly, while all the Indians were gazing
at the sight, Ovando gave the signal, by touching a
gold medal which hung around his neck.   His soldiers
sprang upon the defenceless people, bound the caciques
to the posts of the house, and put them to horrible
tortures to force them to confess their queen's alleged
plot.   The poor caciques said whatever the Spaniards
wished to free themselves from the pain ; but it served

them little, for they were all, eighty-four in number, burned or hung. Queen Anacaono herself was taken in chains to San Domingo. There she had the form of a trial, and was condemned and executed on the forced confessions of her tortured subjects. All her people were massacred or made prisoners to work in cruel slavery, except a few who escaped in their canoes. For months the district of Xaragua was ravaged by the Spaniards ; and the region which had lately been a perfect paradise of beauty and delight was made a place of slaughter and a wilderness. Ovando founded a city in Xaragua, which he called "St. Mary of True Peace." These horrible deeds, crowned by sacrilege, were done in 1503.

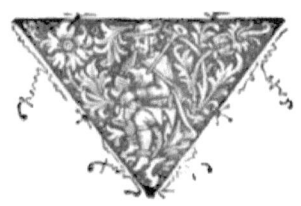

CHAP. VI.—THE CURSE OF AMERICA.

1510.

WHEREVER the Christian religion is taught, there is sure to be a witness against wickedness, even if it is not attended to. The Dominican Friars looked on with horror at the treatment of the Indians, and one of them, Father Antonio Montesino, preached two sermons, setting before the Spaniards the exceeding wickedness of their behaviour in the sight of God. The hearers came to the monastery in a great rage, but they got little comfort there; for these good friars told them that they would give the Sacraments to no man who went out hunting and making slaves of the Indians.

The settlers minded this the less, because the brethren of the order of St. Francis always took the contrary side from those of St. Dominic. The Franciscans said that the heathen men had no right to be free; and that enslaving them was the best

chance of making them Christians.   At last, Brother
Antonio went to Spain, and told the King, to his
face, horrible stories which his governors had kept
from him ; how thirteen Indians had been hung in a
row, how many were hunted and torn by dogs,- how
they were worked to death under the lash in the
mines ; and how, when there were too few left to
work in the gold diggings in Hispaniola, ships were
sent to the Lucayan Islands to persuade the poor
natives to come to the Isles of the Blest, where the
spirits of their ancestors lived !   He told how, purely
in sport, a Spaniard had picked up a little Indian
child, and thrown it over the heads of the by-
standers into the sea, laughing and joking as it came
two or three times to the surface.

   The King's anger was hot when he heard these
things of the people whom his good Queen had loved
and hoped to win for Christ.   A council was held at
Burgos, and laws were made, not taking away the
custom of making the Indians work, but trying to
hinder all the horrid injustice and cruelty.   At the
same time negroes began to be brought to the islands.
Ever since the time when the Portuguese began
sailing to the African coast, they had made their chief
profit from the sale of negroes, whom they had taken,
as the Spaniards did the Indians, under the pretence

of teaching them to be Christians. In 1510, the Genoese merchants brought the first negroes to Hispaniola, and they were soon found to bear work in that climate much better than the Indians; and did not run away, because, poor things, they had nowhere to run to. They were much more tame and less dangerous than the Caribs, and thus the Spaniards preferred them; and the great sin and curse of America was begun, by the constant habit of obtaining blacks from the coasts of Guinea by stealing, or, more often, by buying them from hostile tribes, and carrying them over to work in the West Indies.

The settlements there had begun to spread into the great Island of Cuba. Two friends, a gentleman named Pedro de Rentezia, and a young priest, Bartolome de las Casas, had a grant in Cuba, and a *repartimiento* of Indians. They were good and kindly men, but had not thought of trying to convert their Indians, or troubled themselves about the crime of making them slaves. There was only one other priest in the island, and Las Casas, though he had hitherto been more of a farmer than a clergyman, was sometimes obliged to preach. As he was preparing a Sermon, he came upon the Thirty-fourth Chapter of Ecclesiasticus, and there read: " He that sacrificeth of a thing unlawfully gotten, his offering is ridiculous, and the gifts of unjust men are not accepted. The Most High is not pleased with the offerings of the wicked, neither is He pacified for sin by the multitude of sacrifices. Whoso bringeth an offering of the goods of the poor, doeth as one that killeth the son before the father's eyes." What, then, thought Las Casas, must God think of the treatment of the Indians? He remembered how one of the good friars in Hispaniola had refused to give him absolution while he kept Indians in servitude. He had then been angry, and thought it absurd; but now the good seed had borne fruit, and he resolved, in the first place, to give up all his own Indians. He had, however, to wait till his mate, Rentezia, should return from Jamaica, where he had gone to another Spanish colony on business, and he was very anxious to know whether his friend would consent. Rentezia had been spending Lent there and had gone into retreat in a convent. During this quiet time, it had likewise been borne in on him how great was their sin toward the poor natives. He had come to the conclusion that it was their duty to give up slave-keeping and to try to found colleges and schools, where the young, at least, might be taught the Christian faith.

The two good men were delighted to find themselves thus agreed, and they resolved to sell their farm, and use the proceeds for the teaching of the

Indians.   Las Casas went home to lay the case of the
Indians before the King.   Ferdinand was then an old
man, and he died soon after the arrival of Las Casas,
in 1516.   His poor daughter Juana was mad, and her
son Charles reigned over the kingdoms of Spain and
the Indies.   If edicts at home could have done any
good, the Indians would have been free men, well and
gently trained in Christian ways.   But the isles were
far off, and full of greedy men, who paid no attention to the laws at home.   The only one they cared to
carry out was one that Las Casas had unfortunately
recommended, hoping to benefit the Indians, namely,
that each white man should be licensed to import a dozen
negro slaves.   The good man grieved for it afterwards,
and perceived that to steal and enslave negroes was
quite as cruel and unjust as to do the same by Indians.
He spent his life in struggling hard to teach, console,
and protect the Indians, but always in vain.   He went
from one place to another, tried one experiment after
another, and failed again and again.   As time went on,
the Indian race perished under the savage brutality of
the gold-hunting Spaniards in the West Indian Islands;
while negroes snatched from the coast of Africa filled
up the place they had left empty ; and gangs of black
slaves worked in the gold mines, pearl fisheries, and
plantations of sugar, spices, and cotton.

VASCO NUNEZ ON SHIPBOARD.

CHAP. VII.—THE FIRST SIGHT OF THE PACIFIC.

1513.

THERE was coming out from Hispaniola, under the leadership of a lawyer named Enciso, a fresh party to assist in founding the colony of St. Sebastian on the coast of South America. Alonzo de Ojeda, who attempted that settlement, had invited Enciso to join him, and tendered him the office of alcalde in the new city. The expedition of Enciso had not been long at sea when the crew of one of the vessels were amazed by a large cask which stood on deck suddenly being opened. Out of it came Vasco Nuñez de Balboa, a Spanish gentleman who had been a settler in Hispaniola, and had there got into debt and difficulty, from which he was thus making his escape.

Enciso was not at all pleased with the mode in which this volunteer showed himself, but Vasco overcame his anger, and was the more acceptable since he had the experience of a previous voyage along the coast. The expedition touched at the harbour of Carthagena, where Ojeda met so hostile a reception, but managed to avoid collision with the natives. Enciso was here surprised by the arrival of a vessel in command of Francisco Pizarro, whom Ojeda had left as his deputy at St. Sebastian. The vessel had on board all who survived of the garrison of St. Sebastian, having been compelled by starvation and danger to abandon that post. Enciso, by his authority as alcalde of St. Sebastian, induced Pizarro and his men to return to that post with him. They found the fort dismantled, the climate dreadful, and the natives so fierce that it was no use to stay there. Vasco advised moving on to the river of Darien, where the natives were less fierce, and did not poison their arrows. The advice was taken, the move was made, and the Spaniards drove the Indians from a village on the banks of the River Darien. Enciso took possession of the place, and gave it the name of Santa Maria. The colonists soon divided into factions. Vasco and Enciso quarrelled, and at last Vasco, who was the favourite of the soldiers, threw Enciso into prison, for, as he said, taking the government without proper appointment. Enciso, however, had friends powerful enough to oblige Vasco to let him go back to Spain and plead his cause.

Left alone in the command, Vasco de Balboa made a visit to Careta, Cacique of Coyba, who hospitably received him. He repaid his kindness by returning at night after a pretended departure, seizing the cacique, his wives and children, loading two vessels with plunder, and taking his captives and his booty with him to Santa Maria. He showed to his prisoner his war-horses, armour, and guns, and the Indian was so impressed with the power of the Spaniard, that he offered him his daughter as the price and pledge of peace. Balboa, seeing the convenience of an alliance with a powerful chieftain, accepted the daughter; and a compact was made by which the chieftain agreed to furnish food for the colonists, and Balboa to subdue the chieftain's enemy, with whom he was then at war. Balboa performed his part of the contract, subduing the cacique his father-in-law's enemy, and ravaging his territory. He was royally entertained after his victory by Careta.

Balboa next paid a visit to a friendly cacique named Comagre, who hospitably welcomed him, and showed him his palace. It was a wonderful place, one hundred and fifty paces long and eighty broad, founded on great logs, surrounded with a stone wall, and covered with a beautifully carved roof. It had many chambers for different kinds of stores; and one hall contained the remains of the cacique's family, which had been dried in the fire and then wrapped in cotton, adorned with gold and precious stones, and hung up by cords.   The cacique gave Balboa four thousand ounces of gold made up into ornaments.   Of this he weighed out a fifth for the King's share, and divided the rest in equal shares with his followers.   The cacique was surprised and shocked at their fierce eagerness over the division. He pointed to the south, and told Balboa that if he cared so much for gold, he would find abundance beyond the mountains.   From their tops could be seen a mighty sea, and all the streams that flowed into it so abounded in gold that the kings who reigned there used only golden vessels, and indeed gold was as common among them as iron was among the Spaniards.

He added that the way was difficult and dangerous, and beset with cannibal Indians; but all this was nothing to Vasco.   He sent for provisions and recruits to Don Diego, son of Christopher Columbus, who was then governing at St. Domingo, in Hispaniola.   Meanwhile he received private advices from Spain that Enciso had succeeded in the suit against him, and that he would be summoned to Spain to answer criminal charges.   He was resolved to set forth before the official news should arrive, or factions at Darien prevent him.   He moved on the expedition with one hundred and ninety of his bravest men, a number of Indians furnished by the cacique his father-in-law, and also a pack of bloodhounds. These terrible dogs had been trained by the cruel Spaniards to hunt down and fly at the poor runaway Indians, and were looked on by them with the utmost horror and dread. Vasco Nuñez had one of these dogs, named Leonico, immensely strong, tawny, with a black muzzle; and so brave and so much feared by the Indians, that when his master lent him to a plundering party, he received for him a share of the booty equal to that of a man-at-arms.

The journey was a very hard one. The Spaniards had to climb rugged precipices, and fight with tribes of Indians; and so many men were lost, or had to be sent back to the village of the friendly cacique, that only sixty-seven men were with Vasco Nuñez when, on the 26th of September, 1513, he climbed the last height alone, and beheld before him the unbroken expanse of the mighty Western Ocean. He called his followers to his side, pointed it out, and bade them thank God. A friar who was among them led the Te Deum of rejoicing, and a list was drawn up of those who first beheld this great sight. The names of Ferdinand, King of Arragon, and his daughter Juana, Queen of Castile, were carved on the great trees around.

The Spaniards had still a long way to go before they reached the shores of the great sea. They fought with an Indian cacique named Chiapes, but overcame him, and Vasco Nuñez made him into a warm friend. When at last he came to the shore, Balboa waded into the water above his knees, and took possession of the ocean for the sovereigns of Spain. The spot was in the Bay of Panama, close to the Gulf of San Miguel, the name given by Vasco Nuñez himself, intending to consecrate the mighty ocean to St. Michael, the archangel. After a time Vasco undertook to build a fleet with which to navigate the Western or Pacific Ocean. He caused the timber to be cut and prepared at Acla, a town founded at a port in the country of his father-in-law. Careta favoured his purpose, and accorded assistance. The ship-timber and other material was carried on the backs of Indians over the mountains and across the Isthmus of Darien. It was a cruel scheme, for the work was far too hard for the Indians whom he forced into doing it, supplying their places with others as fast as they died of the toil.

Meanwhile, the representations of Enciso at the court of Spain had resulted in the appointment of Don Pedro Arias Davila, commonly called Pedrarias, as Governor of Darien, with power to depose Vasco Nuñez and call him to account for his treatment of

Enciso. After the sailing of Pedrarias from Spain the messengers from Nuñez arrived there, bringing news of his great discovery, and presents to the King of pearls and golden ornaments. Pedrarias arrived at his new government, and proved harsh and cruel to the Indians. Now Vasco knew how to make them trust him, and be friendly ; and the contrast between the two Spanish commanders added daily to their mutual dislike. Before Pedrarias could attempt to depose a popular favourite, a commission arrived from Spain appointing Vasco Nuñez de Balboa, Adelantado or Lieutenant in the government, in recognition of his valuable discoveries and successes. Pedrarias was implacable. He induced Balboa to leave the Pacific coast, where he had begun to make explorations in his new ships. He invited him to a friendly conference at Acla, where Francisco Pizarro was deputed to arrest him. He was accused as a traitor and usurper of the territories of the Spanish Crown, and of an intention to put to sea with the squadron in the Pacific and defy the governor. Upon these charges Vasco Nuñez was convicted and beheaded, with four of his friends. Thus perished this brave and generally kind and faithful man, one of the most illustrious of the Spanish adventurers, when only forty-two years old, and just about to sail on the great ocean he had discovered.

CHAP. VIII.—THE WAY INTO THE PACIFIC.

1520.

THE kings who had refused to attend to Columbus were much disappointed when they found how far from a mere wild-goose chase his plans had been. Henry VII. of England had sent out an expedition, under a Venetian father and son, named Cabot, who, in 1496–8, touched at the island which still bears the name of Newfoundland, and coasted along the continent of North America, from Labrador to Florida. As no signs of gold were found, nothing more was for some time done by the English.

The Portuguese king, Don Manuel, was also eager to make discoveries. Vasco de Gama had rounded Africa, and Pope Eugene IV. had granted the Portuguese a right to all the new lands they might discover. This power the Popes claimed as Vicars of Christ, because of those prophecies of the Old Testament, which speak of the kingdom of Christ stretching to the east and west, from one sea to another. Ferdinand and Isabella asked also the papal sanction, and Pope Alexander VI. fixed as a boundary a line running from pole to pole, three hundred leagues to the westward of the Azores. All the lands eastward of this were granted to Portugal, and all to the westward to Spain.

An expedition was sent out from Portugal in 1500, under Don Pedro Alvarez Cabral. It was intended to go to India, and was sent off in great state from Lisbon, with solemn blessings by the clergy, the commander receiving a cap sent by the Pope himself. However, when they had passed the Cape Verd Islands, a strong wind drove them away from Africa, across the Atlantic, till they came to what they took for a large island. The natives came down to the beach, wearing crowns of brightly-coloured feathers, but no clothes, and their copper skins were painted in many hues. They had white bones through their ears and cheeks, and a great hole in the under lip, in which some wore a stone and some thrust out the tongue. Their eye-lashes, eye-brows, and beards had all been pulled out. They were spoken to in Negro language and Arabic, but of course answered to neither ; though two, who were afterward caught in a

canoe, did better understand the language of beads and
looking-glasses. For these they gave in exchange
fruit, maize, and the flour of the root of the mandioc
shrub, which we still know as " arrow-root."

On Easter Sunday a large body of the Portuguese
landed, and a solemn mass was celebrated, the natives
hovering about, and imitating the gestures of the
Portuguese. Cabral set up a large stone cross, and
took possession of the country for his king, naming
it Santa Cruz. He left behind him two men. It
was the custom of the discoverers of those times to
take from the prisons men under sentence of death,
and leave them behind among the natives, to take
their chance, learn the language, and prepare for new-
comers.

The ships then went on to India, and on their
return to Portugal, King Manuel sent out three ships
under Amerigo Vespucci. These fell in with a few
more savage tribes, who killed and devoured three
of the sailors, whom they had made prisoners ; one of
them actually in view of his horrified comrades in the
boats, before whom the savages held up pieces of his
limbs. Vespucci sailed along a great length of coast,
and then, as it was late in the year, crossed to Africa.

In 1503, Amerigo, still intending to go to India, sailed
with six ships, and was driven upon the coast which he

had already visited. Five of these vessels were lost, and Vespucci, landing, remained five months, made friends with the natives, and built a fort. One of the five vessels lost was wrecked, and her crew were taken off. The other four were never heard from. In the fort he left twenty-four men who had been saved from the wreck. As before, he took home a cargo of gums and spices, and a red wood, already known to the Portuguese, and much prized by them. It was called, from its colour, *brazil*, or burning wood, and the country came to be named Brazil, instead of the name, given at first, of Santa Cruz. Many adventurers went out thither to obtain this wood, with the abundant gums and spices. Monkeys and parrots were also among the imports of the early navigators into Europe. An expedition was fitted out in Spain to sail for Brazil, under Amerigo Vespucci, but it never set forth. Vespucci had entered the service of the King of Spain, however, and received a liberal salary as principal pilot, preparing charts and sailing directions. He died in 1512, his widow was pensioned, and his son was taken into royal favour. Shortly after his last return from Brazil, he wrote a letter, giving an account of his voyages. This letter was published, not however at Vespucci's instance, and the publisher suggested the name of America for the newly-discovered continent.

It became a subject of dispute between Spain and Portugal to whom Brazil belonged. But as the coast of Brazil was clearly to the east of the line established by the Pope, the Portuguese claimed it; while Spain construed the papal decree to mean that all lands discovered by sailing west belonged to her. In 1511, Don Juan Diaz de Solis sailed from Spain, still hunting for the western passage to India. Sailing along the coast of the continent to the south, he came to what he took for a sea of fresh water, but was really the mouth of a great river, the Rio de la Plata. Going ashore with a small party, he was cut off by the natives, who broke forth from an ambush, shattered the boat with their clubs, killed every man who had landed, then carried their bodies to a place within sight of the ships, cooked and devoured them. The terrified explorers returned at once to Spain.

In 1519, Fernando de Magelhaens or Magellan, a Portuguese mariner in the service of Spain, sailed with five Spanish ships from Seville. He followed the coast of South America, looking still for the western passage to India. In the mouth of the La Plata, where poor Solis had fallen, he thought he had found it, but discovering his mistake he proceeded south. He found some gigantic people, whom he called Patagonians, because he fancied their feet were *patas* or pads, like those of lions or dogs. He passed the straits, which still bear his name, between the land of the Patagonians and a bare volcanic island, which he named Tierra del Fuego, or land of fire. The difficult and dangerous passage occupied twenty days, and he came out into the southern part of the ocean which Balboa had seen from the Isthmus of Darien. He found the ocean so peaceful that he named it the Pacific. Sailing onwards, he did what Columbus had aimed at, for he reached the most eastward of the islands of Asia, and thus nearly came round from extreme west to extreme east. He did not live, however, to tell the tale. Touching at a fruitful group of islands, where his crew were refreshed, but which he called the Ladrones, from the thievish character of the inhabitants, he next proceeded to the group now known as the Philippines. Here, in resisting an attack from a large body of the natives, Magellan was killed, with several of his officers. But the survivors continued the voyage, and visited the Portuguese settled in the East, to their extreme astonishment. One of the fleet of five vessels with which Magellan sailed from Spain reached home again on the 7th of September, 1522; having made the first voyage round the globe in three years and twenty-eight days.

CHAP. IX.—THE AZTEC EMPIRE.

1513.

THE desire of finding the great empire, full of gold, of which the Indians spoke, still drew on adventurer after adventurer. In the year 1518 Fernando Cortes, a Spanish gentleman of Estremadura, obtained from the Governor of Cuba a fleet of seven ships, with a force of five hundred and fifty soldiers, twelve or fifteen horses, and ten brass cannon, wherewith to seek this wonderful place. It was quite true that there was such an empire. Indeed, there were two such lands of gold : one in North America, called Anahuac; the other, named Peru, in the mountains of South America. The inhabitants of Anahuac were called Aztecs. They were not like the wild Indians on the coast, but dwelt in cities, had temples, a priesthood, and a regular form of government with an emperor at its head. They had good roads and regular communication between city and city. Though

AN AZTEC CITY.

they had no alphabet they recorded their history in a sort of hieroglyphic work, painted in brilliant colours on cloth, or on prepared skins, or on paper made from the aloe plant. They had also pictures in feather-work, with which their palaces were hung. Iron was not known among them, and their tools and weapons were of copper, tin, and sharpened stones ; their vessels either of clay, earthenware, or of gold and silver.

They had many gods ; thirteen principal ones, and more than two hundred of lesser rank, with a numerous body of priests. Their temples were sometimes like pyramids, with steps on the outside, and broad terraces at different stages ; but instead of finishing in a point, there was a broad flat space on the top, where stood two towers with the images of the gods in them. In front of each was an altar, and the stone of sacrifice, on which, unhappily, the victims were human beings— generally captives taken in war. They were laid flat on the stone, and their hearts cut out and cast at the feet of the idol. Little children, wreathed with flowers, were carried in litters to the temple of the god of rain, and there sacrificed ; and the corpses were feasted upon in banquets, served up with the choicest cookery and splendid ornaments. It is reckoned that not less than twenty thousand human beings perished each year in this manner.

Yet the Aztecs lived in considerable civilization, and understood many of the sciences, in their own method, especially arithmetic and astronomy. They farmed every inch of land in their mountainous country, growing Indian corn, banana, and cocoa (whence was made chocolate), and the great aloe, or *maguey*. The juice of this plant was fermented into a liquor called pulque. The fibres of the leaves formed thread and cordage; the thorns, pins and needles; the leaves made thatch when whole, and could be pounded into a paste whence paper could be made. The garments of the Aztecs were woven of the thread of the aloe, of cotton, and of hair; but their most beautiful work was in the feather hangings, where the lovely tints of all the tropical birds were used to make exquisite pictures. Their houses were built round large courts, in which beautiful flowers were grown. Their feasts, served in gold and silver dishes, were as regularly conducted and as ceremoniously as any in Europe. Mexico itself, the capital, was one of the most beautiful cities that ever existed. It stood on islands in a great salt lake, shut in with a great circle of mountains. Three broad causeways led to it; and the streets were some of them of water, some of land, some of them with footways bordering canals. Lovely gardens, trees, and flowers adorned it ; the numerous temples, and the splendid palace and garden of the Emperor crowned it.

In spite of their horrible religion, the Aztecs were a well-ordered nation, and loved poetry and art, and all that is graceful and beautiful. They had happy and peaceful homes, and just laws ; indeed it is thought that two nations, one savage and the other gentle, had become blended into one; and that the custom of offering fruits and flowers remained from a better form of worship, which had been overcome by the frightful custom of human sacrifices.

The Aztecs had quantities of writings in their own picture fashion. Though most of these were destroyed, a history was copied from such as were spared. The process was to write the meaning of the symbols in the Mexican language with the letters of the alphabet. This copy was then translated into Spanish. From these records it is known that they had a long line of kings, some of whom had been very wise and just, as well as brave and magnificent. They were religious men, too, who thought much, as even the Greek philosophers did, of the hope that good and virtuous men may be blessed after their life here is over.

Anahuac, at the arrival of Cortes, was divided into three kingdoms — Tezcuco, Tlascala, and Mexico.

Tezcuco had the best and noblest kings, and had been the most powerful kingdom. The Tezcucan kings dwelt on the east shore of the great lake, opposite to the city of Mexico, and had had about three centuries of war and rivalry with the Mexicans till, just before the Spaniards found their way to America, the last of the great and good Tezcucan kings, Nezahualpilli, was overcome by fraud and force by his neighbour Montezuma, King of Mexico, and lost great part of his dominions. When the Tezcucan pined away and died, Montezuma took to himself the title of king over other kings, which the Spaniards translated "Emperor." It was he who was reigning in Anahuac, and at war with the Tlascalans, when Cortes set forth to find the great golden empire.

CHAP. X.--THE CONQUEST OF MEXICO.

1521.

ORTES was preceded by two adventurers in Mexican discovery, Fernandes de Cordova and Juan de Grijalva. Each prepared the way for the next; and it was their reports of the wealth in gold which caused the more powerful expedition of Cortes to be fitted out. Grijalva coasted from Yucatan as far north as Panuco, in the department now called Vera Cruz. The first place at which Cortes landed was at the mouth of the river Grijalva, as it is sometimes called, in honour of that discoverer. It is now marked on the charts as the Rio de Tabasco, from the name of the district which it traverses. As the natives had shown a fierce disposition to repel their previous Spanish visitors, they came down in strong force to oppose Cortes. When the Spaniards fired their guns, the Indians threw dust in the air that the Spaniards might not see the damage they were doing. But victory was sure to be where there were horses and fire-arms. The Tabascans submitted, and brought Cortes twenty girls, as slaves, to crush their maize, and make bread of the flour. One of these girls was an Aztec chief's daughter. She was christened Marina, and became a most useful and faithful interpreter to Cortes. Sailing farther along the coast, they landed at San Juan de Ulua, an island which commands the harbour of Vera Cruz, and which had been visited and named by Grijalva. Here, for the first time, they heard of Montezuma as a great emperor, far inland. He had sent messengers to ask what these strangers were doing on his coast. Cortes answered that they had been sent by their king to treat with Montezuma, and meant to see him. This, the messengers said, was impossible. But when Cortes insisted, they said they would send to their prince for an answer, and began drawing pictures of the Spaniards to send him. Whereupon Cortes had all his troops drawn out, caused his horsemen to make a grand charge upon the sands, and the cannon to be fired ; so that indeed they had some strange pictures to send. He also bade them tell Montezuma that he and his companions had a complaint of the heart which could only be cured by gold. Montezuma refused to see this stranger, but sent him presents that did but whet the appetite of all those who had that dangerous complaint of the heart, namely, a sum of gold and many other precious things.

Cortes was absolutely resolved to make his way to see the emperor; and that no one might be able to turn back, he ordered his ships to be burned. He had founded a city, which he called Vera Cruz, where he left all that he did not want on his march under the charge of the weaker men. It was much in the favour of Cortes that the countries round the coast were held in subjection by the Mexicans, and hated them; so even though they had begun by fighting against Cortes, they were willing to join with him against Montezuma as soon as they had felt his strength. The first thing Cortes always did was to stop the horrible human sacrifices, clear the temples of blood, set up a cross, and charge the priests to guard it, and then to make the people vassals to King Charles of Spain.

Tlascala was a great republic, tributary to Montezuma. It had a large and beautiful capital, with a wall nine feet high and twenty broad, measuring six miles in length. The people became the allies of Cortes, and some thousands of them came on with him on the march to Mexico. There was much fighting on the way, but Cortes held on until he had

reached the great causeway, and from the heights
looked down into the great valley of Mexico. The
sight of the wonderful city, full of gardens rising up
from the lakes, was so marvellously and surpassingly
beautiful that the soldiers stood still, and asked one
another if they were awake, the scene was so like a
dream, or like the enchanted castles and gardens they
had read of in romances.

Montezuma had found it vain to try to stop
these strangers, so he had promised to receive their
leader. Cortes, with all the splendour he could
muster, rode to meet him at the gate, between rows
of Mexican lords, who saluted the new comer by
laying their hands in the dust and then kissing them.
Montezuma stood leaning on the arms of his brother
and nephew, wearing on his head plumes of the royal
green which floated down his back.   He had on gilded
sandals, and a mantle rich with gold and precious
stones, while over his head four nobles held a canopy,
the ground-work of which was of green feathers, with
the richest embroidery of gold, pearls, and precious
stones in fringes and drops.   Cortes, dismounting,
advanced, and was received with princely courtesy.
There was an exchange of presents, a feast, and a
conference, with the Indian girl Marina for an interpreter.   Cortes explained the Christian Faith and the

Divine Law, and tried to make Montezuma accept them. The Emperor was so grandly polite and courteous, and unwilling to contradict a guest, that the Spaniards hoped he was succeeding. But when the Emperor took Cortes to see his great temple, on the platform at the top of many stairs, the Spaniards were sickened and shocked. The place looked and smelt like a slaughter-house ; and before one idol lay five, before another three, human hearts, torn out that morning. Cortes showed his horror, and tried to speak of better things ; but Montezuma was grieved at the dishonour done to his gods, who, he said, gave him victory, wealth, good harvests, and all he needed, and deserved to have offerings made to them. To Cortes it seemed a clear duty to win the country for Christ and for Spain. He did not trust the Aztecs, and he resolved to get their emperor into his own hands. There had been a little fight between the people he had left at Vera Cruz and their neighbours, and this he made an excuse for surprising Montezuma, and keeping him in the Spanish quarters as a hostage for his people. It was one of the most amazing acts of boldness ever done, but it succeeded.

Montezuma was cowed, and finding his only chance of safety was to give his allegiance to Spain, he sent for his nobles, and called on them to consent. They

wept bitterly, but gave way, and for some months
Montezuma continued to be still their emperor, though
closely watched by the Spaniards.   New difficulties
and dangers arose for Cortes.   Velasquez, Governor
of Cuba, had become his enemy, and sent out an
expedition, under Panfilo de Narvaez, to depose and
arrest him.   By fighting and defeating the army of
Narvaez, and winning the soldiers to his cause, Cortes
kept his command.   Returning to Mexico, he found
the Aztecs up in arms against the Spanish garrison.
A massacre of the inhabitants while celebrating a feast
had maddened them.   The Spaniards were besieged
in their quarters, and fearful encounters took place
whenever they ventured forth.   The destruction of a
temple which overlooked the Spanish quarters added
to the fury of the Aztecs ; but from its upper stage
the Mexicans had thrown arrows upon the Spaniards,
and when a Spaniard was made prisoner, his countrymen had seen him dragged up the side of one of these
temples to die a horrid death before the idols.   As
Montezuma had professed allegiance to Spain, and was
still in the hands of Cortes, he could call the rising of
the Mexicans a rebellion.   He brought out the unfortunate prince to address the people.   They listened
for a little while, but then flung stones and shot arrows.
Three struck Montezuma, and in a few days he died

of grief, or of his wounds, the Spaniards having tried in vain to make him confess himself a Christian.

The Spaniards were compelled to leave the city of Mexico, but made their retreat under great difficulty. A new king, by name Guatemozin, was set up, and Cortes had to besiege Mexico, and carry on a dreadful war, before, on the 13th of August, 1521, he finally took the great lake city, and the Aztec Empire, with all its spoils of gold, silver, and pearls, was added to the realms of Spain. The city of Mexico withstood a siege of three months, in which uncounted thousands died by war and famine. Its conquest was effected by the aid of native allies of Spain, enemies of Mexico. The capture of Guatemozin ended the resistance of his subjects. Three years later he was hung by Cortes on a charge of conspiracy. So perished the last of the Aztec kings. The country thus conquered was named New Spain.

CHAP. XI.—THE CONVERSION OF MEXICO.

1529.

DON FERNANDO CORTES, the man who had conquered Mexico, was great, both in patience and ability. However much he might be provoked he never said a hasty word, though one vein in his forehead and another in his throat used to swell with wrath. He was a devout man after his fashion, religious and loyal, who meant to work for the honour of God and the king; and he sent at once for a bishop and clergy to convert the Aztecs, and hold service in the churches. And though he did hard and cruel things at times, it was always in the way of what he thought his duty. But there were ten plagues in New Spain which made terrible havoc of the Aztecs, and were thus counted up by a monk, who was a friend of Cortes: (1) smallpox; (2) the slaughter in the war; (3) famine after the war; (4) Indian and Negro overseers; (5)

the heavy tribute demanded from the Indians ; (6) the
gold mines ; (7) the rebuilding of Mexico ; (8) the
making of slaves to work in the mines ; (9) the carriage of metals from the mines ; (10) the quarrels of
the Spaniards.

The false accusers had gone home to Spain, and
there was terrible jealousy of Cortes. A judge was
sent out to hold a court and try him ; but after waiting
seventeen days not a single charge of any act of dishonesty, selfishness, or disloyalty was brought. However, he went over to see the King of Spain, who had
by this time been elected as the Emperor Charles V.
All falsehoods about him were confuted as soon as the
Emperor actually saw and heard him ; and he went
back to Mexico as Captain-General of the army, though
not as Governor. He took a wife back with him, and
obtained large estates in Mexico. The great Mexican
and Tlascalan chiefs and landowners, who chose to make
friends with the Spaniards and become Christians, were
not deprived of their property ; and the Aztec race did
not melt away, as the Indians of the isles had done,
but a mixed population grew up—Spanish, Indian, and
Negro, mingled together in strange ways.

All this time the great desire of Cortes was to find
the way over the mountains to the southern sea that
Vasco Nuñez de Balboa had seen. The tribes in the

mountains, who had been in the fear of the great Emperors of Mexico, offered submission ; and through their states the Pacific Ocean was reached in 1522, about one thousand miles above the spot where Balboa had first beheld it. Guatemala, which means in Aztec, "the place of decayed wood," a country as civilized as Mexico, situate on the western coast, received and submitted to Pedro de Alvarado, an officer of Cortes. Twelve Dominican and twelve Franciscan friars were sent out from Spain to attend to the conversion of the Aztecs. They were received with great respect by Cortes, who bent his knee and kissed their hands, while the Indians, amazed at his condescension to barefooted men, in rough serge, with ropes around their waists, cried out, "Motolinia," which means "poor." As poverty is said to have been the bride of St. Francis, one of these brethren was so delighted with the name that he took it for his own, and was ever after called Father Toribio Motolinia. He spent his life in teaching, catechising, and converting the Aztecs, and is said to have baptized four hundred thousand of them. Another was a Fleming, Peter of Ghent, who thought himself unworthy to be anything but a lay brother, but who spent fifty years in kind and gentle training of the Mexicans. He built with their help a large school, where he was the first to teach them to read, write, play on musical instruments, paint and carve like the Flemings at home. He could preach if no priest was at hand, and he persuaded many an Aztec to destroy his idols. He was altogether a man of such influence that the archbishop once said, " I am not Archbishop of Mexico, but Brother Peter of Ghent is." In his old age he thought it a temptation of the evil one that he felt the yearnings of home-sickness, and longed above all to hear his native Flemish : but he stayed at his post in Mexico all his life, and died there.

Grievous deeds were done by the greedy Spaniards, and suffered by the natives, as the conquest of Mexico was followed by that of Central America. But, on the whole, things were not so shocking as in Hispaniola and Cuba. Las Casas had come to the mainland, and so testified against the violence of the Spaniards, that for some years he was forbidden to preach. He also published a treatise, in which he declared, first, that the Indians ought to be made Christians by love and good teaching, not by slavery and violence ; and, next, that even if they refused, that did not make it right to make war on them and enslave them. He was laughed at by the Spaniards, and told that his plans of persuasion were mere folly. The Spaniards derisively challenged him to try.

Now there was, near Guatemala, a district where the people were so fierce that the Spaniards had named it the Land of War, for they had three times been driven back from it.   Las Casas actually signed and sealed an agreement with the Emperor Charles V., that he would bring this place to be Christian and to submit to him, if no soldiers, or colonists, or any other Spaniards, except those connected with the Government, were allowed to enter the country for five years.

The first thing Las Casas did was to choose some good Dominicans.   With fasts and prayers they prepared themselves.   Then they drew up, in verse, in the language of the country, an account of the Creation, the Fall, the Redemption, the work of the Holy Ghost, and the Last Judgment.   They taught these poems to some Christian Indian pedlars, who used to carry wares into the land of war every year, and who sang them with all their hearts.   The people listened, and the pedlars then told of the holy lives of the good Fathers who had taught them, and could explain more. So well did these native missionaries do their work, that a young chief actually besought that the Fathers would come to him.   Father Luis Canea, who knew the language best, was sent, and was welcomed with arches of triumph, flowers strewn, and every honour. A church was built for his ministrations, and chiefs

and people came in. With great difficulty the pious
Fathers did contrive to keep out the worst violence of
the Spaniards, and the country which had once been
the land of war, was named Vera Paz, or True Peace,
and the Indians there have ever since been a Christian,
peaceful, flourishing race.

CHAP XII.—THE INCAS OF PERU.

1524.

ANOTHER Spanish soldier, unfortunately of very different mould from Cortes, set forth on another quest for the land of gold, following in the track of Vasco Nuñez de Balboa. This man was Francisco Pizarro, who had already made one of numerous adventurous parties in journeys of discovery; and was fully imbued with that horrid Spanish notion, which the priests and monks were always resisting, that heathen Indians deserved no better treatment than brute beasts.

The country to which he was bent on making his way was Peru, which lies on the western side of South America, sloping upwards from the Pacific Ocean, to where the Andes, the "Giants of the Western Star," rise up into thin air and cold, beyond where man, beast, or plant can live. The people there thought themselves the Children of the Sun, whom they worshipped above all; but not with human sacrifices, like the

Aztecs. They were a much more gentle people, and their principal sacrifice on the chief feast-day was only a black lamb. They thought the moon was the sun's wife, the planet Venus his page ; and they had hosts of other deities, whose golden images filled their great temples. There were great colleges of priests, and of virgins dedicated to the sun. The first studied astronomy, and offered the sacrifices and led the worship ; the maidens prepared the sacred bread that was given out to the people at the feasts, sang songs, and led dances in honour of the sun. The prince of the country was styled the Inca, and was supposed to be the living representative of the sun, his forefather. He could only marry in his own family. The Inca was a sacred person, ruling with such wise, fatherly care, that as we read of old Peru, in the Commentaries of Garcilasso de la Vega, we cannot help thinking that he could only have heard the best side of the story. De la Vega was born in Peru, and his mother belonged to the Inca family.

There was no money in Peru, no private estates. Everything belonged to the Inca, as Child of the Sun ; all the land, the metals, and the flocks of lamas, guanacos and alpacas, which served as horses, cattle, and sheep. Every year the land was freshly portioned out, according to the number of each family, with a reserve for the sun and the Inca. The rent was to be personal service paid to the Inca, in tilling his lands and those of the sun. Their produce maintained the priests, and supplied the sick and helpless, and if there were any remainder, it was stored up against case of scarcity. The animals were distributed in like manner, and their wool was given out by the Inca every two years, to supply the nation with clothing. Some of the tribute of labour was employed in building the temples and palaces of the great city of Cuzco; and some in making and keeping up wonderful roads all over the country, in the heights of the Andes, which were crossed by strings of lamas, bearing gold and silver in baskets on their backs.

The country was like one large family, and, as there was no private property, stealing was unknown. Each household helped its neighbours to cultivate the ground, and public feasts were held every two or three months, to which every one was invited, and where there were songs and dances. Officers were sent forth by the Inca to watch that no one was idle, down to the child of five years old ; and each householder was commanded to keep his doors open when he was at dinner, that the royal inspectors might look in and see whether the family were behaving properly, and living according to their rank.

The Peruvians kept their records by a number of cords, which they called quipus. The colour of threads in a quipu, and the patterns in which they were knotted together, had meanings given them, which made them answer the purpose of writing. In them the laws and history of the kingdom were preserved, and also some poetry. The Peruvians seem to have acted plays at their great festivals; but they had not, on the whole, made so much progress in science and literature as the Aztecs.

The last Inca who had reigned before the Spaniards found Peru had conquered the province of Quito, and had made a most wonderful road along the mountains from thence to Cuzco. He had married a daughter of the lord of Quito, and had a son, whom he named Atahualpa, or Sweet Valour. But this youth had not equal rights with the elder son, Huascar, or the Golden Chain, whose mother was one of the Daughters of the Sun, the only right wives for the Inca.

Atahualpa was, however, a favourite with the people, and obtained his grandfather's country of Quito on his father's death. Huascar took up arms against him, but was defeated by the chief general of Quito, Quizquiz, who made him prisoner, and put to death a great number of the royal race of Cuzco, with a barbarity which does not look as if the Peruvians were quite as gentle as they have been represented.

It was at this time, when Peru was thus disturbed by the quarrel between the brothers, that Francisco Pizarro, a brave, rough man, unable even to write his name, agreed with his friend, Diego de Almagro, to seek for the riches of the south ; and with a school-master named Fernando de Luque, they induced the Governor of Panama, Pedrarias, to let them buy a ship, and enlist men for the expedition. In 1524, Pizarro, with eighty men and some horses, set forth in one ship and two canoes, coasting along southwards, and suffering terribly for want of food ; so that they named one spot where they landed the Port of Hunger. Almagro followed with another ship, and found them in a wretched state. But they were wonderfully patient and resolute, and would not give up their attempt—especially as some prisoners they had made told them of the land of gold in the mountains. At last, after untold sufferings and labours, they became quite sure of the existence of the great empire, and that all that was wanting was the means of winning it. A second expedition confirmed these impressions, and also convinced Pizarro that the needed means and authority must be sought in Spain.

CHAP. XIII.—THE CONQUEST OF PERU.

1532.

FRANCISCO PIZARRO went home to Spain, made his way to court, and told his story of the golden kingdom in the mountains. Nothing in those days seemed to be too wonderful to be true. The old device of Spain had been two pillars, representing the pillars of Hercules—namely, the rocks on either side of the Straits of Gibraltar—with the motto, *Ne Plus Ultra*, "no more beyond." Charles V. left out the *ne*, so that his badge was *Plus Ultra*, or, "more beyond ; " and the ensign of Hispaniola was a horse leaping off a rock into infinite space.

No doubt crossed any one's mind as to the right of attacking these distant kings; or rather, the text giving the Messiah the heathen for His inheritance was mis-interpreted to mean that His supposed representative, the Pope, could give away heathen empires to Christian kings ; nor was there a thought of the cruelty of sending a fierce, hard, ignorant man to be a conqueror and ruler. So Pizarro had the government of Peru granted to him. The schoolmaster, Fernando de Luque, was to be Bishop, and Almagro, Judge, or Adelantado. Pizarro's four brothers sold their Spanish lands and sailed out to share with him ; but altogether, when he had come out from Spain and collected his whole forces at Panama, he had only three ships, thirty-seven horses, and one hundred and eighty-three men. The use of the horses was much more to amaze and terrify the natives than for actual fighting. With this small party he set forth to win an empire on Innocents Day, the 28th of December, 1530.

The point for which Pizarro aimed on his third voyage was Tumbez, near the entrance of the Bay of Guayaquil, which he had visited before, and where he had made acquaintance with the Indians, showing them his power and receiving supplies from Panama. He was obliged to land some sixty miles to the north by head winds, and disembarking his troops marched along the shore, suffering great hardships. Reaching the Bay of Guayaquil, he occupied the Isle of Nuna, where his ships rejoined him. On the isle of Nuna and on the coast of Tumbez he remained over a year, and was joined by Fernando de Soto with reinforcements. From the Indians of Tumbez he now heard of the war between the two Incas. He sent a deputation to Atahualpa, who was encamped near the city of Caxamarca. The deputation returned with an envoy, bringing presents from the Inca, who seems to have wished to secure the assistance of the new comers against his brother Huascar. Without any opposition, Pizarro marched on to the city of Caxamarca, which he found deserted. He took possession of the great square, and thence sent Fernando de Soto and his own brother Hernando, with about thirty horsemen, to Atahualpa's camp.

They found the Inca in his quarters, the only person seated, and wearing on his head what served for a crown, namely, a cap with an enormous tassel of fine crimson wool, like silk, which hung down over his eyes, so that he had to lift it up when he wished to see. He behaved with much pride and stateliness, and said he understood the Spaniards were no great warriors, but that they might go and help his men to subdue a stubborn race of Indians four miles off. He promised to come and see Pizarro in his camp in the square of the city of Caxamarca. On the 16th of November, 1532, the Inca came. Most likely he meant to surround and capture the strangers, and secure their arms and horses, for he brought with him five or six thousand men, apparently unarmed, but with clubs, slings, and bags of stone under their cotton dresses. However, he himself came peacefully, in a litter of plated silver and gold, adorned with paroquets' feathers. Pizarro had placed all his men, except about twenty whom he reserved as his suite or staff, under cover in the deserted buildings, apparently barracks, which opened upon the square. When the Inca halted, Pizarro sent a priest to him to expound, briefly, the whole Christian doctrine; from which the priest deduced the fact that it was the duty of the Inca at once to submit himself to the Pope and the King of Spain. An Indian interpreter made such a rendering of the discourse as he could, and some talk followed, in the course of which the Inca asked for the breviary which the priest held in his hand. After glancing at it he threw it down, and sharply complained of the mischief the Spaniards had done in their advance. Standing up in his litter he made signs, and spoke to his people. He was thought to be calling them to the attack, and Pizarro, with his followers sprang forward with the Spanish war cry. It was responded to by the concealed soldiers, who rushed into the square. Whether they were armed or not the Indians made no resistance, except immediately round the royal person. The bearers of the litter were killed, and the Inca, with all his clothes torn off in the struggle, was dragged from under the litter and made prisoner. A terrible slaughter was made of the Indians, but the only wound on the other side was a slight scratch received by Pizarro, from one of his own men as the conqueror was defending the life of Atahualpa, whom he preferred to take alive.

The plunder of the camp of the Peruvians was enormous, and while Pizarro kept Atahualpa prisoner, Spaniards were sent out to seize and rifle the great cities and temples of Peru. One hundred and sixty men had in fact subdued a warlike nation of eleven millions, by the seizure of their chief. Atahualpa was at first kept as Montezuma had been, and allowed to see his courtiers, and to send out orders. Meanwhile his armies had conquered his brother Huascar, and made him prisoner. It is not certain that Atahualpa actually commanded that his brother should be put to death, but it was done, and though he seemed to mourn, the Spaniards thought his grief was only feigned. An enormous ransom in gold was to be paid by him, and the metal was to be piled on the floor of an apartment about twenty feet square till it reached a line nine feet from the floor. While the ransom was yet incomplete, it was found expedient to divide what had been received. A fifth was sent to the King of Spain, and the rest was shared among the soldiers. Almagro, and a fresh troop of three hundred men, who reached

Caxamarca about this time, found that they were not by any means to share on equal terms with the first comers.

They therefore did not want the collection of the ransom to go on, and wished to be able to plunder for themselves. So they were bent on the Inca's death, and there were continual reports that he was secretly calling on his people to raise an army and deliver him. This was the natural thing for him to do, but the Spaniards called it treachery. One night two Indians came in, and said that a great force was marching on Caxamarca. Thereupon the Spaniards decided upon instantly trying the unhappy Peruvian king, according to the form of their own Spanish law. Of course they convicted him, and then they sentenced him to death, and that by fire, unless he would become a Christian. It was put to the vote whether this cruel sentence should be carried out, and among four hundred Spaniards, there were only fifty to vote for the life of their captive. Atahualpa loudly complained of the injustice and wickedness of the sentence, but in vain. He was led out into the great square of Caxamarca, and there, when he saw the stake and faggots, consented to be baptized.[1] This was done, and Juan de

---

[1] August 29. This day is sometimes kept as the day of the beheading or martyrdom of John the Baptist. For this reason the Inca was baptized Juan or John.

Atahualpa, by which name he was baptized, was then bound to the stake and strangled. He was buried with all the honours of a Spaniard and a Christian.

The royal tassel was given to one of his brothers, who was in the hands of the Spaniards, but who, before long, pined and died of grief, at the hardness with which he was treated, and the miseries of his country. Cuzco, the capital city, was entered with little difficulty, and there the Spaniards perfectly gorged themselves with plunder. Above all they ravaged the great Temple of the Sun, where there was a huge disc of the sun himself. This was seized by a common soldier, and gambled away in a single night's play. There were also figures of men, women, animals, and plants, such as Indian corn made in solid gold, of beautiful workmanship. All alike were the prey of these rude, ignorant men, who melted them down, and gambled and revelled with the price. And as to the cruelties suffered by the people, they surpass all thought or words.

CHAP. XIV.—THE CIVIL WAR IN PERU.

1535.

HONOURS and rewards came forth from Spain to the conquerors of this new empire. Pizarro was created a marquis; and Diego de Almagro a marshal, and governor of all the country to the south; while Valverde, the chaplain, was to be Bishop of Cuzco. While crowds of Spaniards flocked to Peru, soldiers, sailors, and adventurers of all kinds, to enjoy the spoil, a new city was founded by Pizarro, on the coast. He called it *Ciudad de los Reyes*, or City of the Kings, after the three kings or Magi, because it was founded on the festival of the Epiphany, 1535, but it took and kept the name of Lima. There was much dispute between Almagro and the brothers of Pizarro, who held the government of Cuzco, as to whether that city belonged to Almagro's jurisdiction or that of Pizarro. An agreement was reached as the parties were on the eve of blows, and Almagro set out to subdue Chili, the country to the south.

Manco, the brother of Huascar, had appealed to Pizarro as the rightful heir to the throne of the Incas; and the Spaniards went through the ceremony of his coronation, and presented him to his countrymen as their future sovereign. But he was really held in a sort of captivity, and demanded the powers as well as the title of Inca. Making his escape from the Spaniards, he put himself at the head of his people, and made desperate attempts to free the land from the white men, who were cruelly oppressing the whole country, even beyond the wont of their nation, and destroying the temples of their gods. Manco had two large gold vessels full of the native wine brought before him, and called on all who tasted it to pledge themselves that not a Christian should be left alive in Peru.

Then he attacked Cuzco, where the Spaniards found themselves in very great danger, and there was fighting from street to street and house to house, but at last the assailants were beaten off with terrible slaughter by Pizarro's three brothers. Manco surrounded Cuzco with Indian troops, and the Spaniards were besieged there for several months. Sorties were made, and there raged a terrible war, in which Spaniards and Indians killed each other whenever they met; and among those who fell was Juan Pizarro, one of the brothers.   Manco Inca withdrew to the mountainous districts, where he could elude capture, repel assaults, and reject overtures at treaties ; now hold parleys and then could descend and harass the Spaniards.   One of the Spanish visitors at his camp, named Gomez Perez, who was teaching him to play at bowls, on some dispute about the game, threw a bowl at his head, which caused his death, thus ending the dynasty of the Incas.

During these disturbances Almagro came back from Chili.   He had made a miserable journey through the frozen passes of the Andes, and had met with no empire and no gold.   So he persuaded himself and his men that Cuzco was part of the government which the emperor had assigned to him.   He came to the walls, and summoned Fernando Pizarro to give it up to him. Of course Fernando sent down to Francisco, the marquis, at Lima, for orders ; but before instructions could arrive, Almagro crept into the town by night and filled it with his men.   Fernando and Gonzalo Pizarro defended themselves in the palace of the Incas, till it was set on fire and the roof began to fall in on them, when they yielded and were put in chains. Almagro then prepared to descend to the sea-coast, and establish a port for himself.   He took Fernando Pizarro with him, leaving Gonzalo under guard in

Cuzco. On his march he learned that Gonzalo had escaped and joined his brother Francisco, at Lima. A correspondence now took place between Francisco Pizarro and Almagro; an interview was appointed to be held at Mala, and the dispute to be submitted for arbitration to a single umpire, Fray Francisco de Bovadilla. The two old partners met, but not in the most affectionate manner. Meanwhile it was discovered that Gonzalo Pizarro was moving on Mala with a body of troops. The conference had become very like a quarrel, when one of the cavaliers present gave Almagro notice by singing from an old ballad:

> "Time it is, Sir Knight, I say,
> Time it is thou wert away."

Another brought a horse to the door, on which Almagro mounted and galloped off. The marquis declared that he did not know of his brother's advance. Almagro did not believe him; and when Fray Bovadilla decided that Cuzco must be surrendered to Pizarro until a scrutiny should determine the question, and that Fernando Pizarro should be set at liberty on condition of his leaving the country, the Almagro party declared that it was an unjust judgment, and that Almagro should not submit to it. So furious were the threats of Almagro's men, and so great was the danger of Fernando, that Francisco Pizarro conceded that Cuzco should remain in the hands of Almagro, and Fernando was liberated. The Pizarros and Almagro held an exchange of civilities, the agreement was ratified, and Almagro was persuaded that a cordial settlement had been made. But the marquis instantly set about preparations for renewal of the war. He notified Almagro that the treaty was at an end; he persuaded his brother Fernando to break his pledge to leave the country, and gave him command of the army. Fernando Pizarro marched to recover Cuzco. He met the army of Almagro at a place called Salinas, or salt pits, near the city. There was a fierce battle in which Almagro was defeated, the city was taken, and Almagro made prisoner. He was thrown into prison, brought to trial, and put to death on the 8th of July, 1538.

Francisco, the marquis, it is said by his friends, did not know what was going on in Cuzco till all was over; and wept bitterly for the old friend who had turned into a foe. Fernando soon afterward went home to Spain; and there, being called to account by the relatives of Almagro, was imprisoned for twenty-three years. He was at last released, and lived on his own estate to be a hundred years old.

The Marquis Francisco Pizarro, was for the present

undisputed governor, for Almagro's son and other friends were waiting for a judge from Spain, who they expected would take vengeance for the marshal. Pizarro sent his master of the horse, Pedro de Valdivia, to subdue Chili ; and the names of a province, a river, and a sea-port town still witness to the success of that leader. Gonzalo Pizarro was sent to act against the natives of Charcas, and there won an exceedingly rich country, where the mines of Potosi were afterward discovered. He was appointed Governor of Quito, beyond which he was told there was a country full of cinnamon trees. In search of this he set out with three hundred Spaniards, and four thousand Indians. They crossed the mountains through frightful snow and ice, and at last arrived at a province called Sumaco, where they did not find good trees, and where they are said to have been very cruel to the Indians. Pushing on eastward, they came to a perfect net-work of rivers, with marshy country between them ; and wonderful trees, creepers, and ferns through which they had to cut their way. At last they stopped and built themselves a barque, which carried the sick and the baggage down the river Coca, while the rest went along the bank, cutting their way with hatchets. After two months, when they were almost starved, they came to some Indians, whose language the

Peruvians understood enough to know that they said that this river joined another very large one ten days off, and that there would be plenty of food. Gonzalo therefore resolved to send the barque down the river, with a brave captain, Francisco de Orellana, and to wait himself for its return.

In three days, going with the stream, Orellana came to the junction of the Coca and the Napo, but he found no food; and as he declared he should be a year forcing his way back up the rapid current, he persuaded his men, not without difficulty, to abandon their comrades to their fate, and go on down the river till it reached the sea. Only two men, a priest and a knight named Sanchen de Vargas, were faithful enough to refuse, and were left behind to perish in the forest. Orellana safely reached the sea, having made his way down the mighty flood called the Marañon, which has taken the name of the Amazon, because he saw some women with bows and arrows on the banks. It was in 1541 that this traitor was the first to cross the continent. Gonzalo, after waiting long for him to come back, followed the course of the Coca down to its junction with the Napo. There they found young Vargas, who told them the course Orellana had taken. The party then turned back, and struggled through horrible miseries to Peru again. The return march occupied more than a year. When, half naked, sick, and starved, the survivors of the expedition, less than half, reached Quito, it was to hear that Francisco Pizarro had been murdered in his own house in Lima, by conspirators, friends of Almagro, on the 26th of June, 1541, after defending himself bravely.

A judge named Vaca de Castro had arrived from Spain just before the death of Pizarro, with a commission to assist the marquis in tranquillizing the country, and in the event of the death of Pizarro to succeed him. He had not entered upon his duties, or even reached Lima, when the assassination took place. But he instantly assumed the direction of matters, civil and military, conquered the adherents of the son of Almagro, who had risen in arms, and executed that young man with others, his associates. He was an upright, honest man, and Gonzalo Pizarro consented to lay aside all further thought of revenge or ambition, and retired to the estate near Potosi which his brother had assigned to him.

CHAP. XV.—PROTECTION FOR THE INDIANS.

1542—1566.

THE poor Peruvians, once so rich and happy, had suffered grievously among all the wars of their conquerors. The good Las Casas, the friend of the Indians, went home to Spain to plead their cause with the emperor ; and a set of rules were authorised for their protection in all the Spanish colonies. These were called the " New Laws." The *repartimiento* of Indians was not to pass to a man's heirs at his death, but it was to go to the king, which meant release. No *repartimiento* was to be held by any bishop, abbot, or officer of the crown ; all lands were to be forfeited by those who had been concerned in rebellion, and no personal slavery was to be exacted from the Indians.

Good and humane governors were chosen to enforce these laws in the isles, in Mexico, and in Peru. In

Hispaniola, however, there was hardly an Indian left alive ; and Negro slavery was fast coming in, and it was much the same in Cuba and Jamaica. On the continent, the Spaniards thought the New Laws the height of injustice ; and when the new governor arrived in Mexico, they had nearly resolved to go out and meet him in mourning. He found that if he endeavoured to carry out the New Laws there would certainly be a rebellion which he could not repress ; and he sent letters back to represent the matter to the Emperor.

In Peru, Vaca de Castro, whose wise measures are related in the last chapter, was succeeded by Blasco Nuñez Vela. When the new viceroy arrived at Lima, the first thing he saw was a placard : " Him who comes to thrust out of my estate I shall thrust out of the world." Vela was not terrified, but very angry, and he was determined to carry out his orders. He did hasty deeds, and made many enemies, who all went over to join Gonzalo Pizarro, making him the head of a rebellion against the New Laws and their enforcement. Gonzalo procured the support of the people as Captain-General of Peru ; and Blasco Nuñez was compelled either to surrender his authority or to assert it by force of arms. He was hunted down, defeated, and killed, an old personal enemy causing his head to be struck off even while he was dying of his wounds. Gonzalo Pizarro remained Governor of Peru, hoping to be confirmed in his power by the Emperor.

A lawyer priest named Pedro de la Gasca was appointed to bring Peru into order. He bore a conciliatory message from the emperor directing Pizarro to co-operate with him in restoring order. Pizarro refused to receive the imperial clemency, and raised the standard of rebellion. The only way of reaching Peru was, then, to cross the Isthmus and sail from Panama ; and Gonzalo had plenty of time to prepare. He had nine hundred Spaniards who were ready to join with him in fighting for the Province. He gained one great victory ; but after that he was defeated again and again, and forced to yield himself a prisoner. He was tried, found guilty of treason, and executed in the year 1548. Two of his brothers had before died deaths of violence. The other of the four was in prison in Spain. The great conquest had brought little good to the conqueror and his family. Bloodshed brought on bloodshed, and the death of Atahualpa was visited on them.

Gasca had put down rebellion from Panama to Chili, and had an enormous spoil in his hands, including the newly discovered mines of Potosi—the richest silver

mines in the world. All the lands were to be redis-
tributed ; and his arrangements, which were meant to
be merciful and just, raised in some directions a spirit
of discontent and some disorder. But the mutinous
spirits were appeased or vanquished, and the authority
of the King of Spain was at last firmly established
about the time that Charles V. abdicated, and Philip
II. became King of Spain in 1555.

The Peruvians accepted the Christian faith, and the
church was endowed with great splendour. Indeed
the clergy deserved all praise for the steadfast efforts
they made for the protection of the Indian races ; and
it is owing to their constant witness against cruelty,
and appeals to the sovereign against the wickedness
of the colonists, that there is still a considerable native
population in Peru.

Las Casas was offered the bishopric of Cuzco, but
would not accept it. However, when he was offered
the bishopric of Chiapa, the chief of the Dominican
Order insisted on his taking it, since otherwise there
would be no one to see that the New Laws were
carried out, and the Indians saved from oppression.
Chiapa is that portion of Central America which lies
south of the peninsula of Yucatan, and it had been
settled by Spaniards who hated Las Casas beyond
all measure. There was hardly a white layman in

the New World who did not look on this good man
as his enemy, and think that the notion of saving
Indians from slavery was as absurd as declaring that
oxen and horses ought to be free.   If he went out of
the capital, Ciudad Real, they closed the gates against
him; they fought against him, abused him, tried to starve
him, and threatened him ; but all this was vain against
one who lived like the poorest of monks, and would
have been glad to die as a martyr.   He held his
ground till he had set up various convents of Dominicans, who were sure to protect the Indians ; and he
only licensed as confessors men who would only give
absolution to those who abstained from wanton injustice and cruelty to the natives.   Even the wildest and
fiercest Spaniard thought with horror of going unab-
solved, and thus these confessors really were able to
prevent much cruelty.

There was to be a great Synod of the clergy at
Mexico, and thither Las Casas went to attend it.   But
the news of his coming raised such a tumult among the
Spaniards, who hated him for hindering their cruelties,
and interfering with their gains, that the Government
bade him wait till men's minds were calmed down.
However he came safely in, and the Synod was held.
There four great rules were laid down.   First, that
heathen kings had as much right to their lands as

Christians ; second, that the Pope had given the New
World to the kings of Spain, not to make them richer,
but that the Faith might be spread ; third, that the
Indians were not to be despoiled of their lands or
riches ; fourth, that the kings of Spain were bound to
pay the expenses of missions to them. These were
excellent decisions, and Las Casas set out to carry
them to Spain. He never returned, finding he could
do more for the Indians, by pleading their cause with
the king, than by struggling with the colonists.

He did so with effect. Once, when Philip II.
needed money, he was told that if he would do away
with the claim of the Crown to all a man's Indians at
his death, each colonist would pay largely. But, on
the showing of Las Casas that this meant making them
slaves for ever, he refused. Tributes were laid upon
the Indians, and they underwent much harshness and
ferocious cruelty ; but the great Las Casas saved them
from absolute slavery. The bishops, priests, and
friars watched over them, and hindered the Spaniards
from the horrors they had practised in Hispaniola and
Cuba ; and thus the Indian race was saved from utter
extinction in Mexico and Peru, and became Christian.

Las Casas lived chiefly in a convent in Spain, always
watching to hinder any measure which would bear
hardly on the natives. He wrote a history of the

Indians, and, when ninety years old, a treatise on
Peru. Two years later he came to Madrid to beg the
king to give the people in Guatemala a court of justice
of their own. The journey was too much for him, and
he died at ninety-two years of age at Madrid, in 1566,
leaving a noble name behind him.

CHAP. XVI.—ENGLISH NORTH AMERICAN DISCOVERIES.

1524—1580.

ALL the discoveries in the New World had hitherto remained in the possession of Spain, except Brazil. By the demarcation line of the Pope that country belonged to Portugal, and was claimed under the accidental discovery of Cabral, in 1500. The boundaries of Brazil, as arranged by treaty between Portugal and Spain, were the Amazon on the north, and the Rio de la Plata on the south. Subsequent treaties varied the boundaries, especially on the west. As the valuable mines of Brazil were not discovered until a century later, there was the less reason for dispute. In 1580 Philip II. of Spain claimed the crown of Portugal, and annexed that kingdom to Spain.

In 1524 Francis I. of France, protesting that he " did not think that God had created these new countries only for Spain," authorized an exploring expedition in behalf of French interests. The commander was Giovanni Verazzani, a Florentine. He coasted the northern continent from the tract now known as the Carolinas up to Nova Scotia, and took possession of it under the name of New France. The disturbed condition of France prevented the immediate further prosecution of discovery. Ten years later, Jacques Cartier made his first voyage to the northern portion of the continent. A second was made immediately after his return, and a third in 1541. These voyages accomplished little but geographical discovery.

In 1555 a party of French refugee Reformers attempted a settlement in Rio Janeiro. The bad character of their leader and dissensions among themselves brought the colony to the verge of ruin, and the Portuguese completed its destruction. In 1562 the distinguished French Huguenot, Coligny, obtained from the French crown permission to plant a colony of Huguenots in the New World. A first attempt was made on the coast of Florida, near its northern limit, and abandoned. A second was undertaken under the same auspices, in 1564, but, in its tragical termination, furnishes one of the darkest passages in colonial history. The site chosen was at the mouth of the St. John's River. Though the promoters of the colony professed religious motives, the colonists included desperate men, who engaged in piracy against the Spaniards. Jacques de Soria, a Huguenot pirate from La Rochelle, captured a vessel with forty Jesuit priests, who were on their way to act as missionaries to the Indians, and murdered them all, peaceful men though they were.

Spanish jealousy was aroused. An expedition under Pedro Melendez de Aviles was fitted out for the colonization of Florida. Melendez landed at St. Augustine, so named by him, claimed the continent for the crown of Spain, and laid the foundation of the city in 1565. From St. Augustine, Melendez marched through the forests to the French colony on the St. John's. The garrison was surprised, and in the massacre which followed nine hundred persons are said to have been murdered, though Spanish accounts give a less number. In 1567 Dominic de Gourges, a native of Gascony, fitted out an expedition to avenge the fall of the French colony. He surprised the Spaniards who had erected forts on the site of the Huguenot settlement, hanged his prisoners, and departed. The French Government disowned the expedition, and gave up all claim to Florida.

The English had, in the time of Henry VIII., sent out Sebastian Cabot, who had discovered New-foundland. Their first notion was, that as Magellan had found a passage to India by the south-west, and Vasco de Gama by the south-east, they would try what could be done by the north. In the time of Edward VI., in 1553, Sir Hugh Willoughby had tried a passage to the north-east, but had been overtaken by the winter, and was found frozen to death, with all his crew, on the pitiless rocks of Russian Lapland.

In this same year a company of merchant adventurers was formed in England, both for discovery and for traffic. They fitted out various ships, and among their most noted members were two Devonshire brothers, William and John Hawkins, sons of a captain who had once traded with Brazil. Their first voyages were made for the purpose of catching Negroes on the coast of Guinea, to sell to the Spaniards in Hispaniola. Thus began that share in the slave trade which remained the shame of England for two centuries, but which was in those days thought no crime, as it was held that wild savage natives might be brought into bondage, if they were taught Christianity. Such voyages opened to John Hawkins and his comrade, Francis Drake, the way to what was then called the Spanish Main. After having made four voyages as a slave-trader, Drake resolved to make his fifth as a plunderer.

There was, indeed, no war between **Queen** Elizabeth and Philip II., **but they** bitterly hated **one another,** and the English had heard enough of Spanish cruelty to think it a virtuous thing to hunt down a Spaniard. The city of Nombre de Dios, **on** the Isthmus of Panama, was the place where **the** silver and gold collected from Mexico and Peru was received and embarked in heavy vessels, called galleons, to be taken **to** Spain.

In 1572 Drake sailed with two ships, to try to plunder these riches, hoping to surprise this place. However, the Spaniards had been warned, and were on the alert, and the English vessels were beaten off, though not before they had secured a great deal of booty. They entered the Gulf of Darien, taking several treasure ships by the way. Here Francis Drake landed, and climbed a high mountain whence he could see the waters of the Pacific. He made a resolution that on the western ocean he would sail an English ship.

In 1576 Martin Frobisher tried to get into the Pacific by the north-west. His ship, the *Gabriel,* reached a long channel, which leads from Davis's Strait to Hudson's Bay. He called it Frobisher's Strait, which name it still bears. He thought it would certainly lead to the great western sea ; but he lost

his boat and five men, who were taken by the Esqui-
maux, and was forced to come back.   A bit of black
stone which had been picked up on the shore was supposed to be full of gold ; and he made a second voyage
with three ships to penetrate the passage and bring
home more gold.   Of course the passage to the Pacific,
through Hudson's Bay, was never found ; and though
plenty of stone was brought home, no gold was ever
got out of it, and Drake's way of getting the precious
metal by plunder was much preferred.

In 1577 Drake set forth with five ships and one
hundred and sixty-four men to make the circuit of the
earth.   They preyed on all Spanish and Portuguese
ships as before, and thus obtained their stores.   They
crossed toward Brazil, looked into the Rio de la Plata,
then coasted along Patagonia.   There they came to a
gibbet where Magellan had hung some mutineers, and,
strangely enough, Drake had to use this very same
gibbet for the execution of a man named Doughty, who
had been stirring up the crews against him.   After
much prayer for protection the ships safely passed the
Straits of Magellan ; but a storm afterwards blew them
so far south that the voyagers were the first European
navigators who beheld Cape Horn and the Antarctic
Ocean.   One ship was lost, and the others were
separated.   One went back to England, but Drake, in

the *Golden Hind*, went northward up the coast of Chili and Peru. In Callao, the port of Lima, he plundered seventeen vessels.

His notion was to try to enter the north-west passage on the western side, and so come home ; but he found it impossible, on account of sickness among his crew, to get much farther north than California, which he never guessed to be a gold country. And then, striking across the Pacific, he touched at various of the great groups of islands south of Asia, which were mostly claimed by the Portuguese. Then he crossed the Indian Ocean, rounded the Cape of Good Hope, and came safely to England on the 26th of September, 1580, having made one of the most wonderful voyages ever accomplished. Queen Elizabeth at first doubted whether she ought to reward a man who had certainly been a pirate—doing much harm to a king with whom she did not profess to be at war ; but at last she decided that, as every one looked on the Spaniards as fair game, she would go with the stream. So she knighted Drake, dined on board the *Golden Hind*, and had the vessel kept for a show ; while every spirited young man longed to go and fight on the Spanish Main, and the galleons sailed from the West Indies in fear and trembling of the terrible Englishmen.

CHAP XVII.—DISCOVERIES ON THE EASTERN COAST.

1536—1634.

WE have seen how the Portuguese were gradually settling Brazil, and drifting into that portion of South America which projects to the eastward of the longitudinal boundary line between the grants of the Pope to Spain and to Portugal.

When Francisco de Orellana returned to Spain with accounts of the great river of the Amazons, down which he had sailed, he was sent out with four ships and four hundred men to make a settlement and subdue the country. He died on his passage out, and no Spanish footing was made in the land of the Amazons. There were no great kingdoms like Mexico and Peru on the Atlantic coast of South America, only wild Indian tribes with caciques living in little villages. Gold and silver were much harder to obtain, although the great river southward of Brazil had been named by Sebastian Cabot, the Venetian, the Rio de la Plata, or River of Silver, because of a little he obtained from the natives.

In 1534 Don Pedro de Mendoza, in the service of Spain, set forth to make a settlement on this river, and to look for the silver. He began to build a city on a site which he thought so healthy that he named it " Nostra Señora de Buenos Ayres." But the air did not agree with him ; his people could get neither silver nor food ; and in searching vainly for a way of getting across to Peru they came upon an enormous serpent, forty-five feet long, and as thick as a man's body. After four years of misery this settlement was given up, and Mendoza died on his way home.

The city of Buenos Ayres was again occupied, and again deserted. Each governor of the province of the Rio de la Plata strove to find a passage to Peru. But they only succeeded in partly establishing the Spanish power in Paraguay, which settlement was declared to be attached to the vice-royalty of Peru. They founded a city called Asuncion, or Assumption, which is still the capital of Paraguay. Another settlement, with a bishopric, was founded at Tucuman. In this manner, founding settlements and defining their jurisdiction, the Spaniards had traced out nearly all the western coast of South America, claiming the possession.

They had small settlements here and there, wherever there was gold, or silver, or spice to tempt them. Conquest spread southward from Peru, and the city of Valparaiso, or the Vale of Paradise, was founded as the capital of Chili.

That long peninsula which hangs down from the eastern coast of the northern continent, and shuts in the Gulf of Mexico, had first been seen, as long ago as 1512, by Juan Ponce de Leon. This gentleman fancied that in the West Indian Islands there was a fountain, the water of which would make people young again. In sailing in quest of it he came upon this peninsula, which he took for another island. He saw it first on Palm Sunday, which the Spaniards call Pascua Florida, and thus it took the name of Florida. Afterwards parties of Spaniards went slave-catching there, since it was understood that all Caribs or cannibals might be enslaved ; and it was easy to say that all natives they wanted to seize were such. But Florida slaves were sure either to starve themselves to death, or to die of home-sickness. Several attempts were made at forming a colony in Florida, but sickness or war generally destroyed all the settlers. One man, named Cubeca de Vaca, who was made prisoner, became a sort of god to the Floridians, who thought him a child of the sun, worshipped him, and carried him about on their shoulders, in awe and trembling, till he made his escape into Mexico. He tried to teach them the true faith, but did not understand enough of their language. However, at last a settlement was made in Florida, but the Spaniards never spread any farther to the northward, partly because it was too cold for them, and partly because there was no promise of gold.

The settlers on the Rio de la Plata and in Paraguay had a different character of natives to deal with. The Araucaninian Indians were desperate warriors, and had a cacique, Carpolican, who made a resistance so brave that a poem was written on him. Nor have these Indians ever been entirely subdued ; they remain still free, under their own government.

The Bishop of Tucuman invited the Jesuit priests to assist in the conversion of Paraguay. This order was at that time composed of the most ardent of missionaries among the Europeans, and eight of the Fathers came out, mostly Spaniards and Italians, but one Scotch by birth. They had learned something by the failure of some missionaries, and by the success of Las Casas and the Dominicans with certain wild tribes in Mexico, in making the Land of War the Land of Peace. The plan of the Jesuits was to go about in pairs, after having learned the Indian language, and

make little settlements with churches and schools, a
dwelling for the cacique close to the priest, and cot-
tages and gardens for the Indians, who were to be
trained in cultivating their land, and in all good
Christian knowledge.   If Spaniards came amongst
them they were to be civilly treated, but sent away
after a day or two, and no one was to be allowed to
strike an Indian.   Their watchword was to be : " Love
one another, even as Christ hath loved you."

They wonderfully fulfilled it.   Whatever were the
errors of the Jesuits at home, their work among the
Indians of Paraguay was carried out in the spirit of
peace and love.   Many villages sprang up, which made
a perfect garden of the country round the Rivers
Paraguay and Uruguay.   The whole community
assembled for mass in the church in the morning,
then the youths were taken out to work in the common
fields, and the children sent to school.   The men
worked in their gardens at home, but there was a
public store of crops from the common land, whence
the sick and the widows were maintained.   The Jesuit
Father of the village took all care and thought on himself, and the gentle, docile people lived happily under
him, almost without a vice, in simple obedience.   The
only fault in the system seems to have been that it did
not train the Indians to think or act for themselves,

but kept them as children all their lives, generation after generation dependent on a foreign order of priests. Yet perhaps this was because few Indians were capable of being highly trained, there being, for the most part, a want of substance in their character.

The Jesuits were highly educated men, and made many discoveries in the new country, which was most fertile in their hands. Maize or Indian corn, potatoes, cotton, and tobacco were already cultivated and used in America. Turkeys (called, in French, dinde), were first found in Mexico; and several important plants, for use or medicine, were now made available, in especial caoutchouc, or Indian rubber, and chinchona, or quinine—the great remedy for ague or marsh fever. This last was long known as Jesuit's bark.

CHAP. XVIII.—ENGLISH SAILORS ON THE SPANISH MAIN.

1584—1596.

WHILE Francis Drake was on his voyage round the world, another Devonshire man, Sir Humphrey Gilbert, proposed to found a settlement in Newfoundland, whence the Spaniards might be more effectually harassed. He made the attempt twice, but, though he was allowed to read out to an assemblage of tradesmen and fishermen the royal commission giving him possession of the territory, both times failed. Newfoundland was not fit for a set of men entirely inexperienced in guarding against the cold and hunger of that barren, fog-bound coast and terrible climate, and Gilbert was forced to sail on his return, in 1584, with only two ships. A storm overtook them, and the last the other ship heard of him was his voice shouting through the tempest: " Do not fear, God is as near by water as by land."

The scheme was taken up by his half-brother,

SIR HUMPHREY GILBERT READING HIS COMMISSION.

Walter Raleigh, who thought that it was useless to settle in the cold north, but that it would repay the colonists to make a home on that temperate coast which the French had surveyed. In 1584, then, he sent out a party to the land bordering on Carolina—a tract which still preserves the name which originated with the Huguenots. Raleigh named his grant Virginia, in honour of the virgin Queen, Elizabeth. Sir Richard Grenville took out one hundred and eight settlers, whom he landed on the Island of Roanoke, on the coast of Carolina, leaving Sir Ralph Lane as their governor. They mapped out a city which was to be called Raleigh, and built a fort and some dwellings. But, instead of saving grain, and planting fields, these foolish settlers roamed about in search of mines, and quarrelled with the Indians. In consequence, when, a year later, Sir Francis Drake touched there to see how they were getting on, he found them nearly starved, and harassed on all sides by the Indians, and, to save their lives, they could only be carried home. A few days after their departure a ship despatched by Raleigh with provisions arrived, but had only to take the cargo back to England. And yet a few days later Sir Richard Grenville came with three ships, and, finding the island deserted, left fifteen men to garrison the fort, and sailed away. Lane had found the Indians in the habit of rolling up certain leaves and smoking them. He brought some home and gave them to Raleigh, and this was the first introduction of tobacco into England. The root called by the Indians *batah* was also brought home, and first grown on Raleigh's estate in Ireland, under the name of potato, and thus first made known in Europe.

In that same year, 1586, Raleigh sent out another party, who had to fight their way with the Indians before they could land. The new-comers found the fort on Roanoke in ruins, and nothing of the garrison of fifteen men but their bones. Nevertheless there were some friendly Indians, one of whom was christened and honoured with the title of Lord of Roanoke. The governor of this new colony was named John White. With him came out his daughter and her husband, a gentleman named Dare. In about a month after the arrival at Roanoke Mrs. Dare bore a daughter, who was christened Virginia. Virginia was the first white child born in North America; but her fate is unknown, for while her grandfather went home to England for supplies, the whole colony vanished. They were probably taken captive by the Indians, for none of them were ever seen again. The Island of Roanoke is now almost uninhabited, but the traces of the fort may still be found.

By this time there was open war between England and Spain, and the bold English sailors went as the Queen's officers instead of as adventurers. Moreover, the whole of South America was claimed by Spain, for the direct line of kings of Portugal had failed, and Philip II. of Spain had claimed the kingdom and all its colonies, in right of his mother, a Portuguese princess. Brazil was therefore in his hands, and his strength and dominion seemed immense, but the English seamen knew better, and said he was only a Colossus stuffed with clouts.

In 1586 Sir Francis Drake and Martin Frobisher, with twenty-five ships, and two thousand three hundred men, set sail for the West Indies. They touched at Dominica, where the natives were as yet undisturbed, and at St. Christopher's, which was uninhabited; and then they fell on Hispaniola, the oldest settlement of all, and full of riches. They seized the gates of San Domingo, got into the citadel, and called on the Spaniards to ransom their city, declaring that they would every day hang several prisoners, and burn a part of the city, till the governor came to terms. At last £7,000 was paid them, large stores of provisions were furnished, and they sailed away, having held the place thirty days. They had been amused by finding on the wall of the palace a painting of a horse leaping off the globe, with the inscription "The world is not enough."

Next, in like manner, they fell upon Carthagena, on the mainland, and after hard fighting gained the harbour ; and did what they called " scorching," as at San Domingo, every day, till they obtained a still larger ransom.   But there was a bad fever among them, and their wounded died of lock-jaw, so they sailed north, into a more temperate climate, to see after the Virginian settlement, taking the ships of the Spaniards by the way, and harrying their towns in Florida.   They found the party at Roanoke in a sad state—as has previously been mentioned—by their own fault.

Plunder of the galleons as they came to Spain, and of the Spanish settlements on the coast, was thought the most honourable mode of serving the Queen and making one's own fortune ; and, of course, the Spaniards thought of the English pretty much as the old Saxons thought of the Danish sea-kings, as mere sea-robbers. On each side there were grievous cruelties, for Roman Catholics thought the English heretics, and worthy to be hanged or burnt, and the English were full of bitter, savage revenge.

When in 1580 the King of Spain claimed the crown of Portugal and its colonies, there was some resistance, but eventually, for sixty years, all the Christian portion of South America acknowledged fealty to the crown of Spain. But the colonies received little protection from that Government, while they were invaded and attacked by its enemies. The Portuguese were even raided by their Spanish neighbours, to reduce them to a submission for which they could hardly understand the reason. The Indians in Brazil were faithful allies of the Portuguese settlers; and in 1594, a party of Indians armed only with arrows, and led by a Jesuit Father, repelled the landing of a Spanish privateering expedition. In 1592, they cut off a plundering party of twenty-five men, sent inland by an English adventurer, Thomas Cavendish. Four years later, Sir James Lancaster, in command of a squadron fitted out by the London merchants, took numerous prizes on the coast of Brazil. France was at this time also at war with Spain, and engaged in raiding upon the Portuguese as Spanish colonies.

Sir James Lancaster, joined by five French privateers, descended upon Recife, now called Pernambuco. He took possession of the fort, and seized all the treasure in the place. The Portuguese colonists made great rafts, set them on fire, and sent them down one of the rivers at the mouth of which Pernambuco stands, in hopes of destroying the English

fleet. But Lancaster's brave men, with their weapons
and all about them wrapped in wet clothes, grappled
the rafts and sent them safely out to sea. At last
the eleven vessels left Pernambuco, loaded with spoil
of treasure, timber, spices, and the like, which was
fairly shared among them. The squadron returned
home without disaster, Lancaster giving thanks as
having done a good work under Heaven's blessing.

Sir John Hawkins and Sir Francis Drake had also
gone on a plundering expedition to the islands, with
twenty-seven ships, though Hawkins was then seventy
years old. They did much harm to the Spaniards,
but without gaining much themselves, and the two
leaders grew angry and quarrelled. After some hot
words with Drake, Hawkins fell ill and died at sea,
near the island of Porto Rico, in November, 1595.
Drake attacked the place, was repulsed, sailed away;
and, after plundering several settlements, went to
Nombre de Dios, on the Isthmus of Darien, whence
the fleet was driven away by the breaking out of a
deadly disease. Drake was among the victims, and
died just as his fleet anchored at Porto Bello, on the
coast of New Granada, December 27, 1595. His
death is said to have been caused as much by grief
and disappointment as by disease.

CHAP. XIX.—THE FIRST NORTHERN COLONIES.

1604—1618.

AFTER the deaths of Drake and Hawkins there were no more great plundering expeditions. The minds of the Europeans were, however, still possessed with the notion of a great golden city, which they called El Dorado, somewhere in the interior of South America, to be reached from the River Orinoco. Troughs and boxes were thought to be made of gold there, and the people were said to powder themselves with gold dust. Most likely these notions grew from the reports which the natives of the eastern coast made of the wealth of Peru. Sir Walter Raleigh believed in them, and in 1595 made an attempt to find his way to El Dorado, taking the island of Trinidad, at the mouth of the Orinoco, and making its governor prisoner. He forced his way up the river as far as he could in boats, making friends with the Indians, but finding nothing but dense forests full of wonderful plants and birds, and picking up specimens of ore. He had seen no golden city, but he still believed that through Guiana was the way to overflowing wealth.

Elizabeth died in 1603, and James I., who succeeded her, made peace with the Spaniards, and discontinued all attacks on them. English sailors did not, however, leave off their robberies of Spanish ships and settlements, and there were men from other nations who joined them. The French Huguenots had, for many years past, a piratical fleet at sea, and now that Henry IV. had won his crown, he wished much to favour seamanship, and there were numerous privateers sailing under the French flag. The Dutch who had revolted from Philip II. of Spain, and furnished some of the best seamen in Europe, were resolved on wresting from Spain some of her western riches. The Spaniards called all these enemies Boucanieros, from *bouc*, beef cut in strips, and smoked, which was their usual food when they camped on shore. As these buccaneers soon came to consist of the worst, fiercest, and most cruel men of all nations, they were a horrible scourge to the whole Spanish Main. They had stations for their ships at the Keys, or little uninhabited islands in the West Indies, where they kept their treasures, and whence they went out to seize

merchant ships, or burn villages on the land. The
crews of their prizes were slain, or driven overboard,
and such vessels as were not needed were sunk.

However, James I. was permitting more peaceful
and reputable settlements. A new London company
and a Plymouth company wished to make another
attempt at North America, and he gave them a charter,
allowing them to make laws, and appoint officers.
There were to be two settlements — the London
company had Maine, the Plymouth company Virginia ;
and a space of a hundred miles was to be kept clear
between them to prevent quarrelling. The first colonists in Maine soon abandoned the settlement, and did
little more than give the name which the district has
retained. The Virginian colony fared better ; and, after
a period of suffering and dissension, was established
securely under Sir Thomas Dale, who assumed the
government in 1611. The laws were very severe,
being, in fact, a code of martial law ; but so many
attempts at settlement had failed from unruliness and
improvidence, that perhaps severity was necessary.
So a man was liable to death if he killed any cattle,
even his own, without leave from the governor ; a
baker who cheated had his ears cut off ; a laundress
who stole linen was flogged. The chief settlement of
Virginia was Jamestown ; not much of a town, for

the houses were of rough timber, with seats of trunks of trees, and the church was an awning stretched between the trees, with a bar of wood nailed between two trees for a pulpit. The settlers cleared away the trees, grew maize for themselves and tobacco to send to England, and were called planters.

The famous Captain John Smith was one of the settlers in Virginia. His was a life of adventure, by land and sea. He had served as a soldier of fortune in different lands ; and as a maritime discoverer had traced the coast of North America up to Maine, and gave the country the name of New England. His services were invaluable to the colony of Virginia, and he was sent on expeditions for forage and discovery among the Indians. On one of these expeditions he was made prisoner by the Indian chief, Powhatan. He was tied to a tree, and was about to be made a mark for the Indian tomahawks, or hatchets, when the chief's young daughter, Pocahontas, threw herself between Smith and the tomahawk, and begged for his life. He was spared, and on his return to the colony, the Indians made friends with the planters, and brought them skins and maize in exchange for red cloths and other articles. Among the bearers of these native commodities Pocahontas frequently came with her basket. These visits resulted in her baptism and

PRESENTATION OF POCAHONTAS.

marriage to a man named John Rolfe, who took her to England. There the red-skinned woman is said to have carried herself like a princess. After being the fashion for a time, it is also said that she met with many troubles, fell into great poverty, and died at the early age of twenty-one. She bore to her husband one son, who returned to Virginia, where proud families trace their descent from the Indian princess.

The English claimed the Caribee, or Cannibal Isles, which the slave-hunting Spaniards had nearly emptied of people ; and in 1608 the Earl of Carlisle obtained from James I. a grant of the Island of Barbadoes. It had been discovered by the Portuguese, and was called the island of the Barbadoes, or bearded natives, but these had all perished. Barbadoes was the first English West Indian settlement.

In 1617 Sir Walter Raleigh, then a prisoner in the Tower, persuaded James I. to let him sail to Guiana, the second time, to find his way to the Golden City, or at least a gold mine. He had twelve ships, and his hopes were high. He was welcomed by the Indians, whom he had made friends with before, but he was an old and broken man. His health was not equal to the toil of exploring these unwholesome rivers, and he had to send a party forward with his son. However, the Spaniards had formed settlements on the way to the supposed gold mines. There was peace between England and Spain, but Raleigh had grown up when peace at home meant warfare on the Spanish Main. The Spanish town of St. Thomas, on the River Orinoco, was attacked and won ; but Raleigh's son was killed, and the party had soon to return to England. James I., angered at the attack on the Spaniards, executed Raleigh ; not for that, but on the former charge of treason, under which he was in prison when released to make this unfortunate expedition. So died the last of Queen Elizabeth's great seamen and foes to the Spaniard.

The great French king, Henry IV., was bent on forming colonies in that further north which Cartier had surveyed. It is said that the Spaniards had looked at the place, saw no gold there, and said, "*aca nada*"— "here is nothing"—whence it was called Canada. But as Canada is an Indian word for a great plain, this is more likely to be the meaning of the name ; and the French called it *Acadie.*

Under a leader, whose name still appertains to Lake Champlain, the country was explored, and found to be very fertile, though the winters were far colder than in the same latitudes in Europe. Large numbers of French came out, and settled on both banks of the River St. Lawrence. The city of Quebec was founded in 1608, and the French settlers were content to live as farmers, not seeking mines, but becoming very prosperous. They behaved better to the Indians than did either the Spaniards or the English. The clergy who came out with them made many converts, since the Red Indians had little actual misbelief, and were ready to hear more about the "Great Spirit" from the "Black Robes," as they called the French priests and friars.

The Dutch were making their attempts likewise. In 1609 they hired a gallant English sailor, named Henry Hudson, who had already made two voyages to try to find the north-west passage. He tried again, and went surveying and touching here and there, from Greenland to Virginia. Thence, turning northward, he put in at the mouth of that beautiful wide river which still bears his name, and was delighted, as well he might be, with its lovely shores, and the friendly Indians, who came in bark canoes, and exchanged grapes, pumpkins and furs for knives and beads. When the river became too shallow for his ship he sent a boat on a little further, and then turned back, having named Staten Island after the States of Holland. His next voyage was again in search of the north-west passage. He entered that great watery opening now called Hudson's Bay, but his men, frightened and angry, rose against him, put him in a boat, tied hand and foot, with his son and one or two more, and left him to perish in the ice.

After this another Dutch expedition, under Adrian Blok, or Block, in 1614, explored both the Hudson and the Connecticut Rivers. He passed through Long Island Sound, and gave the name to Block Island. He lost his ships, and spent the winter on Manhattan Island, where the city of New York now stands. There he built a vessel, which he named the *Unrest.* Manhattan Island was bought of the Indians by the Dutch for beads worth £24, and a settlement was begun called New Amsterdam. Tracts were taken up in the interior by men called Patroons, or patrons, a title conveying baronial dignity. They came out each with fifty colonists, with leave to buy sixteen miles of land from the Indians, and to import Negroes from Guinea to work for them. Slaves had also begun to be used in Virginia to attend to the tobacco plantations, which the colonists would keep to a great extent; though wise men warned them that they would wear out the soil.

The Dutch cared more for the East than the West Indies. It was in trying to find the south-western passage without passing through the Magellan Straits, that, in 1615, Captain Schouten, of the Dutch city of

Hoorn, passed outside of the island group of Tierra del Fuego, and named another Staten Island. The *Hoorn* was wrecked, but she left her name to the southernmost point of the southernmost island. Her captain was considered a buccaneer, because he had disobeyed the Dutch East India Company, and his remaining ship was taken from him and forfeited when he arrived at the Dutch settlements in India. Five nations now had settlements in America—Spain, Portugal, England, France, and Holland.

CHAP. XX.—THE PILGRIM FATHERS.

1620—1637.

KING JAMES I. was resolved that in England strong Church principles should be carried out, and that religious services should closely keep to the Prayer Book, and that every one should attend them. There were fines and punishments for those who refused. Now ever since the Reformation there had been persons who wanted to do away with all forms that they fancied were like those of the Roman Catholics ; and rather than conform to the Prayer Book rules they fled to Holland. When these fugitives numbered about one thousand they resolved, instead of living as exiles among foreigners, to go out to the New World, and make a home there. They sent to the king to beg for a charter by which to govern themselves, and for a grant of land. James would not give them a charter, but he said they might have the land if they behaved well and molested no one else.

So in 1620 one hundred and twenty were told off to

LANDING OF MARY CHILTON.

go and prepare the way. They sailed from Delft in two ships, the *Mayflower* and the *Speedwell*, touching at the old English Plymouth; but the last-named vessel proved unseaworthy, and only the *Mayflower* made the voyage with about one hundred passengers, among whom Miles Standish was the most noted. They meant to have gone to the beautiful Hudson River, but missing that, they came to a harbour which they named Plymouth, after the port they had last left. The day of their landing was the 22nd of December, and a young girl, named Mary Chilton, was the first to step on the new land. Then they built one great log-house, where all might sleep, and divided it in partitions for the nineteen families. A shed was built for a store-house, and another house for the sick. They built a fort with a flat roof and battlements, on which four cannon were mounted. It served also for a "meeting-house," and was fitted accordingly for religious worship. William Brewster was their Elder; and as no clergyman came out with the first colonists for several years, he consented to preach, but never administered the sacraments. They sowed corn, but till it grew they had to live by hunting and fishing, obtaining deer, turkey, eels, lobsters, and shell fish; and often they suffered grievously from hunger, for cattle and farm stock were not imported into the colony till four years later.   Half of the colony died during the winter.   The graves were levelled with the ground, and in the spring sown with quick-growing grass, lest the Indians should see how many were lost.   The *Mayflower* returned the next year, bringing supplies and more settlers, and they began to get their heads above water.

Scattered settlements were made at different points in the district bearing the Indian name of Massachusetts, or " Blue Hills."   Among the most important of these was the settlement at Naumkeag, made by Captain John Endicot in 1628.   He acted in the interest of certain gentlemen in England, who were organizing a company.   Prior settlers objected at first to the assumption of government by Endicot, but the reconciliation of the difficulty, which was " quietly composed," induced these Bible-studying Puritans to call their settlement *Salem*, the " city of peace."   In 1629 a charter was granted by Charles I. to " The Governor and Company of the Massachusetts Bay in New England."   In June of that year the *Mayflower* was again on the coast with four vessels more, bringing to Salem colonists sent out by " The Governor and Company."   Seventeen vessels sent out by this company landed fifteen hundred persons in the colony. They sailed at different times, and all arrived safely at Salem and Charlestown in the year 1630.

Boston, so named from Boston in Lincolnshire, became the capital. These colonists were Puritans like those at Plymouth, but they came direct from England and not from Holland. Their governor was John Winthrop, and very strict and stern were the laws, both in Plymouth and Massachusetts. The strictest possible rules were applied, and every effort was made to enforce them. Tradition exaggerates the severity of these rules, but the following are specimens. People who stayed away from public worship were fined, and if they remained away for a month together were put in the stocks, or in a wooden cage. Light, foolish conduct was punished by the sentence to stand upon a stool in "meeting" with a label pinned about the neck. A scolding woman's tongue was fixed in a cleft stick, or else she was ducked. Worse crimes were met by whipping or the pillory, and many by death. It was needful, above all, to be watchful and vigilant, for the Indians could not but look with dread and suspicion on the white men who came to spoil their hunting grounds. They were ready to fall on the intruders on any provocation.

The settlement in Virginia felt this when their friend Powhatan died in 1618. All through his time the Indians had come and gone freely among the colonists, selling and buying, and the English clergy-

men who had come out had many plans for teaching
and converting the Indian children. But in 1622 a
planter quarrelled with a chief and was killed. His
servants avenged his death by killing the Indian, and
the tribe resolved on vengeance. The whole of the
colonists, between two and three thousand in number,
were to have been slain by the Indians in one night;
but happily one man who had been converted gave
warning, and there was time to arm and prepare. As
many as two hundred and fifty English were killed,
but the others were saved, though for a long time they
had to keep a most anxious watch, and the outlying
farms had to be given up. In 1625, just before his
death, King James called in the charter, and took
Virginia under his own government. The settlements were spreading very fast. King Charles made
many grants to persons as governors. Lord Baltimore was one of these. He settled the country
on the Chesapeake Bay, north-east of Virginia, and
named it Maryland, after Queen Henrietta Maria, who
was usually called Mary in England. He was a
Roman Catholic, and seems to have intended Maryland for a refuge for English Roman Catholics, as
Plymouth and Massachusetts Bay were for Puritans.
But toleration and equality were secured in Maryland
for all Christians. Maine was granted to Sir

Ferdinand Gorges, and is said to have been named after the Queen's French Duchy. A small Swedish settlement was begun on the Delaware.

There came to Massachusetts in 1631 a young Welsh dissenting minister, named Roger Williams. He thought the strict laws regulating doctrine and worship too narrow, and that law should only deal with crimes, not with opinion. These views were deemed very dangerous, and Williams was several times cited to appear before the magistrates ; and at last the General Court or Legislature of the colony of Massachusetts pronounced against him the sentence of exile for teaching doctrines which tended "to subvert the fundamental state and government." It was resolved to send him to England in a ship then just ready to sail. But he made his escape, and in January, 1636, fled on foot from his house in Salem, and for fourteen weeks wandered in the forests before he reached the Plymouth colony. There he got together a few friends, and was about to make a settlement. But Governor Winthrop of Massachusetts, who thought him ill-treated, sent him help, and wrote to him, advising him to make a new home on Narragansett Bay outside the claims of other colonies. He embarked with five companions in a canoe in June, 1636, dropped down the Blackstone River, and landed at the head of Narragansett Bay, where he founded the city called Providence. He obtained from Canonicus and Miantonomoh, Narragansett chiefs, a large grant of land, with the islands in the bay, the largest of which he called Rhode Island, and named his settlement Rhode Island and Providence Plantation. He made his colony a refuge for all those whose opinions had caused them to be exiled. It used to be said that whoever had lost his religion would find it in some village in Rhode Island. He was a generous man, and when he found that a warlike tribe of Indians, called Pequods, were trying to persuade his friends, the Narragansetts, to unite with them in falling upon the Massachusetts settlers, he went to the chiefs at the peril of his life, and persuaded them to let the Pequods stand alone. Both Narragansetts and Mohicans, the two chief Indian tribes, became allies of England, but the Pequods remained at enmity, burning homesteads and torturing travellers. The settlement of Connecticut had been commenced, and the men of that colony, in 1637, united with Massachusetts, made war upon the Pequods, burned their fort in a night attack with six hundred people in it. The whole tribe were hunted down like wild beasts till most were slain—women, children, and all. Their country was laid waste, and the few survivors were made slaves.

CHAP. XXI.—MISSIONARIES IN NORTH AMERICA.

1626—1655.

THERE was some endeavour at converting the Indians. It had begun in Acadie, the French settlement. In 1626 three Jesuit Fathers went to Quebec, intending to carry the faith to the Huron Indians. There was, however, war between England and France, and therefore between their colonies. Only two years after the Jesuits had come out, Quebec was taken by the English, under Sir David Kirk, and the French Governor-General, Champlain, and all the French inhabitants, were sent home.

After peace was made in 1632, Quebec was restored to the French, and two priests, called Le Jeune and La Moue, came back, and going to a hovel in the woods, set themselves to learn the language of the Algonquin Indians. The cold in the winter was frightful, the rivers were frozen over, and water froze at night close before the fire. These patient priests not only endured all this, but went about in Indian camps, amid all the filth, the noise, the smoke, the dogs, and the savagery, learning the Indians' ways of thinking and trying to win them over to listen to Christian teaching.

Five more clergy then came out, and three of them, of whom Jean de Brébeuf was the chief, went out on a mission to the Hurons, who had come in their canoes to confer with Champlain, at Quebec. The French governor committed the Fathers to the chief, and bade him take care of them. At first they found that the Indians resorted to them only as healers of the sick and owners of strange and wonderful things, such as a watch and a compass; but gradually the nobler spirits were gained one by one, and large numbers came in after them. The Jesuits did not attempt too much civilization, or try to make these wild men live like Europeans; but they only received such converts as would give up scalp-hunting, murder, and cannibalism, and would content themselves with only one wife. No one who had not some real knowledge of the faith, except little children, was baptised. One favourite resort for baptism was the lovely little lake called by the Indians Horicon, by the missionaries St. Sacrament, and now known as Lake George.

Father Brébeuf translated into the Huron language

JESUIT MISSIONARIES AT WORK.

a catechism for the converts. About this time arose a Protestant Missionary, John Eliot, who came out from England in 1631, and became minister of the church in Roxbury, near Boston, in the following year. About thirty years old at the time of his arrival, he lived to fourscore and seven. Very soon after his settlement in Roxbury, he conceived a strong passion for Christianizing the Indians. The venerable Dr. Cotton Mather, his junior and survivor, says of him : " The remarkable zeal of the Romish missionaries, compassing sea and land that they might make proselytes, made his devout soul think of it with a further disdain that we should come any whit behind in our care to evangelize the Indians." The Pequod war, or massacre (1637), in which " a nation disappeared from the family of man," strengthened his purpose and quickened his zeal. Nearly fifty years of his life was given to this good work. In New England he is spoken of to this day as the " Apostle to the Indians." Edward Everett, the New England scholar, statesman, and orator thus speaks of him: " The Apostle—and truly I know not who, since Peter and Paul, better deserves that name."

Father Brébeuf, as noted above, translated a catechism for his converts. The Apostle Eliot translated, first, the Ten Commandments, and a selection of texts;

next, the New Testament, published in 1661; then, in
1663, a grammar of the language of the Massachusetts
Indians, and a translation of the whole Bible. The
Indian title of the book may serve for an exercise in
pronunciation. It is " Mamusse Wunneetupamatamwe
Up-Biblum God Naneeswe Nuk kone Testament kah
wonk Wusku Testament." A new edition was published in Boston in 1822, with notes and an introduction by two eminent American experts in the Indian
languages, Du Ponceau and Dr. J. Pickering. Eliot's
Bible was originally published at Cambridge, Massachusetts. He translated also Baxter's "Serious Call,"
and several other devotional works, and a catechism ;
and he made an Indian metrical version of the Psalms.
Most curious of all, he wrote " The Logic Primer for
the use of Indians." The use of this is, however,
apparent when we read that to Haward College, in
Cambridge, founded in 1636, there was annexed a
building sufficient to accommodate twenty Indian
students. Several schools were established at different
points, and the Indian college was designed for the
education of Indian preachers. There were at one
time four and twenty Indian ministers of the gospel,
besides several white missionaries in Massachusetts,
who preached in the Indian tongue.

Eliot fully believed that the devil was the Red man's

master, and the " Great Spirit " that they worshipped.
To prepare himself for their conversion, he spent
nearly fourteen years before he ventured in 1646 to
preach to the Narragansetts the first sermon to them
in their own tongue. The number of towns of " praying Indians " grew up, by the year 1674, to fourteen,
and over these Eliot seems to have presided, in a way,
as bishop, without the title. The principal Indian
town was Natick, on the Charles River, which Eliot
tried to rule by a constitution as like that of the
Israelites under Moses as he could make it, and where
he was gradually taming and civilizing the natives,
and making them good men. He received some
small aid from England, had influential supporters in
the colony, and the sympathy of the best of the settlers
was with him. But the Indian chiefs, with few exceptions, and their " medicine men " or priests, were his
determined enemies, and only their fear of the English
preserved his life. As to the converts themselves,
they were under a ban. The Indians drove out from
their society all who favoured Christianity, and put
them to death when it could be done secretly or safely.
But for the dread of their protectors, the English,
all the converts would have been murdered. The
colonists could not but live in dread of such trouble-
some neighbours, and if to some of them a "praying

Indian " was only an Indian after all, it is not to be
wondered at. What farther became of the Apostle
Eliot's efforts will be noted in a future chapter. We
have anticipated events somewhat, in order to give a
concise view of his labours and his character. And it
may be proper here to remark that English-speaking
people have not relaxed their efforts—subject of course
to unhappy interruptions—to Christianize the Indians.
Christians of all names are at work among those who
remain, both in the British dominion and in the United
States. As we have spoken of translations, it is due
to the Chief Brant of the Mohawks, who figured in the
last century, to say that he translated the Book of
Common Prayer and St. Mark's Gospel into his native
language. The mission and Bible presses of to-day
issue Bibles and religious publications in the Indian
languages, and there is at least one missionary paper
published in English and Indian at one of the western
missionary stations.

Alas, Dutch emulation of the Jesuits took a different
form from that of the Apostle Eliot. Under Philip II.
of Spain, Holland had been so cruelly treated by the
Roman Catholic Church, that her sons revenged themselves on priests and Spaniards wherever they found
them, even if engaged in the most pious and innocent
work. At the Dutch settlements on the River Hudson

fire-arms were freely furnished to the Iroquois, a fierce
and warlike tribe, who bitterly hated the Hurons and
Algonquins, the Indian allies, or subjects of the
Catholic French. The Iroquois roamed about the
banks of the St. Lawrence, and seized a large party
of Christian Indians, with two French priests. The
tortures they made them suffer were beyond all
measure, and cannot be dwelt upon. One priest,
Goupil, was killed. The other, Isaac Jogues by name,
escaped, though one mass of scars, his fingers gnawed
off by dogs and men, and his left thumb sawn off with
a clam shell. He came back at last to France, and
the Queen, Anne of Austria, kissed these hands with
deep reverence. The Iroquois had sworn to root out
the nation of the Hurons. No Frenchman was safe
outside the walls of Quebec and the towns of Montreal
and Three Rivers. Yet Isaac Jogues went back again
to his post, and there he was taken again by the Iroquois ; and, after having strips of flesh cut from his arms
and back, was murdered at last with a hatchet by an
Indian who, two years later, came and begged for
baptism. The whole Huron country was devastated,
the Christians were hunted down, shot, or burnt.
Those taken were tortured in the most frightful ways,
especially all the " Black Robes." Father Brébeuf
was tied to a stake, with a necklace of red-hot axes

hung on his shoulders. Lamenant was surrounded
with a girdle of pitch-smeared bark, and set fire to.
Boiling water was slowly dropped on their heads, strips
of flesh were cut off their limbs and eaten before their
eyes, but they never flinched. When Brébeuf's breast
was finally torn open, the chiefs flocked to drink the
blood of so valiant an enemy, thinking it would inspire
them with courage. The remnants of the tribe, eight
thousand in number, with a few chiefs, took refuge on
Great Manitoulin Isle, in Lake Huron. There they
were safe from all but starvation in the summer, but
they were horribly attacked as soon as the winter set
in. They were able to keep the island, but were shot
down if they hunted in the woods on the mainland, or
fished in the lake. Hunger and sickness destroyed
those who were not slain, and at last only three hundred Hurons were left alive, when, with their French
clergy, they escaped to Quebec.

Then came the times of the Commonwealth in
England. A good many of the cavaliers or royal party
took refuge in Virginia, where they built stately manor-
houses, and brick churches, in the taste of the seventeenth century.

During the war which Charles I. maintained against
the Parliamentary forces, he commissioned his nephew,
Prince Rupert, to command a regiment of horse.

Prince Rupert, brilliant in attack, was deficient in steadiness and in discretion. He surrendered the city of Bristol to the Parliamentary forces, and was dismissed. He was recalled in 1648, and given command of the royal fleet. With such of the squadron as adhered to the royal cause, and with some of the cavaliers who had served with him on land, he kept afloat until 1651, nearly two years after the death of Charles I. In that year the parliamentary admiral, the famous Blake, defeated him, destroying most of his ships. With the few that remained he made his escape to the West Indies, where, with his brother Maurice, he led the life of a buccaneer. Prince Maurice was drowned in a storm off the Caribee Islands. Prince Rupert eluded the ships sent to capture him by Cromwell, and took refuge in France.

Fleets were despatched by the Parliament, both for the repression of Prince Rupert, and to secure the allegiance of the American colonies. This was effected with little difficulty, Virginia submitting with the rest. Oliver Cromwell, though not formally at war with Spain, resolved to send out a fleet to put an end to the Spanish claim to a sole right in the west. Admiral Penn and General Venables, with about ten thousand men, attacked Hispaniola, but were driven off. However, in May, 1666, they took Jamaica, which has remained an English island ever since, though the first English colonists had to live a life of hard fighting to keep off the Spaniards. The Negro slaves of the expelled Spaniards got into the hills, and lived a wild, outlaw life. They were called Maroons, and were much dreaded for many generations. Port Royal, the capital of Jamaica, was the favourite harbour of the Buccaneers, who used to put in there to sell their prizes, and spend in riot their ill-gotten wealth.

Under Cromwell, magistrates in Ireland and Scotland were directed to seize all idle and disaffected persons they could lay hands on, and ship them off for Jamaica. Before the taking of Jamaica, thousands of prisoners of war had been sent as slaves to the island colonies ; and it is stated that no less than seven thousand Scotch prisoners, after the battle of Worcester, in which Charles II. was defeated, were sent to Barbadoes. That island was wonderfully rich and prosperous, and was sometimes called Little England.

CHAP. XXII.—SPREAD OF FRENCH POWER.

1635—1675.

THE seventeenth century was the period of the power and prosperity of France; first, under Cardinal Richelieu, the minister of Louis XIII., then under Colbert, the minister of Louis XIV. Though Roman Catholic, the French heeded the Pope's grant of the west to Spain no more than did the English and Dutch. They made a settlement in Hispaniola itself, and granted the Isle of St. Christopher's, with three lesser ones, to the Knights of Malta. De Poincy, one of these knights, ruled well and wisely at Basse Terre, in St. Christopher's, for twenty-one years, sitting under a great fig-tree to administer justice, once a week. There were three other French groups of islets, the chief of each cluster being Guadaloupe, Martinique, and Grenada. The great value of the Antilles for growing sugar was beginning to be discovered. The

Moors in Spain had grown the cane, and the Venetians had brought it from the East. But it was the Portuguese who first began to cultivate it in Brazil, where it flourished so much that the Dutch made an attack on that country, and gained Pernambuco and half the coast, in 1624. They held these lands forty years, and would have kept them longer but for the parsimony of the merchants, who would not keep up a proper army, and vexed the people with their exactions.

The sugar cane was soon introduced into the islands, and it flourished, especially in Barbadoes; but the English planters only used the juice to make a refreshing drink, until a Dutchman, coming from Brazil, taught them to make sugar. At the same time De Poincy, in St. Christopher's, was, by study and experiment, greatly improving the art of growing and refining sugar. Coffee was likewise introduced by the French, as soon as it had become the fashion in Europe to drink it. A ship was sent out with young plants, but it was becalmed on the way, and fresh water ran so short that all the coffee trees died except one, which was saved by the person in charge, who suffered agonies of thirst for its sake. It was the parent of all the numerous coffee plantations in Martinique and the rest of the West Indies. Cocoa and ginger were also grown, but, unhappily, none of these industries could be carried on without Negro labour, and there was a constant importation of slaves, stolen from the coast of Africa. Not one of the Christian nations was guiltless in this matter, but the French were said to be kinder slave-masters than the rest.

The group of islands near Florida, called the Tortugas, had been a resort of buccaneers, chiefly of French birth, and these growing tamer came under the parent government. In the island of St. Vincent, one of the Antilles, the Negroes who had run away from their masters were called Maroons, as in Jamaica. They put themselves under French protection, and France began to be one of the strongest powers in the West Indies.

Spain was fast growing weaker. Portugal, in 1640, had shaken off the yoke of Spain, and Brazil followed the example of the mother country. After this the Dutch were turned out of Pernambuco, but allowed to settle in Guiana, on the northern coast of the continent. The French likewise had settlements there, and called their colony Cayenne. Low, swampy, and full of forests, the country was baleful to human life, but very good for rice, sugar, spice, and pepper, and thus valuable to people who did not care at what price they grew rich.

The French never made their colonists pay taxes,

and even lent them money in bad seasons, taking
pains to guard them from pirates. They also greatly
encouraged missions. The Jesuit missionaries in
Canada, who undauntedly prosecuted their work, were
extending their teaching far and wide among the
Indians. The French settlers made friends with
the natives, often married squaws, and were on better
terms with them than any of the other nations. In
1673 Jacques Marquette, a Jesuit missionary, found
his way from the great lakes down the river Wis-
consin to the Mississippi, that mightiest of rivers. He
followed the Mississippi down the mouth of the Arkansas, and then, turning back, took the river Illinois
on his return, having voyaged in canoes nearly three
thousand miles in four months. Following in the
track of Marquette, La Salle, a fur trader, a man of
wonderful courage and endurance, reached the Gulf
of Mexico, by the Mississippi River, in 1682. He
had held the plan in mind even before Marquette's
expedition, and contended for years against opposition and jealousy. He returned to France, bearing
tidings of his discovery, and the country was called
Louisiana, after Louis XIV. The French contem-
plated a chain of forts along the banks of the great
river, to connect Louisiana with Canada. Direct communication was held, by sea, between France and

Louisiana, but the first settlement would appear to have been made, in 1699, at Biloxi. From that point the colonists, starved out, attempted the settlement at New Orleans in 1706. The colony languished. Upon the failure of John Law's great Mississippi scheme, the colony passed, in 1718, into the hands of Bienville, who is considered the founder of New Orleans.

During the prime years of Louis XIV. the English king, Charles II., was led into wars with the Dutch, in which the colonies took part. Indeed, the colonists began their wars in 1664, while the mother countries were at peace. The English declared that they had the first claim to New Netherlands, as the Dutch had called their settlement on the North River, and an English fleet summoned the chief city, then named New Amsterdam, to surrender. The governor, Stuyvesant, whose nickname was Hard-headed Peter, tore the letter to pieces ; but the citizens made him join the bits together, and, thinking it impossible to hold out, forced him to surrender, though he declared he would rather be carried out dead. The Dutch claim was divided into two provinces—one called New York, in honour of James, Duke of York ; the other, New Jersey, in compliment to Sir George Carteret, one of the grantees, sometime governor of the channel island Jersey. The city of New Amsterdam became the city of New York. The Dutch settlers remained, and kept their own language and habits. The titles of land were not disturbed. The Patroons still kept their manors and privileges. Dutch was taught in the schools. To this day many of the oldest families show their parentage by their names, and Dutch words remain in the language.

Among the religious movements which preceded and accompanied and followed the establishment of the Commonwealth in England, was the rise of the " Society of Friends," founded by George Fox. The founder of the society says in his journal, " Justice Bennett, of Derby, was the first that called us Quakers, because I bade them tremble at the name of the Lord." The "Friends" maintained that spiritual worship forbids all sacraments, all forms, and all ordained ministers; they bound themselves to the utmost plainness of speech and of dress, and also to use no weapon, even in self-defence. If, even in England, their innovations in worship and their defiance of laws, now happily obsolete, subjected them to persecution, and even to popular obloquy, it is no wonder that in Massachusetts they fared ill. The Quakers at their beginning were as yet not the logical and quiet people that they became under the teachings of Barclay and of Penn. They were not at first, as they now are, inoffensive to others, asking only peace for themselves. The laws of Massachusetts at the date when the people called Quakers ventured into the colony imposed stern restrictions upon *all* the people, and specially directed the modes of public worship and the tenets of religion as the founders of the colony held their faith and worship. To permit the Quakers and the Baptists to set the magistrates and the laws at defiance would have been, as the Puritans thought, to subvert the State, and release all from obedience. Severe laws were added to those already in existence. The meetings of Quakers and Baptists were forbidden. Their books were burned, and they themselves were flogged. They were banished the colony, and if they returned the law imposed on them the penalty of death. It does not appear that more than four executions took place under this barbarous law. A fifth victim was convicted and sentenced in the year 1659. But the inutility, as well as the cruelty, of persecution began to be acknowledged, and a public opinion, more merciful than the law, required a stay in these wretched proceedings. The condemned man was spared and set at liberty, as were also twenty-seven of his companions. About this time came a royal order from England that the persecution of Quakers and others should cease, and thus the death of the four Quaker martyrs inaugurated toleration. In England, too, the Quakers were winning favour in the people's minds by their earnestness and their simplicity, so unlike the luxurious and ambitious splendour that Louis XIV. of France had made the fashion. William Penn, son of the Admiral Sir William Penn, became a member of the society. Born to wealth, of high connections, with official preferment open before him, he cast in his lot with George Fox; and never did a new sect obtain in one person a more valuable accession. The irritable old sailor beat William as a boy, and turned him out of doors, after he had been expelled from Oxford for consorting with "Friends" and "Non-conformity." Recalling his son, the father tried the experiment of giving him a tour on the continent in distinguished company, among whom the future Quaker was quite a cavalier in dress, pursuits, and manners, and was pronounced on his return a "most modish fine gentleman." He had even a captaincy in the army offered him, which but for his father he would have accepted. But the young man returned to his first love — he became a pronounced Quaker. His father forbade him his house. His mother conveyed to him privately an allowance, and William Penn became an industrious controversial writer and preacher. He was imprisoned nine months in the Tower on a charge of heresy, and his release was obtained at last by the influence of his father with the Duke of York. Again he was arrested, and fined for contempt, the jury failing to convict. His father paid his fine. During his long imprisonment in the Tower his father, respecting the firmness he could not subdue, was his frequent visitor. The old admiral gave him his dying blessing, and William Penn became heir, among other things, of a demand of sixteen thousand pounds against the royal exchequer. Charles II. was very willing to procure the cancelling of this by the gift of a tract in the New World. The king called it *Penn-*Sylvania, though that word, without the prefix, was Penn's choice. A time had now come, with the restoration of the Stewarts, whose sympathies were with the Roman Church, that others desired toleration as well as the Quakers. Penn's broad, tolerant mind entertained sympathy for all, insomuch that some bigots of his time accused him of being a Jesuit. His hopes were directed to a " holy experiment," the establishment of a government " in which perfect toleration should prevent religious persecution, and well-defined civil rights secure to all men equality." A refuge for the Quakers, Pennsylvania was also opened to all who called themselves Christians. Penn's charter was granted in 1681. The first settlers under it sailed in the same year, and on the 8th of November, 1682, Penn landed in Philadelphia, the City of Brotherly Love. The future city was at that time but a collection of wigwams or huts, and there were even dwellers in hollow trees and in caves. The advantages of the site, the character of the laws, and reputation of the founder, built up the city and province. Soon after William Penn's landing he had a conference with the chiefs of the neighbouring tribes, and made friends with them so firmly that for years it was the highest praise an Indian could give to a white man to say he was like Onas, which was Penn's Indian name.

CHAP. XXIII.—INDIAN WARS.

1675—1704.

AFTER the cruel extinction of the Pequod Indians
in 1636, there was generally peace with the
Indians in New England until 1675. During that
period the labours of the missionary Eliot, as noted
in Chapter XXI., had been unremitting. The Indian
towns generally, near Boston, were about fourteen, and
the congregations of "praying Indians" are said to
have been no less than thirty. Several sachems were
amongst them, but the great body of the Indians were
jealous and suspicious of the converts ; and some
powerful tribes resolutely proclaimed their determination to abide by the customs of their fathers. Indeed, Massasoit, the first Sachem with whom the
colonists made treaties, wished to insert a clause that
the English should not attempt to convert the Indians.
Of course this was not assented to. And what a treaty
meant was little understood by the Indians. The

Indians considered themselves allies, the colonists claimed jurisdiction. Individual Indians made sales of land which their sachems disallowed, and the decisions of the English courts only farther aggrieved the natives. The Christian Indians were suspected of furnishing information or repeating rumours to the disadvantage of their race ; and as the hunting grounds of the natives passed from their possession, quarrels were constantly rising between the Indians and the border settlers. An unfortunate condition of mutual exasperation existed, which at last broke out into war.

Massasoit died about the year 1653, at an advanced age, having been, from their first arrival, the friend of the English, though he never would consent to Christianity. About that time his two sons, Wamsutta and Metacom, came to Plymouth, and in open court professed their friendship for the English, and desired that names should be given them. Wamsutta received the name of Alexander, and Metacom was named Philip. By these names they are usually spoken of. Alexander succeeded his father, but upon an accusation that he had made war upon certain Indians, subjects of the English, he was summarily seized by the authorities to be taken to Plymouth to answer the charge. He died within three days of fever, or mortification. This was in 1661.

Philip, the younger brother, succeeded Alexander, and appeared at Plymouth to profess his friendship, and obtain recognition as Sachem of the Wampanoags, that being the chief tribe under his rule. But the indignity—if no worse—that Alexander had suffered deepened the mutual distrust between the Indians and the English till, in 1675, the famous King Philip's war broke out. The colonists had become convinced that Philip was organizing an alliance among the various tribes against them, and preparations for war were reported among the Indians. Conferences between Philip and the Plymouth men were held, in which he promised everything demanded of him. Still the colonists were in a state of great alarm and uncertainty.

Philip was summoned in the spring of 1675 to appear at Plymouth, and submit to an examination in regard to his conduct. And here comes in the name of an Indian who, whether designedly or not, caused the outbreak of hostilities. John Sassamon, belonging to a family of "praying Indians," received the advantages of Eliot's educational provisions, and went from Cambridge to Natick as a teacher. On account of some misdemeanour, it is said, he left Natick. However that may be, he renounced Christianity, and carried the exercise of his gifts over to King Philip, whom he served as a competent secretary. Again he veered in his professions, principles he could have had none, went back to Natick, and gave such evidences of repentance that the venerable Eliot received and employed him. After this, Sassamon, under one pretext and another, visited King Philip's tribe frequently, and reported to the English what he heard and saw, and probably what he imagined. About the time that Philip was cited, Sassamon made one of his visits to the Wampanoags. It was his last. His body was found thrust through a hole in the ice, with his neck broken, and his hat and gun near by, as if he had committed suicide. A jury was empannelled, who decided that he had been murdered. Three prominent Indians were seized, convicted of the murder on the single testimony of another Indian, and forthwith hanged. The young men of their tribe instantly retaliated by an attack on the settlement of Swanzey, which was burned, and in and near it several persons were slain.

Thus began King Philip's war. It lasted over a year, and not one open battle took place. Everywhere in the out-settlements, and near the villages, the savages pounced upon their victims, or shot them from their ambush, and all New England was kept in terror.

The list of disasters and burnings is too long to give ; the result in loss to the colonists was the death of more than six hundred men in the prime of manhood, besides women and children. There was scarcely a family but lost a member. Twelve or thirteen towns were destroyed, and one in every twenty families was burned out of house and home. On the side of the Indians, between two and three thousand were killed or made prisoners, and of the captives, against the protest of Eliot, large numbers were sold as slaves ; in the isles where the tropically born Indians had already been worked to death. Within a month from the beginning of the war Philip was driven from his home at Mount Hope, and from that time he was to the English a nearly invisible enemy, inciting the Indian tribes to sudden but disconnected attacks. He had many narrow escapes ; but at last determined to return to the home of his tribe, a hunted man. His own tribe now began to plot against the ruined chieftain. Once more he narrowly escaped, but his wife and only son were captured. "Now," he said, "my heart breaks, I am ready to die." A few days afterward he was shot by a faithless Indian. His son was sold as a slave in the Bermudas. So ended the last of the Wampanoags ; and with the end of King Philip's war the hostile spirit of the Indians in Massachusetts was quenched.

In Maine, the tidings of the Indian rising in Massachusetts was the signal for war by the Indians upon the settlers. But there was no general rising of the tribes. The sailors of an English ship were guilty of outrages upon the Indians, and they avenged themselves upon the settlers. Among these lawless acts it is recorded that a party of sailors seized a canoe, in which were an Indian woman and child, and, having heard that an Indian baby could swim like a duck, they threw it into the River Saco. The mother dived and rescued it, but it died directly after. The father, a considerable chief, vowed vengeance, and a war, or series of forays along the whole border, commenced, and lasted for nearly three years. The tradition of the early days of Maine are full of Indian horrors. At Norridgewock the Indians attacked a farmhouse, where the men were absent, leaving, unprotected, fifteen women and children. A brave girl, named Tozer, set her back against the door to keep it fast while the others escaped. All saved themselves except the brave girl and two poor little children who could not get over the fence. The Indians cut through the door with their hatchets, and left the poor girl for dead, but her friends found her, and she recovered.

For the most part, the French had suited themselves much better to the Redskins than the English had done. Not only had their clergy done their best as missionaries, but the settlers, with their merry good

humour, had adapted themselves to their habits, and
been adopted into their tribes, and the Governor of
Canada, Count de Frontenac, learned the war dance
and danced with the chiefs. Nova Scotia, with very
indefinite boundaries, was ceded back to France in
1667, and Frenchmen settled far down in Maine.
Baron de Castin had a trading station on the Penobscot
River, at a point where his name is still preserved.
He married the daughter of a sachem, lived like a
sachem, and was obeyed as one. Like the other
traders, he made no scruple of selling arms to the
Indians, and thus the struggle was prolonged and
enmity was stored up against the French. Peace at
last was made by a treaty, in which it was stipulated
that in return for their security the English should pay
an annual quit-rent of a peck of corn for every English
family.

Tribe hatreds were strong among the Indians, and
were increased by their siding with this European
nation or that. The friends of the French, the
Hurons, Abenaquis, and Algonquins were the ancient
foes of the Iroquois, who were formerly called the
Five Nations, because they consisted of five tribes—
the Cayugas, Mohawks, Oneidas, Onandagas, and
Senecas. Another tribe, the Tuscaroras, afterward
joined, and the confederacy is now usually spoken of as

the Six Nations. But as the Tuscaroras did not come
in until 1712, the old name may still be used. The
Five Nations were the friends, first of the Dutch, then of
the English, and both the French and Dutch furnished
the Indians. Even when there was a treaty between
the European powers, their red allies carried on their
own quarrels, and thus involved the whites. In 1687,
the French entrapped a number of Mohawks, and
shipped them off to work as galley slaves in France.
The Mohawks in revenge burned and destroyed
French settlements in Canada. In 1690, war between
France and England having followed the Revolution
of 1688, and the accession of William III., the
French governor of Canada, Frontenac, despatched
three expeditions, in midwinter—one against New
York, one against New Hampshire, and one against
Maine. The white and red allies worked together.
Much mischief was done, including the destruction of
Schenectady. The English colonists invaded Canada
in return, and this kind of warfare went on for years,
till the peace of Ryswick in 1697 put a temporary end
to it. It was conducted with more savagery than one
can bear to think of. The tribes who had listened to
the missionaries were beginning to give up the practice
of torturing their captives ; but the state of things was
so terrible, that a price was paid on both sides for the

head or the scalp of a hostile Indian. Every village
in the north of the colonies lived in constant alarm.
After the treaty of Ryswick there was a lull, but it was
of short duration. In 1702 the English and French
were again at war, and the old enmities of the whites
and Indians were revived. On the last night in
February, 1704, a party of French and Indians came
from Canada to the little town of Deerfield, in the
Massachusetts. The settlers had been warned by the
Mohawk Indians of their danger. A stockade had
been erected and sentinels placed, but they had retired
as morning broke, and the people were waked from
their sleep by the war whoop. The enemy was within
the place, no resistance was possible. Forty-seven
were killed, over a hundred in number were carried off
as prisoners. The village was set on fire, and all the
buildings except one house and the church were
burned. In an hour after sunrise, before the few who
escaped could give the alarm, the stealthy savages
were on their return. The wretched captives had
their clothes taken from them, and no food given
them except nuts and acorns and scraps of dogs' flesh.
The weak who could not keep up with the rest were
killed, except such children as pleased the Indians,
and for them they made sledges. All who could walk
were forced to carry burdens. Such as reached

Canada were sold to the French as slaves, but were kindly treated and allowed to be ransomed by their friends.

Among the captives were John Williams, the pastor of Deerfield, his wife and five children. The wife was killed by the Indians on the way. Mr. Williams was released in 1706, and on his return published "The Redeemed Captive," a narrative of his sad adventures. His wife Eunice deserves a name among the saints. She did not leave her Bible behind, and the wondering savages looked at her as, when they rested, she turned to its pages for consolation. At last she could go no farther, and sank down to die. Her husband cheered her with the hope of the "house not made with hands, eternal in the heavens." She "justified God in what had happened," and commended her five children to God, and their father's care. A tomahawk ended her sufferings, and her husband said : "She rests in peace, in joy unspeakable and full of glory." Of her children three sons became ministers of the Gospel, and one daughter, having been adopted by Christian Indians in Montreal, would not leave them. She married a son of the family, and when years after she visited her friends in Deerfield, it was in an Indian dress, which with Indian customs she never laid aside. She clung to her husband and children. Others of the children of this captivity became hunters and trappers.

In the thirty years after the outbreak of Philip's war the " praying Indians " kept their loyalty to the English. The Government trusted them, but the people were jealous of them, and not quite just or merciful. In the stern Old Testament idea of national policy, the Indians were to them Hivites and Jebusites and children of Ammon. All through the time from the days of Philip, dreadful incidents were happening like those we have been reading; and when there was no public war, which was seldom, there would be private quarrels. All these things were against the conversion of the Indians, but efforts still were made. Services were held for them in the English church at Albany, and Easter Day was a great holiday for the Mohawks who came to the communion. The praying town of Natick was broken up by the war with Philip. The Indians whom the people distrusted were removed to Deer Island in Boston Harbour, where during the winter they suffered piteously. One party was plundered on the way by some English soldiers; was plundered of all they had, even to their poor pewter Communion chalice. After the war they crept back to Natick, and as long as Eliot lived, which was till 1690, they kept their character as "praying Indians." After his death, from the hatred of their own race, and the jealousy of the whites, they faded away.

The sale of "fire water" was not restricted, and it became the Red man's curse as well as the white man's. Under its influence, Indians made sales of land, which, when sober, they denied. The white settlements spoiled the Indian hunting grounds. The Indian was warned off and roughly treated; he retaliated by stealing cattle, if not children, and burning houses. He was shot at like a wild beast, then he fell on the Englishman with the cunning and cruelty of a fiend. So along the borders the Indians were nearly driven off, and those who remained withered away under the influence of dirt, brandy, despair, and a cramped life. This has been going on for two hundred years, and, though it cannot be said to be over yet, the consciousness of strength now makes the white merciful, in cases where weakness and fear then made him desperate and cruel.

The Six Nations in New York sided with the English in her war with her colonies. Their service was accepted, in spite of the indignant protest of the Earl of Chatham, and the opposition of other high-minded Englishmen. The massacres of Wyoming and of Cherry Valley, and the murder of farmers near

Fort Schuyler, with the devastation of miles around, show their course, and these are but leading incidents. In lesser atrocities they spared neither friend nor foe. A portion of the Senecas remain on a reservation still in New York ; the Mohawks retired to Canada after the war ; and both are thriving under Christian influence. The Mohawks have the Bible and Prayer Book ; but of Eliot's " praying Indians " there was not one alive at the beginning of this century who could read the Indian Bible.

CHAP. XXIV.—THE ENGLISH CONQUEST OF CANADA.

1732—1762.

THE English settlements were but a narrow line along the coast of North America, for a thousand miles, with the French to the north of them, and the Spaniards to the south; and they were in great dread and jealousy of both. Whenever there was war in Europe the colonists attacked one another; and, as Florida became fuller of Spanish settlers, it was thought to threaten Carolina. James Edward Oglethorpe, a brave English gentleman, who had served on the staff of Prince Eugene, and on his return to England entered Parliament, was appointed a commissioner for the relief of insolvent debtors, and inquiry into the state of prisons. People were then imprisoned for debt, and as of course they could do nothing to pay what they owed, there they lay for life in a hopeless state of misery and neglect. General

Oglethorpe persuaded King George II. and Parliament that it would be a good thing to have another colony between Carolina and Florida ; and to permit him to hold land in trust for the poor, peopling it with the most deserving of these poor debtors, and with other unfortunate persons. In 1733 Oglethorpe landed with his first party of emigrants, and laid out and founded the city of Savannah ; and " the humane reformer of prison discipline became the father of a state, the place of refuge for the distressed people of Britain, and the persecuted Protestants of Europe." After about a year's sojourn in his colony, during which he established friendly relations with the Indians, Oglethorpe returned to England, and in 1736 went out again with a new party of emigrants. Among them were a company of Moravians, and John and Charles Wesley, the founders of Methodism. After Wesley, followed Whitefield four years later, another of the Methodist pioneers. He visited all the English colonies, from Florida to the northern frontier. His great object was help for Georgian orphans, whose parents had been sometimes solely recommended by poverty, without energy. Whitefield made many voyages, and many land journeys, and died in 1770 at Newbury in Massachusetts. His bones repose in the crypt of a church in Newburyport, where they may be seen by visitors ; a rare, perhaps unique, instance of respect to Protestant relics, and certainly without a parallel in the United States.

The Moravians who went out with Oglethorpe were the reinforcement of a larger body who had gone out before. They claimed their origin from John Huss, and claimed also a succession of bishops. Persecuted on the continent of Europe, the Society for the Propagation of the Gospel, seconding the enterprise of Oglethorpe, invited them to settle in Georgia, as the colony had been named. They received free passage, provision for a whole season, allotments of land, and all the privileges of native Englishmen. Scottish High-landers, who, after the failing of the Jacobite risings, could no longer live at home, joined the colony, and volunteers from many directions came in. Oglethorpe trained his colonists to fight bravely against the Spaniards, and promoted habits of industry. He thought the climate of Georgia good for silk worms, and brought them into the colony, choosing as its arms, a family of these little creatures, with the motto, " Not for themselves but others." His laws allowed no slavery ; but after his surrender of his charter and colony to the crown, in 1752, slavery crept in, and Negroes were owned by the rich colonists of Georgia, as well as everywhere else in America.

The Spanish power was weak. It was the French that was really alarming. The chain of forts was spreading, which was to connect Louisiana with Canada. Along the northern border there was constant petty warfare; the French Canadians invading New England, and the men of New England and Canada, and the Indian allies of each, committing atrocities on their neighbours. When in 1712 peace followed the war between England and France, which had lasted nine years, Acadie, or, as we call it, Nova Scotia, was yielded to the English, but the boundary was not fully made out, and the border war went on. It was principally in the hands of the Indians, who could not understand how they were made, by treaties in which they had no voice, subject first to one European power and then another.

There was a brief interval of quiet, but the war in the colonies broke out with double force when George II. and Louis XV. went to war in 1740 about the accession of Maria Theresa. In 1744, Annapolis, an Acadian city, whose name had been changed in honour of Queen Anne, was threatened by a French expedition, which surprised an English garrison on the Strait of Canseau. Annapolis was not taken, but the French plundered the port, and carried off some prisoners to Louisburg, a fort on Cape Breton, so strong that it

was called the American Gibraltar, as it commanded
the mouths of the River St. Lawrence.   These
prisoners, upon their release on parole, told Governor
Shirley, of Massachusetts, of some weak points in the
fortification, and an expedition was fitted out by New
England men alone—without help from England—
which actually mastered this fort, and thus saved their
own country from an invasion.   The expedition was
commanded by William Pepperel, a merchant of Maine,
who for this exploit was knighted.   The colonists
were greatly disappointed and angered, when, two
years later, at the peace of Aix la Chapelle, their
conquest was given back to the French.

The French forts continued to spread at the west,
beyond the Alleghany mountains.   No English
colonists had yet made homes there, and each nation
claimed the country—the French, because Marquette
and La Salle had first discovered it; the English, as
having bought it from the Indians.   In 1749 a charter
was granted to certain colonists of Virginia and Maryland, under which was formed the Ohio Company, for
the settlement of the Ohio valley.   Here began quarrels with the French, who drove back the settlers, and
even established forts in the borders of Pennslyvania.
Governor Dinwiddie, of Virginia, resolved to send a
messenger to expostulate with the French officers.

He selected for this purpose George Washington. He was a Virginian, born February 22nd, 1732, of one of the old families, who lived in the colony like English squires. His father died when he was ten years old, and he was largely indebted to his elder brother Lawrence for his education and the formation of his character. In his education the practical was uppermost, and Lord Fairfax, the grantee of an immense tract in Virginia, noticing the exactness of his work in his exercises in surveying near his home, employed the lad of sixteen to survey the Fairfax domain. So well was the work done that Lord Fairfax procured for him, at eighteen, the appointment of public surveyor. The Ohio troubles had awakened a military spirit in Virginia, and when the colony was divided into military districts for the training of the militia, George Washington, at the age of nineteen, was appointed one of the adjutants-general, with the rank of major. His brother Lawrence, one of the chief men in the Ohio Company, no doubt influenced these appointments; and the conduct of the younger brother vindicated the elder's choice. George Washington was twenty-one years of age when, in the beginning of the winter of 1753, he started on his mission, travelling with Indian help through dangerous forests, and crossing the rivers in canoes, swimming the horses. After all, the French gave no redress, but showed plainly that they meant to have the whole Ohio valley. The return journey was still worse. They counted on crossing the rivers on the ice, but found the Alleghany frozen solid only a few rods from the shore, and were obliged to construct a raft. The current was full of floating blocks, one of which struck Washington's setting pole, jerking him into the water. He saved himself by catching hold of the logs of the raft. After a night of suffering, the party managed to cross the river on the drift ice which was wedged together.

The Virginians resolved on the defence of the frontier. There was peace between France and England, but each power sent armaments to America to defend its frontiers. Virginia asked help from the other provinces, but none would give it but South Carolina. The French could not be hindered from establishing a fresh post, Fort Duquesne, at the confluence of the Ohio and Monongahela, which completed the line of sixty from Quebec to New Orleans. Then General Braddock was sent with an army to help the colonists. He was cautioned by Benjamin Franklin, now from a printer's boy become a prominent official, and he was warned by others, of the character of Indian warfare. Disregarding advice, he proceeded in his own way into the forests. George Washington, after a campaign with Virginian settlers, had resigned his colonial commission; but he accepted an invitation from General Braddock to join his staff. On the 9th of July, 1755, within seven miles of Fort Duquesne, while following a path only twelve feet wide, but in martial array, the English marched into an ambush. The French and Indians were much fewer in number, but numbers were of no use in such a place ; and the English soldiers were confused and dismayed by this mode of fighting, with the enemy hidden among the trees. Braddock retreated, mortally wounded, and Washington, the only one of his staff who was unhurt, had to do his best with his Virginian rangers to cover the retreat. One half of the English force were killed or wounded. Three companies of Rangers had only thirty men left alive. Out of eighty British officers, twenty-six were killed and thirty-six were wounded. Of Washington, the Indians said that the great Manitou guarded him. Two horses were killed under him, and four balls penetrated his coat.

The Indians thought that luck went with the French, and the border burnings and desolations were worse than ever. At the north the English claimed that Nova Scotia included all the tract now known as New Brunswick, as well as that now known as Nova Scotia. The French claimed that the Bay of Fundy was the

dividing line. Nova Scotia, which had been for thirty
years a British province, had, in its population, seventeen or eighteen thousand French settlers, who were
excused from bearing arms against France, and were
called " French Neutrals," but were suspected, with
more or less justice, of being ready to favour any
movement to restore their ancient allegiance. The
dispute about the boundary between New France and
Nova Scotia, carried on by protocol in Europe, was
brought to a point by the French in America, who
erected two forts on the peninsula at the head of
the Bay of Fundy. Massachusetts furnished three
thousand men, the commander of which force was
subordinated to an English officer who joined the
Massachusetts men there on landing. The two forts
were taken without difficulty, and in the garrisons
were found three hundred French Neutrals. To disperse the soldiers was easy enough, but to manage the
fifteen or twenty thousand Acadians was not so easy.
The Governor of Nova Scotia, the Chief Justice of the
province, and two British admirals, at a council held in
July, 1755, determined on the deportation of the unfortunate Frenchmen. They were taken off in ships,
and landed at various ports, every colony receiving its
quota. Some escaped, but the number actually transported is estimated at from seven to ten thousand.

THE EMBARKATION OF THE ACADIANS.

Their country was laid waste, and their houses were burned, and great hardships attended their removal. It was a harsh and cruel measure, the only excuse for which was what was deemed a military necessity. The sympathy of the world has been with the Acadians; and Longfellow's poem, "Evangeline," is founded on the story of these exiles. After the peace of 1763, those who survived were permitted to return; but only some thirteen or fourteen hundred were found to accept the permission. The colonial Assemblies, in many instances, had provided for the passage of the exiles to France, Canada, St. Domingo, and Louisiana.

War between England and France was declared in 1756; and the hostilities of the colonies endorsed by the mother countries. Things went ill with England nearly all through 1757, but in 1758 the tide began to turn. Washington, under Brigadier-General John Forbes, assisted in driving the French out of the Ohio Valley. Fort Duquesne was taken, and renamed Fort Pitt: it is now the city of Pittsburg. Fort Niagara, near the Falls, was taken with other posts, and the great line of forts was broken.

Ticonderoga, an advance post which the French had established in New York, surrendered to the British arms, after having twice repulsed them. Louisberg, on Cape Breton, was recaptured, General Wolfe here winning the title of "the hero of Louisberg." But the great exploit of the war was the capture of Quebec. Wolfe was sent in 1759 against the city with only eight thousand men. Quebec stands on a steep rock, in the fork of the rivers St. Lawrence and St. Charles, and was one of the strongest places in the world. General Montcalm came with an army to protect it, and repulsed Wolfe, who was nearly in despair, when he was told of a steep path, leading to the Heights of Abraham above the city. He sent his troops in transports up the River St. Lawrence beyond Quebec, thus deceiving the French; and on the night of September 12th, 1759, the troops descended the river in boats, drifting with the current, without sail or oar, climbed the heights to the plateau called the Plains of Abraham, and the French in the morning beheld an army above them. Montcalm, whose camp was outside of the city, advanced and gave battle. Each general received a death wound. As Wolfe, mortally wounded, was carried to the rear he heard the cry, "They run!" "Who run?" he asked. "The French," he was told. "God be praised!" he said; "I die happy." Montcalm, on the other hand, said, on being told that his wound was mortal: "So much the better. I shall not see the surrender of Quebec." The famous citadel did surrender, without waiting for an assault ; and though the French tried to retake it, they could not, and the next year had to surrender Montreal, their stronghold.

The English fleet was very strong at this time, and Lord Rodney took St. Lucie, Tobago, Guadaloupe, and the Western Caribean Islands, as well as Martinique, the strongest of all. Spain was, in 1761, drawn into the war, as an ally of France, partly by a Bourbon family compact, partly by disputes with England about the Spanish Central American colonies. England made war upon Spain as an ally of her enemy France. Admiral Keppel captured the great city of Havana, the capital of Cuba. Treasure ships were taken, as in the days of Elizabeth. Peace was reached in 1763, by the treaty of Fontainebleau.

CHAP. XXV. — EXPULSION OF THE JESUITS FROM SOUTH AMERICA.

1750—1773.

THE Portuguese had always been the allies of England; and Brazil and all that depended on it took part against Spain. But in the year 1750, a treaty was made between Spain and Portugal, which traced out the boundaries of their American possessions, and defined the borders of Brazil.

The River Uruguay became part of the boundary line, and all settlements which had been made to the eastward, or Portuguese side, by grants from Spain, were to be broken up. All moveable goods might be taken away, but all the houses, churches, and lands were to be given up, and the people themselves to remove to the Spanish possessions. It was like the removal of the French settlers of Acadie. The kings and their ministers, who sat at home, and looked at their maps, had no notion of the cruelty of their orders to all these living beings; for on the Uruguay were seven flourishing Jesuit settlements, where thirty thousand Guarani Indians were living, as their fathers and grandfathers had lived before them, as farmers and planters—a peaceful, civilized Christian life, looking on the land as their own, which it was.

The Jesuits sent to the two courts all sorts of representations of the misery that would be inflicted; but the Marquis of Valdelirios, who had been sent out to see the treaty enforced, allowed no delay. The Jesuits were accused of having done much harm in Europe by their perpetual interference on behalf of the Pope; and though here on the Uruguay they were quite in the right, and were defenders of the weak, they suffered for the dislike their order had excited. Because they had tried to obtain from the governors a delay long enough for tidings from home of the result of their appeal, the Bishop of Buenos Ayres forbade them to administer the sacraments; and because they tried to induce their poor natives to submit patiently to what could not be prevented, they were accused of having sold their settlements to the Spaniards, and were treated like prisoners even by the Guaranis.

The Jesuits knew that resistance would be of no use and that the Guaranis were not fit to fight, having lost all the spirit and dash of their wild forefathers. But

there was no hindering them from taking up arms to
defend their homes, and this put an end to all hopes of
mercy for them.   The Spanish and Portuguese armies
joined together and routed the gatherings of these
poor people, killing some, plundering the rest, and
absolutely driving them out, to revert again to the
savage life from which their ancestors had been re-
claimed.   The Jesuits were accused of having incited
them to rebel, and even of having taught them cruelty
to the wounded.   But this was disproved by the
evidence of the Guaranis themselves, who declared
that the Fathers had never taught them anything but
to submit, and that they would not have rebelled, had
time been given them to remove their property and
cattle.   In a few years more, the Courts agreed to
change again the boundary line, the Guaranis returned
to their homes, and the mission work began again,
though some of the younger and stronger men, having
once tasted the delights of savage liberty, could not be
brought back.

At home, however, feeling had set strongly against
the Jesuits.   They had done much harm as well as
much good, and alike for the evil as for the good, the
Roman Catholic Kings and their Ministers were determined to put them down.   The foremost in the attack
was the Marquis of Pombal, the Prime Minister of the

King of Portugal. He hated all Monks and Friars, and
the Jesuits most of all, and he seems to have honestly
thought that the Indians of Uruguay, Maranham, and
Paraguay were kept by them in an inferior state;
ignorant, half-clothed, and working to enrich the Order.
So directions were sent out that no ecclesiastic should
hold any Indians under his power, and that the Jesuit
mission stations should be made into towns, with
magistrates like those of Portugal and Spain. Pombal
had never seen, and therefore could not understand, the
state of things, and that these natives really could not
take care of themselves like white men, and that to take
away the Fathers, who knew how to deal with them,
was to give them up to ruin and savagery. He drew
up long instructions to directors, who were to take
charge of them, make them learn industry, teach them
to speak Portuguese, and, in short, to make them just
like Europeans. This was to take effect from the
River Amazon down to the River Paraguay, wherever
the Jesuit Fathers had missions and settlements of
half-reclaimed Indians.

At the same time, the Pope was entreated to send
out a commission to inquire into the conduct of the
Order in South America, and to see whether they
were not like merchants, soldiers, and little kings all
along these borders of Brazil. Just as the inquiry

had begun in 1758, King Joseph was shot at and wounded in the streets of Lisbon, in his carriage, and a plot amongst the nobles of Portugal was discovered, in which some Jesuits were said to be concerned. Probably this was untrue, but they suffered for the sins of their predecessors. Father Juan Mariana had published long before, in 1599, a treatise in which it is maintained that it is lawful to compass the death of a tyrant. The book had been condemned by the General of the Order, but it drew on the Jesuits an odium of which their enemies were not slow to take advantage. The Order was suppressed in Portugal, and in its American possessions. Every Jesuit was sought out, they were brought together and shipped off—one hundred and sixty-eight from Bahia, one hundred and forty-five from Rio. The sick were taken from their beds, they were stripped of all their books and papers, and kept between decks like Negroes in a slaver, till the ship's doctor declared they would all die, and that the fever would spread to the crew. Some were kept in prison in Lisbon for eighteen years, till Pombal's death ; the others were turned adrift in the Pope's dominions.

Misfortunes oppressed them. In Martinique, a great Bank which had been established under their management for the convenience of the commerce of their settlements failed, and many persons were ruined. The Order was sentenced to make good the losses. A madman tried to stab Louis XV. of France, and this, too, was supposed to have been contrived by them, so that the French king also turned against them.

In Spain a popular tumult frightened the king, Charles III., into supposing the Jesuits were concerned in it, and he followed the example of his neighbours in expelling them from all his dominions; from Mexico, Peru, Chili, and the Isles wherever he had possessions, these missionary priests were driven out, with not quite so much violence and cruelty as by the Portuguese, but to the bitter grief of the poor natives, whose best friends and guides they had been. They counselled submission, and did all they could to help them for the future; but in the year 1773 the Pope was persuaded to suppress the Order altogether.

There were plans for educating and civilizing the Indians without the aid of the Jesuits, but no one would take the trouble to see these provisions properly carried out, and the Indians were not willing to obey the new comers. So the natives fell back gradually into savage life, and the garden-like lands they had cultivated fell back into being wildernesses. The clergy, being very little looked after by the European church, grew more and more sluggish, selfish, and vicious ; the settlers more lawless and indolent, mingling with their religion gross superstition.   In Spanish South America, in particular, every kind of evil habit prevailed ; and though the towns had wealthy and civilized inhabitants, the country around became full of wild, fierce, ruffianly riders, whose chief business was to pursue, catch with lassos, and kill cattle, great herds of which roamed at large.

CHAP. XXVI. — THE THIRTEEN COLONIES.

THE peace which was signed at Fontainebleau in 1763, between England, France, and Spain, left the northern continent of America in a very different state from that in which it had been at the beginning of the war. All the French possessions east of the Mississippi were given up to England, except the city and vicinity of New Orleans, which were assigned to Spain; all Canada and Acadia; and nothing was left to France but the right to fish on the shores of New-foundland and in the Gulf of St. Lawrence, with the little islets, St. Pierre and Miquelon, to shelter the ships; but no more than fifty soldiers were ever to be on them, and there were to be no fortifications. The French Canadians were to be left free to live as Roman Catholics under English laws; but no fishing vessel or other from France was to come within fifteen leagues of the shores of Cape Breton. In the West Indies, France gave up the Isles of Tobago, Dominica, St. Vincent, and Grenada ; but the English gave her back Martinique, Guadeloupe, Marie Galante, and Desirade.

To Spain was conceded, under the treaty, all Louisiana west of the Mississippi, with an indefinite boundary to the north ; and she had New Orleans, as already noted, which is on the east bank of the Mississippi. She gave up Florida to the English, in exchange for Cuba, which was restored to her. She gave up the right to fish for cod off Newfoundland ; and she gave to the English permission to land in the Bay of Honduras, to cut mahogany and log-wood, and to build houses, warehouses, and quays, as long as they built no forts. This peace put an end to the last remains of buccaneering in the West Indies, and established the bounds of the national languages there.

The English had still to fight with the Indian allies of the French. The Indians were much attached to those bright, kindly men, and were told by the Canadians that the King of France was only dead for a while, but would come again. Pontiac, the chief of the Ottawas, who is said to have led that tribe in the battle in which Braddock fell on the Monongahela,

declared, " I am a Frenchman, and will die a Frenchman." He sent messengers through the tribes, offering
them the tokens of war—a belt of red and black shell-
beads, called "wampum," and a tomahawk. All
accepted them, and it was agreed to unite and drive
the English from the Ohio, and the country along the
Lakes. Very cunning was Pontiac. He tried to
surprise the post of Detroit, on the strait between
Lakes Huron and Erie, by gaining admission to show
an Indian dance, with thirty or forty of his warriors,
who had tomahawks hidden under their blankets. A
woman, however, gave warning in time, and when the
dancers were admitted, they found the soldiers under
arms. At another fort, some hundred Ottawas played
at ball outside the walls, till the soldiers came out to
watch them. Then the ball was flung close to the
gate, and as the Indians rushed after it, each squaw
handed her husband his hatchet, and he fell upon his
man. Only twenty soldiers escaped. In the Ohio
Valley every fort except Pittsburg was taken ; more
than one hundred traders killed and scalped. The
Indians massacred women and children ; and five
hundred English families were forced to wander in the
woods. Pittsburg and Detroit held out through this
fearful five months, though Detroit was subjected to a
new thing in Indian warfare—a regular investment

and siege. Relief for the English arrived, and as winter approached at length Pontiac could no longer keep his wild warriors together. The French behaved admirably through the difficulty. The Indians spared their traders, and the French, whether official or private, took no part, except to shield and protect prisoners, and to use their influence to explain the treaty, and persuade the Indians to submit. One of the French officers, almost the last to leave his post, sent belts and messages and pipes of peace to all the tribes, telling them to bury the hatchet and make friends with the English, for they would never see him more. Pontiac said he accepted the peace which his French Father had sent him, and submitted. He was killed a year or two later, while in a fit of intoxication, by an Illinois Indian.

The colonies which had gone through this war called themselves the " Old Thirteen." They were— New Hampshire, Massachusetts, Rhode Island, Connecticut, New York, New Jersey, Pennsylvania, Virginia, North and South Carolina, and Georgia. The first four of the colonies, with the district of Maine, belonging to Massachusetts, made up New England. James II. attempted to consolidate all the colonies north of the Delaware ; and in 1686 Sir Edmund Andros appeared in Boston as Governor of all New

England, including New York, and New Jersey as an appanage of New York. After the accession of William and Mary, the consolidation was no more heard of; and, in the popular language of the United States, New York is not included in New England. Maine is now a State, and with Vermont, carved out of the rival claims of New York and New Hampshire, makes up the six New England States. The inhabitants of this territory were chiefly English, and about this time began to be called by the nickname of Yankee, which is either the Dutch Yankin, the contraction of John, or else the Indian form of the word English. In America the term is applied to New Englanders only, though in England it is used for citizens of all the States. Probably the Indians use the same designation; for an Indian chief a few years since, who was conducted over the ships and forts to reconcile him to submission, was overheard, in his broken English, to curse the "Yangheese." The New Englanders were mainly Independents or Congregationalists, and had built for themselves solid churches and schools. They had a University at Cambridge, near Boston. Yale College, in Connecticut, was founded in 1701; and among its early patrons was Berkeley, afterward Bishop of Cloyne. The New Englanders were a hardy race, and had many thoughtful, resolute men among them. They had strict laws and observances, dreading such amusements as theatres, races, and balls; and they led a hearty, wholesome country life, though laborious; their wives and daughters working at all farmhouse arts and domestic manufactures. The nature of their land taught them the thrifty habits for which Yankees are proverbial. New Jersey, though settled in part by "Friends" or Quakers, had a strong New England character given to it by emigration. Princeton College was founded by Presbyterians in 1746.

Emigration is apt to run on lines of latitude. The upper part of New York received thus a somewhat Yankee tinge; but the Dutch element, from the beginning of the settlement, kept its hold, and modified New England Puritanism. The Patroon system and the better soil gave New York farmers larger holdings, and their handsome country houses and farms employed a limited number of Negro slaves, who, of course, led easier lives than on a Spanish *repartimiento*. Slavery existed, indeed, in all the colonies, though rather tolerated than encouraged in the northern settlements. The New York settlers never were so rigid in their mode of life as their neighbours. They were Protestant, the Dutch Church and its kindred Presbyterian bodies having early possession of the ground ; but the Established Church of England had an early footing. Dutch manners prevailed, and the families, especially in Albany, made the broad doorstep of the house— stoop, they called it—a reception room in the evening and a sitting place for the family, as they used to do in Hamburgh. On New Year's Day the ladies received all their male acquaintances ; and the custom still lingers, though it is becoming evident that village fashions are inconvenient in great cities.

Most of the colonists had fought with the French and Indians, and they rather looked down upon their neighbours in Pennsylvania, who had hung back. Pennsylvania had her own peculiar embarrassments. She had a proprietary interest, a colonial, and a British contending with each other, and the peace doctrines of her founder were in the way of military measures. Benjamin Franklin, Boston born, but Philadelphian by adoption, printer, philosopher, man of science, and politician, was active always in public matters. It is said that he procured the passage of a bill through the Assembly for the purchase of grain and hollow ware —the grain being gunpowder, and the hollow ware guns. The frontier settlements of the province had received large accessions of settlers other than Quakers, and these settlers, organized into military companies, gave the first repulse to the savage foe in the Pontiac war. In that war Pennsylvania was among the chief sufferers, but the benevolence of the Friends, who would not aid war, but who would relieve its victims, restored comfort and prosperity.

The Virginians were more like country squires living on their estates, except that instead of tenantry they had swarms of Negroes, who worked their plantations of tobacco and were their household servants; though they were not quite so plentiful as in the Carolinas, where black men were much more numerous than white. Among the whites in the last two colonies there was an admixture of French Huguenot families. The Virginians, among whom Washington was conspicuous, had borne themselves bravely in the French and Indian wars, and all felt that they deserved honour from the mother country. However, there was a foolish narrow jealousy in the policy of those times, and there was a fear of the colonies getting too strong and powerful and taking away the English trade. And far-seeing statesmen began to fear that the peace of 1763, by relieving the colonies from the outside pressure of colonial and Indian wars, would increase the difficulty of governing them according to the narrow colonial policy.

The adherents of the Church of England, who were

numerous in the southern colonies, begged for an English Bishop. They were refused, because it was then supposed that a Bishop must be a wealthy, powerful man, a member of the House of Lords, and this England thought impolitic. So the American parishes were held by clergymen ordained at home and invited out to the colonies. No one could be confirmed, and no church consecrated. It is curious that money was so scarce that these clergy were paid in tobacco to export instead of coin.

There were plans for uniting all the colonies under the same government. At a Congress of Commissioners appointed by the British Board of Trade to treat with the Indians in 1754, Franklin was present as one of the deputation from Pennsylvania. He introduced a plan for a President - General to be appointed by the crown with executive power, and a council, chosen by the colonial legislatures. Here was the germ of the future constitution of the United States. But the project was difficult. The constitutions and laws of the Provinces, not being alike, were hard to reconcile, and there was an opposition made at home lest by becoming one the colonies should become too strong. The proposition was too democratic for the crown, and had too much royal prerogative for the colonies. Another misfortune was that, each government being small, it was too often given to some poor hanger-on at court at home; and these governors, not always being men of honesty, ability, or good sense, misrepresented the Americans to the English, and the English to the Americans. Still the colonists loved the old home, drank the health of King George with all their might, and were ready to fight to the death against any foreign enemy.

The war had been very costly, and as it was in their defence, the Home Government felt it just that the cost should be partly borne by the colonists, who had never been laid under any system of imperial taxation, though they made grants to the royal exchequer from loans and taxes raised by their own Assemblies. The law in England had long been that wills, deeds, and receipts should always have a government stamp to make them valid; and in 1765 it was decided in Parliament to extend this Stamp Act to the colonies. But, in the days of Edward I., the Commons of England had established their claim to have no tax laid on them unless their representatives consented to it in Parliament; and the colonies in America considered that unless they were allowed to send members to Parliament they ought not to be taxed. They resisted so resolutely that the Stamp Act was the next year repealed, but the main question was left undecided.

CHAP. XXVII.—THE AMERICAN REVOLUTION.

1765-1776.

THE Bill repealing the Stamp Act was accompanied by another affirming the authority of Parliament over the colonies in all cases whatsoever, and declaring the opposite resolutions of the Colonial Assemblies to be null and void. So the repeal settled nothing. The question between England and the colonies was still left open. The Stamp Act had brought the discussion of these difficulties to a point. It had given official force and expression to the claim that the colonists, as Englishmen, ought not to contribute to the revenue without their own consent, any more than their kindred at home who sent members to the House of Commons. And it had produced a Parliamentary denial of that claim, but disbursed in the form of Crown patronage. By the laws of trade, the Thirteen Colonies were cut off from all the world but England. Even trade with the British Islands was subjected to duties which were almost prohibitory. Industry in the colonies was repressed for the advantage of English manufactures.   Under such a system the colonists were under a much more despotic authority than if they had stayed at home.

It was felt that the time had come for making a stand, and Virginia took the lead.   In the Assembly of that colony a young man named Patrick Henry brought forward a series of resolutions affirming the rights of the colonists as Englishmen.   In the course of the exciting debate Henry said, " Cæsar had his Brutus, Charles the First his Cromwell, and George the Third——"   Cries of " Treason ! " interrupted him and he ended with, " May profit by their example." It was voted that taxation could only be fixed by the General Assembly of a colony.   The Assembly of Massachusetts, approving this principle (as indeed did all the colonies), invited their representatives to assemble and unite in remonstrances.   Nine sent deputies to the Congress which met in New York, two though not present assented, and thus eleven colonies agreed in drawing up a " Declaration of Rights " and a Petition.   These were sent, the Petition to the King, and the Declaration to the Parliament, in October, 1765.   Some of the greatest statesmen, such as William Pitt, afterward Lord Chatham, thought the Americans in the right, and if their counsel had been followed, means might have been found of keeping the colonies free, yet still loyal to the crown. But there were other advisers who believed the honour of the crown concerned to put down all resistance. The result was the repeal of the Stamp Act, but with the aggravating accompaniment which left the questions of taxation, of the army, of appointments to office, and the laws of trade still open. In the mean time farther provocation was given.

Boston was the foremost American town in showing discontent with the Government. "Liberty Poles" were set up, and frequent occasions taken for exhibiting the spirit of resistance. The quartering of British regular troops in the colonies was everywhere protested against; and in Boston there were perpetual quarrels between the people and the soldiers, whom the mob called "lobsters" and "bloody backs." These encounters were with clubs and stones, the soldiers not carrying arms when not on duty. One of these disturbances resulted in the affair popularly called the " Boston Massacre." For two days there had been rioting between parties of soldiers and the labourers in a rope walk. On the evening of the second day a sentinel was assaulted while on duty. Six men and a sergeant were ordered for his protection, and the captain of the company followed, in all, seven men.

The crowd, presuming on the English law that no soldier may fire upon a crowd except under orders from a civil magistrate, pressed upon the soldiers, assailing them with taunts and missiles. Somebody gave the command "Fire," and a volley was discharged, killing three men and wounding five. Warrants were instantly issued by justices of the town—the soldiers were arrested and committed for trial. The citizens demanded in town-meeting that the garrison should be withdrawn, which was acceded to, and it was removed to Castle Island. The seven soldiers were tried, and all acquitted except two, who received slight punishment for "manslaughter." John Adams and Josiah Quincy, both names of note, and among the most zealous of popular leaders, were assigned as their counsel, and did their duty for their clients. Of course this "massacre" was made much of, and added to the excitement of discontent. While the soldiers as individuals were exonerated, the Government was held accountable.

Over the whole country the use of the taxed imported articles was given up. The ladies took to spinning and weaving, and said they would wear sheep-skins rather than buy their goods of people who insulted them. Non-importation agreements were entered into, and merchants who declined to join the agreement were placarded as objects of public scorn. College boys graduated in homespun. This universal resistance produced its effect. The obnoxious taxes were removed on everything except *tea*. Commercial intercourse was resumed, though tea was still contraband with the republicans. The duty on this was continued, as the Stamp Act repeal was loaded with an obnoxious rider, to assert the principle against which the colonists contended, the right of Parliament to tax the unrepresented colonies. To meet the non-importation agreement, a drawback or remission in England of all duties was granted to the East India Company on all teas which they would send to the colonies to pay duty there. Consignees were appointed to receive and dispose of the cargoes. Philadelphia led the way in protesting. Boston followed, and added action to her protest. Three tea-ships arriving at that port, public meetings were held, and the popular leaders harangued the people. The immediate sending away of the tea was demanded. The consignees not being able to comply, the ships were boarded at night by men dressed up as Mohawk Indians, and the chests were broken up and the tea emptied into the water. The harbour was said to have become one great teapot, for what was called the Boston Tea Party. At other ports the cargoes of tea were sent back or destroyed.

In much indignation the Home Government appointed General Thomas Gage commander of the forces in America, and commissioned him also as Governor of Massachusetts, thus giving him in his double capacity the legal right to fire upon the people, and additional troops were ordered out to support him. The port of Boston was closed by Act of Parliament till the tea should be paid for, which, by the way, was never done. The port was effectually blockaded; no vessels could come in and none go out, none which were building could be launched from the stocks. Even water carriage between wharf and wharf was forbidden; the ferry service across the Charles River was stopped, so that from Salem, the nearest port, goods could not be obtained. The town of Boston was reduced to the last extremity, and all industries were paralyzed. The colonies vied with one another in liberality; but all supplies which came by sea had to be landed at Marblehead, thirteen miles distant from Boston by water, thirty miles by the circuitous land route. British troops were as of old a continual provocation in a city, the very boys of which were rebels. General Gage adjourned the Legislature to Salem, which was declared the seat of Government. The Salem people, like those of other towns, declared they would not profit by Boston's misfortune. The first thing the

Legislature did in June, 1774, was to make such a reply to the Governor's Message that he refused to hear it through. The next was to recommend a General Congress to meet in Philadelphia in September, and resolutions were also passed recommending entire discontinuance of the use of British goods, and all articles subject to Parliamentary duty. General Gage, finding what was going on, sent his secretary to dissolve the Assembly. But Samuel Adams—whom with John Hancock, Joseph Warren, and others, Gage was instructed to seize as rebels—had locked the door of the hall, and the secretary read the Governor's proclamation on the steps outside. This was the last session of the Legislature or General Court of Massachusetts under British rule. Henceforth the people acted for themselves, as did also the other colonies. The proposition for a Continental Congress, which met as Massachusetts appointed, had already been proposed in New York, and seconded in other places.

The colonists were determined to fight it out. A year of troublous time passed without any serious encounter. Boston held fast, and had the sympathy of all the colonies. But in the spring of 1775, General Gage, having discovered that military stores were deposited at Concord in Massachusetts, sent a force of eight hundred men to destroy them. The expedition left Boston at midnight on the eighteenth, and was intended to be secret. But the watchful colonists detected the movement, and despatched messengers to alarm the country side. Among these messengers was an ardent, popular leader named Revere. "Paul Revere's Ride" is the subject of a vigorous poem by Longfellow. At Lexington the British found sixty or seventy men drawn up on the village green. They were ordered to disperse, and, hesitating, were fired upon. Eight of these militia-men were killed, and several wounded. They were dispersed, and the British moved on toward Concord. Meanwhile, the news had sped, and on their arrival they found the greater part of the stores removed. Two cannon were found and spiked, sixty barrels of flour were stove, and a few hundred pounds of shot thrown into a mill-pond. A bonfire was made of the liberty pole and some gun-carriages. A skirmish took place between the militia and the regulars, in which two were killed and some wounded on each side. The regulars, finding the country roused, retreated; but the retreat as far as Lexington was rather a rout, for enemies beleagured them on all sides. At Lexington they found about a thousand troops sent out to reinforce them. Even thus strengthened, they were so hunted and beset all the way back that they lost, in

THE RETREAT FROM CONCORD.

killed and wounded, near three hundred men. The loss of the colonists was ninety, of whom half were killed. And thus, on the 19th of April, 1775, began the "War of Independence." On this day was fired the gun which "echoed round the world."

The Continental Congress had become a perpetual body, and assumed the responsibility of enlisting and organizing an army, and appointing a commander-in-chief. Meanwhile General Gage, threatened by the concourse of militia gathered in the vicinity of the town, and shutting him in, decided on occupying the eminences which commanded the town. Bunker Hill in Charlestown, near Boston, was one of these; and the Americans, finding this out in time, set forth to prevent it. On the morning of June 17th, the British ships in Boston Harbour found themselves confronted with earthworks six feet high on Breed's Hill. That was the point taken and fortified, as nearer Boston. Twelve or fifteen hundred men, under Colonel William Prescott, had thrown up the works during the night. The ships opened a fire upon the works, and a battery on a hill in Boston played upon them. The Americans continued the labour of entrenching, their colonel and other officers walking on the battlements amid the fire to inspirit the soldiers. At one o'clock the regulars landed in Charlestown, and undertook to march up the hill. Twice they were repulsed with fearful slaughter. The third time the advance was made with less show of contempt for the Americans than the first, and with more regard to military tactics. The Americans having exhausted their ammunition were forced to retreat. The exact time from the first discharge of the musketry to the last was an hour and a half. The Americans lost, in killed, wounded, and missing, four hundred and fifty men ; the British, over a thousand. The Americans withheld their fire till their assailants were within destructive range, or, as it was said, till " they could see the whites of their eyes." The Americans lost one of their most promising officers, Joseph Warren, a volunteer just appointed, but not yet commissioned. On the British side, seventy commissioned officers were wounded and thirteen killed, for they distinguished themselves by their courage in an affair which cost General Gage his military reputation. Charlestown was burned during the engagement; but the defeat of the Americans, after having shown so much courage, was as useful as a victory would have been.

Franklin wrote to his English friends, " England has lost her colonies." When George Washington heard how the Americans had borne themselves, he said, " The liberties of the country are safe." The Continental Congress had already unanimously elected him

Commander-in-chief of the army. On Monday, the 3rd of July, being then forty-three years old, he assumed the command, standing under a great tree in Cambridge, still known as the Washington Elm. His men, though staunch and brave, were undisciplined. The defence of Breed's Hill had been rather by agreement of purpose than by discipline. There was also a great want of powder, and a great need of tact to conceal the deficiency, to reduce volunteers to a sense of obedience, and to reconcile jealousies. Bunker Hill remained in possession of the British. But Dorchester Heights, the other commanding position, was still unoccupied by either ; till, on the morning of the 4th of March, 1776, the British in Boston were surprised by seeing the Heights crowned by fortifications thrown up in a night. The city could not be held, nor could ships remain in the harbour, under such conditions. The idea of an attack was entertained, but abandoned ; and by an informal agreement the British were allowed to evacuate the town unmolested. This they did on Sunday the 17th. About twelve hundred persons who held to their old allegiance went with them. In many places there were those who continued loyal to the British Crown, and they mostly took refuge in Nova Scotia, whence they hoped to return when the war was over.

Meanwhile, in the Continental Congress, steps had been taken which showed that the contest was no longer a struggle about taxation. The British determination was, on the other hand, declared to subdue the rebellion at any cost. Congress, in February, passed a resolution that the United Colonies had a right to contract alliances with foreign powers, and the ports were declared open to vessels of all nations, Great Britain excepted, thus reversing the colonial rule ; it was declared irreconcilable with reason and good conscience for the people of the colonies to take the oath of fealty to the British Crown, and necessary that every exercise of authority under that Crown should be suppressed ; and that adherence to the King of Great Britain was treason against the colonies. Meanwhile, a resolution that the colonies were, and of right ought to be, free and independent, was under consideration delayed by the lingering doubts of some of the members as to the propriety of a step so positive, though the leading spirits had come to the conclusion that they must break altogether with the mother country. The postponed resolution of Independence was reported from a committee, of which Thomas Jefferson was chairman, on the 1st of July. On the 2nd it was passed. On the 3rd, the DECLARATION explaining and vindicating the resolution was taken

READING THE DECLARATION OF INDEPENDENCE.

up, debated and amended ; and on the 4th was passed.
In this paper the word Colonies is set aside for " Free
and Independent *States*." The sole authorship of this
paper is conceded to Thomas Jefferson. It was referred
to the " States," and accepted by all.

The Declaration was received by the people everywhere with demonstrations of approval. It came at
a propitious time. The evacuation of Boston, and a
repulse of the British sea and land forces at Charleston, South Carolina, left the States free from the
presence of any royal army, though the British fleets
hovered on the coast. Generally the people were
orderly in their demonstrations, though " Tories," as
the loyal colonists were called, were in some places
insulted and roughly treated. In New York, a leaden
equestrian statue of George III. was thrown down,
and the lead cast into bullets. This statue had been
placed in the Bowling Green by the citizens of New
York themselves when the Stamp Act was repealed.
Since the Declaration of Independence the 4th of July
has been the great national holiday in the United
States.

On the first day of this year, 1776, Washington displayed at his headquarters, near Boston, what he
termed the " Union Flag." The field had thirteen
stripes ; the upper corner, the blended crosses of St.

George and St. Andrew. Congress adopted the flag, with the change of thirteen stars for the crosses; and it remains the flag of the United States, except that for every new state a star is added.

The French Canadians, who had been conquered chiefly through the New Englanders, would have nothing to do with them, though invited by Congress, and thus Canada remained firm for the Home Government; and its loyalty was reinforced by refugees from the States. But the French Government and statesmen, sullen under the humiliating treaty of 1763, were delighted at anything that could weaken England. Other nations shared the jealousy of her power. There were, moreover, enthusiastic youths who were charmed at the thought of a battle for freedom. The cause of America had able advocates in Europe in the American commissioners who had been sent over by Congress. Prominent among these was Benjamin Franklin. The commissioners could not even, at first, provide a passage for volunteers. The Marquis de Lafayette, a young French nobleman, twenty years of age, ran away from home to join the Americans, for whom he fitted out a vessel at his own cost. The French Government not only forbade his departure, but despatched vessels with orders to arrest him in the French islands, should he touch there. He avoided his pursuers, and landed in South Carolina in April, 1777; where his first act was to present Governor Moultrie with clothing and military accoutrements for one hundred men, as a token of his appreciation of the gallant defence of Charleston, when, in 1776, that port was attacked by Sir Peter Parker with his fleet, co-operating with Sir Henry Clinton. Several of the Poles, whose country had just been divided between Russia, Austria, and Prussia, came to fight in the cause of freedom; and among them the famous patriot Kosciusko, and Count Pulaski. De Kalb, Steuben, and many more European officers, were volunteers; so that Washington had at his side, including his own countrymen, both enthusiasm and experience.

The discussion of the Stamp Act had developed the purposes of the British Ministry, and the repeal did not surrender them. The resolutions of the Assemblies had still their moral force. In addition to the expenses of the late war, a standing army was proposed for the colonies; its officers appointed by the Crown, and the expenses of the army to come from the British Treasury. The judges of the Courts were to be appointed in England, as well as other officers, and all were to be independent of colonial support; the payment for these expenses being levied on the colonies by taxation.

CHAP. XXVIII.
THE WAR OF INDEPENDENCE.

1776—1778.

THE Americans had declared their independence. But there was plenty of sharp fighting to come, for bold and firm as they were, they had to learn to meet disciplined troops, and to submit themselves to discipline. It was an arduous work for Washington to meet the exigencies of his position. His difficulties could only be entrusted to his safest counsellors, and many times could not be confided even to them. Much of the burthen he had to bear alone, and only subsequent revelations have brought out the full and evenly balanced character of the "Father of his country."

After his repulse at Charleston, Sir Peter Parker sailed with his squadron to New York. Thither General Washington had repaired after the relief of Boston, and held the city. In no part of the country had the cause of the Crown more supporters and adherents, and there was a plot discovered, and averted, to seize the American Commander-in-chief. The British were encamped on Staten Island, in New York Harbour, and their fleet was anchored in the bay. The troops which had held Boston, together with fresh arrivals from Europe of English and Hessians, and the troops under Sir Henry Clinton, made up the British force of upward of twenty thousand men. About this time overtures were made to the colonies for a reconciliation. But as they were made informally, and Lord Howe, the bearer, would not recognize the official character of those whom he addressed ; and as the proposition was to pardon rebellious subjects, not to treat with independent States, it was not entertained. Had the offer come a little earlier, or the Declaration of Independence been a little later, the tender would have divided the counsels of the Americans.

On the 22nd of August the British troops landed on Long Island, about fourteen thousand strong, thence to march to the ferry opposite New York. On the 30th, Washington's forces, which had opposed their progress, retreating before them, safely landed in the city. The British followed two weeks later, and by the end of September were in possession of the lower part of Manhattan Island, on which the city of New York stands. There was constant fighting, but no general engagement. On the 16th of November the last post held by the Americans surrendered, and Washington retreated across the State of New Jersey. On the 8th of December, still closely followed by the British, he crossed the Delaware at Trenton, having previously sent over his sick and wounded and stores. He had previously seized or destroyed all boats above or below, and thus cut off pursuit. This retreat through the Jerseys ranks among the most masterly in history, and would alone establish Washington's claim to the character of a true general.

Washington established his headquarters at Newtown, Pennsylvania, nearly opposite Trenton, New Jersey. From thence, in the early morning after Christmas Day, he despatched a force of between two and three thousand men, to surprise the Hessian force stationed there in the midst of their festivities. It was a complete success. The Hessian commander Rahl was killed, about twenty men were killed or wounded, and nearly a thousand taken prisoners. With his prisoners, twelve hundred stand of arms, six field pieces, and all the standards of the brigade, Washington immediately returned across the Delaware.

On the 29th of December Washington entered New Jersey again, and from that time till July there were various engagements, a battle at Princeton being most noteworthy. By the 1st of July the British forces were all withdrawn from the State, and the march by land to Philadelphia across New Jersey was abandoned. Troops were embarked on the 23rd for the capture of Philadelphia, and landed at Elk Creek on the Chesapeake on the 25th of August. On their march to Philadelphia, they were opposed by Washington at a ford on the Brandywine River. While the battle was going on the British found another passage, and the Americans were forced to retreat. In this engagement the loss of the British was six hundred, and that of the Americans nine hundred in killed and wounded. Among the wounded was Lafayette. On the night of the 20th of September an outpost of the American army, under General Wayne, was surprised at Paoli, and Wayne was compelled to retire with the loss of three hundred men. Washington was unable to resist the passage of the British over the Schuylkill River, and on the 26th the British forces entered and occupied Philadelphia. Congress had previously adjourned its session to Baltimore, and thence to other places. From Elk Creek to Philadelphia is about sixty miles ; and the time occupied by the British army in its march was thirty days. When Franklin, then in France, heard that the British had "taken Philadelphia," he said, that was not the way to state it—"Philadelphia had taken the British."

The warlike stores of the Americans had been removed before the entry of the British forces. Washington encamped at a point about twenty miles from Philadelphia. The British established a chain of posts above Philadelphia, from the Delaware to the Schuylkill, the main encampment being at Germantown. On the 4th of October Washington attempted a surprise. The British pickets were driven in upon the main body, and at first the attack seemed almost a victory. But the steadiness of the trained British regiments, as they rallied and were reinforced, compelled him to retire. The loss on each side was heavy, about eight hundred, but the returns are disputed. It has been said of this battle, that the British at the beginning were so nearly defeated as to learn respect for the Americans; and that the Americans were so nearly routed at the end, as to learn the absolute need of discipline.

Meanwhile stirring events were in progress at the north. In June, 1776, General John Burgoyne led a British force from Canada to invade the United States. The Canadas had now become a good base for operations. Their adherence to Great Britain had been confirmed by an invasion made by an American force under Benedict Arnold and Richard Montgomery, in the winter of 1775–76. Chambly, St. John's, and Montreal were taken, and Quebec attacked. Before the latter place Montgomery fell. The invaders were demoralized and retreated, relinquishing all they had gained ; and the remainder of their force got back to the United States. Montgomery's name figures in the geography of the United States as the name of counties and of towns ; and a monument is erected to his memory in St. Paul's churchyard, New York, whither his remains were removed nearly fifty years afterward.

Burgoyne's first step was to summon a council of the dreaded Six Nations of Indians, a large body of whom he took into the British service ; but he found these wild allies did him more harm than good. They brought in scalps as the first evidences of their loyalty; and with all that Burgoyne could do he found it impossible to keep them in order in battle, or to hinder them from savage deeds in the settlements ; all which made the British name still more hated. He took Ticonderoga, but soon fell into difficulties, having neglected to keep open his communication with Canada. His way led through difficult roads and marshy grounds, over which he could carry no supplies. He sent a large detachment to capture the stores of the Americans, said to be at Bennington. The force was attacked by General John Stark, who, it is said, called out to his men : " There are the red-coats ! We must beat them, or Sally Stark will be a widow ! " Mrs. Stark was not a widow. The red-coats were beaten off. The battle of Bennington took place on August 16th. The Americans took four or five hundred prisoners, a thousand stand of arms, and four pieces of artillery. The British loss is stated at nearly two hundred in killed and wounded, the Americans less than one hundred. About the same time a British detachment assaulted Fort Schuyler, the western American post in New York, and were repulsed. The Indians ran away, and the British commander was forced to retreat. These wild allies were continually deserting, while their barbarities led crowds of volunteers to join the American army.

On the 13th of September Burgoyne crossed the Hudson, about thirty-five miles above Albany. It required six days to move ten miles, rebuilding bridges and repairing roads. On the 19th Burgoyne reached the camp of General Gates. It was laid out by Kosciusko, the Polish general, and its site was almost unassailable. After two days of fierce fighting, in which the advantage was with the Americans, and several days of skirmishing, Burgoyne was obliged to fall back to Saratoga; and there, on the 17th, he surrendered. His supplies were intercepted, and his men were starving. His retreat was cut off, and the Americans were coming to the aid of Gates by battalions. There was no place in Burgoyne's camp which was not covered by the artillery of the Americans; and it is said that while the council of war was debating in the general's tent a cannon ball swept across the table. The plan of the campaign had been that General Howe was to take Philadelphia, and march to the north, to meet Burgoyne coming south. But Burgoyne was defeated before Howe entered Philadelphia; and though Sir Henry Clinton tried to reach him from New York, his hopes in that quarter failed. Burgoyne had no choice but to capitulate. The Americans suffered the troops to keep their personal baggage, and return to England on condition of their never serving again in America. The prisoners were nearly six thousand; the previous loss of men was over three thousand; and the arms, artillery, and camp equipage were the property of the captors. Lady Harriet Acland went through the whole of this dreadful campaign in the English army, and when her husband was wounded passed into the American camp to nurse him, showing wonderful bravery and resolution throughout.

Though General Howe entered Philadelphia in September, it was not till late in November that he was able to open communication with the fleet on the Delaware; which river the Americans had obstructed by forts and ships and sunken obstacles. The American army went into winter quarters at Valley Forge, where they suffered severely for want of supplies and clothing. Even officers came often upon parade wrapped in old blankets, and the feet of the shoeless soldiers left blood stains in the snow. Nevertheless, they kept up such a show of strength, that they were left unmolested by the British. In their winter quarters in Philadelphia, with the countenance of such inhabitants as were still loyal to the crown, the winter passed in a round of festivities.

The battle of Saratoga was the turning point of the war. It made the French think the colonists no longer rebels, but people worth helping. Franklin, who had been in France with two other commissioners over a year without official recognition, now obtained it, and in February a treaty of amity and commerce was concluded between France and the United States. This treaty was coupled with another of eventual defensive alliance. In the following month Franklin was received by the King. The other commissioners wore the court dress; the sturdy Franklin adhered to his republican simplicity. He was the popular idol of the Parisians ; and at his reception by the Academy of France, he was addressed as the man who had "wrenched the lightning from the clouds and the sceptre from tyrants." Sick, perhaps, of their own pomp and vanity, the Parisians were in a perfect fever of admiration of Franklin's straightforward simplicity.

CHAP. XXIX.
THE WAR OF INDEPENDENCE.

1779—1781.

THE eventual treaty between the United States and France soon came in force. The French ambassador in England announced to the British Ministry, in March, 1778, that the United States were in full possession of independence, that a treaty of commerce and amity had been concluded, that the King of France was determined to protect the lawful commerce of his subjects, and had taken measures for that purpose in concert with the United States. This was regarded as establishing a state of war. The British ambassador was recalled from Paris. The British statesmen, in office and out, were divided. The great Earl of Chatham, who had opposed the war, was wakened to oppose what he deemed a dishonourable peace; and when the Duke of Richmond advocated the withdrawal of the British troops, the Earl of Chatham, who had come down to the house, aware of what was to be done, ill and broken, rose and protested against yielding an inch of British ground. In the midst of his speech he tottered and fell back, in a fit of apoplexy, of which shortly after he died.

In June, 1778, the British evacuated Philadelphia, crossing over to New Jersey, and marching to New York. The crossing of the State occupied a little over two weeks, and Washington followed, harassing the British. On this march occurred the battle of Monmouth, one of the most severely contested during the war. The British had the advantage during the early part of the day, the Americans later. Both armies remained on the field ; but during the night the British retreated with such silence and skill, that their disappearance was not known till daylight. During this march, the British lost two thousand men, including desertions. The retreat was inevitable, for a powerful French fleet, under the Count D'Estaing, was already on its passage. Had he found Howe in Philadelphia, and his fleet in the Delaware, the position would have been a serious one. D'Estaing arrived in July, and undertook to co-operate with the Americans in the siege of Newport, Rhode Island. Disputes arose between the American officers of the army and the commander of the French fleet. D'Estaing withdrew, and the siege was raised.

There was much distrust of the French among the Americans. Perhaps as citizens of the new republic, they had not quite forgotten their traditional dislike as British colonists often at war with their French neighbours. Heated debates took place in Congress, the undefined powers of a legislative body without an executive head causing frequent disputes. Meanwhile, in the progress of the war, savage things were done on either side. The country was, in many districts, demoralized. Marauders ranged themselves for plunder and the purposes of hate under both flags. An American, named John Butler, organized early in the war a band of traitors, Indians, and vagabonds, who dressed and painted like Indians, with which he harried the borders. In July, 1778, he attacked the settlement of Wyoming, Pennsylvania, with his band of " Rangers," as they called themselves. The settlers were overpowered, the Indians took nearly three hundred scalps, and, having capitulated, the survivors— men, women, and children—were permitted to fly, though savage ferocity murdered many fugitives. The houses were burned, and the settlement desolated. All along the frontier, the Indians were incited to attack the Americans, though some of the tribes refused to attack, and even joined them.

In the spring of 1780, Charleston, South Carolina, surrendered to Sir Henry Clinton, and the State was assumed to be again under the Crown. But while many were willing to submit, or obeyed under constraint, the spirit of resistance was still alive; and Generals Francis Marion and Thomas Sumter, the former of whom was called the "Swamp Fox," crept about in the woods and marshes annoying the British out-posts, and attacking convoys and detachments. These men were more than mere partisans, and their names are historic. As the tide of success ebbed and flowed, the British treated as deserters those among their prisoners who had been forced previously into the British service, or who had accepted submission, or taken the oath of allegiance. All these things maddened the south, and indicated the final defeat of the British arms. Meanwhile, at sea, British transports and private ships were captured by American privateers. Congress early in the war had both built national vessels and authorized and commissioned privateers. Among these privateers, the most noted —a terror of the seas—was John Paul Jones. One ship which he commanded was named, after Franklin's "Poor Richard," almanack-maker, *Bonhomme Richard.*

Washington had to be extremely patient and cautious, and to bear with many murmurs of those who complained that he did not gain any great victories, like Gates at Saratoga—forgetting that Washington's policy in preventing General Howe from reaching Philadelphia through New Jersey, and in impeding his march from the Chesapeake, had made Burgoyne's defeat possible. There were jealousies too among the generals, but in only one case did it rise to treachery. Benedict Arnold, a brave but fierce and selfish man, was long a subject of distrust; and, as he claimed, of neglect. He had even been tried for dishonesty. But his undisputed military talent procured for him the command of the fort at West Point, on the Hudson River. It was a most important point, commanding the approach to New York, then held by the British army, and keeping open the communication between New England and the west. Arnold opened a correspondence with Sir Henry Clinton, who had returned from Charleston to New York; on the 23rd of September Major John André, an English officer, was stopped by three American scouts, as clad in citizen's clothes he was riding towards New York. His manner and replies aroused their suspicions, his offer of a large ransom confirmed them. He was searched, and concealed in his stockings were found a plan of the fortifications at West Point, a memorial from the engineer on the attack and defence of the post, and returns of the garrison cannon and stores. These were in Arnold's handwriting. André was detained, but permitted to send a letter to Arnold, who made his escape. Washington, returning from Connecticut, turned aside to examine the condition of the works at West Point, and there first heard of Arnold's treachery after his flight. The first duty was to provide for the safety of the post ; since the preparations for the completion of the plot, including the capture of Washington himself, were already in progress. On the 29th André was brought before a board of officers, and unanimously adjudged a spy. The execution of the sentence was delayed until the 2nd of October at the request of Clinton that representations might be made in behalf of the prisoner. The overtures were for an exchange. The answer was that no one but Arnold could be received in exchange for André. This could not be, and André suffered. If the purpose of a spy be to obtain damaging information, by covert means, he had done it. Washington did not sit in the board which tried him. His remains were taken home to England, and buried in Westminster Abbey. He was a youth of promise and much beloved. So also was Nathan Hale, a graduate fresh from Yale college, who was executed as a spy in 1776, having been found within the British lines. In character and in standing they were equals, and their sad fate was the inexorable rule of war.

Troubles came thick and fast on the Americans in the winter of 1780–81. There was neither pay nor food to be had for the soldiers. The Pennsylvania troops in their winter quarters in New Jersey revolted, from sheer suffering; but were won back to their allegiance, and a large number discharged, as they claimed was their right. Two British emissaries sent from New York to corrupt them were hanged as spies. The New Jersey troops followed the bad example; but it was deemed necessary to adopt sterner measures. Their camp was surrounded by a detachment of loyal troops; three of the ringleaders were tried by drum-head court-martial, of whom two were shot and the other released.

Gates, who had been appointed to the command of the American army in the south, had "changed his Northern laurels for Southern willows." In August, 1780, he was routed by Cornwallis at Camden, South Carolina. He was superseded by General Nathaniel Greene. Greene was the son of a Quaker preacher in Rhode Island. At the beginning of the Revolution he renounced his Quaker principles, studied military tactics, and commanded the Rhode Island troops who joined Washington at Cambridge, which under his drill and discipline were among the best troops in the field. He deserved, gained, and kept the confidence of Washington, was early promoted, and had distinguished himself in most of the leading battles in the war. He worked in boyhood as a blacksmith, but by diligence in study supplemented the little he had learned in a common school. When Greene reached his command in North Carolina with about four hundred men, he found the skeleton of the Southern army, without artillery, stores, or discipline. To restore the last required vigorous measures. The whole country was suffering under the cruelty of the partisan rangers, on both sides.

A detachment of Greene's army, under General Daniel Morgan, encamped at a place called Cowpens in South Carolina, was attacked by a British force under General Tarleton, January 17th, 1781. The rout of the attacking force was complete, so skilfully were Morgan's men posted and led. The American loss in killed and wounded was less than a hundred ; the British, over three hundred, besides five hundred prisoners, and a large amount of military stores. Notwithstanding the victory, the Americans were compelled to retreat before the superior force of Cornwallis.

So ill shod were they that the ground was tracked with the blood from their wounded feet, the supply of blankets was one to four men, and that of food scanty and irregular. Greene halted at Guilford, North Carolina, and there, on the 15th of March, was attacked by Cornwallis. The British gained the victory, but with such terrible loss that it did them as much harm as a defeat.

The pursuers now became the pursued. The royalists were dispirited, and the undecided rallied to the support of the Americans. Harassed by Greene, Cornwallis reached Wilmington, a seaport of North Carolina, with the wreck of his army, where a body of troops sent from Charleston awaited him. Greene left Cornwallis in Wilmington, and pursued his course to the south, now successful, now defeated; till, by the month of September, the British held in three States— the Carolinas and Georgia—only the three seaports, Wilmington, Charlestown, and Savannah. In Charleston the British commander completed the disaffection to the crown by the execution on the gallows of Isaac Hayne, a man widely known and esteemed. After the fall of Charleston, Hayne had accepted British protection. When the British were shut up and could no longer protect him, he joined his countrymen, was taken in arms, and hanged.

In the beginning of 1781, Arnold, now holding a royal commission, was sent to Virginia with sixteen hundred men. Lafayette had made a visit to France, and had been received at home with high honours, being followed by the most hearty official commendation of the American Government. He returned to America; not, as at first, a fugitive, but with high military rank and reputation. To Lafayette, Washington entrusted the checking of Arnold. That traitor's stay was only long enough to burn Richmond and indulge in a brief exhibition of ferocity. Cornwallis arrived upon the scene, and, having no desire for his company, ordered him to New York. He obtained the command of an expedition to Connecticut, where he burned New London, took a small fort by storm, massacred more than half the garrison after the surrender, killing the commander with his own hand. And that is the last to be said of Benedict Arnold, except that the British officers, to their honour, never would receive him as a comrade. In St. John's, New Brunswick, where he tried to reside, he was hung in effigy. A British officer whom he challenged stood unhurt before Arnold's fire, and declined to return it. " I leave *you*," he said, " for the hangman."

Cornwallis, reinforced, made war on the Virginians.

Lafayette, reinforced, contended with him. Virginia became the last battlefield. The French contingent, under Rochambeau, marched in by land. Cornwallis was driven to Yorktown, on the Chesapeake, but the French fleet under De Grasse appeared in the bay, and cut off both the chances of relief and of escape. Washington, who had sent troops forward, himself hurried to join the army, spending one night at his own home, Mount Vernon. On the 9th of October, 1781, the siege batteries against Yorktown being completed, Washington himself applied the match to the first gun. The two allied armies pressed the siege. Once the British forces attempted a sally, but in vain. As a last resort, it was proposed to cross the York River and push to the north, but that was abandoned ; and to save useless bloodshed Cornwallis capitulated on the 19th, with seven thousand men as prisoners of war. The ships and naval stores were given to the French. The loss of the British during the siege was about five hundred ; that of the Americans, three hundred men. The investing armies numbered sixteen thousand men, seven thousand of whom were French. So closed the serious work of the war, though Indian raids and partisan difficulties continued on the western borders somewhat longer.

The news came to Philadelphia at night. It is said

THE SURRENDER AT YORKTOWN.

that the officer who brought the intelligence was taken up for knocking too loud at the door of the residence of the president of Congress. In those days the watchmen called the hours, and the city was waked with the cry, " Past twelve o'clock, and Cornwallis is taken!" An aged door-keeper of Congress is said to have died of joy.

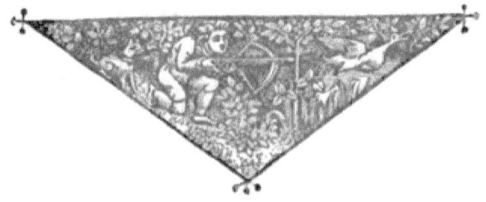

CHAP. XXX.—THE AMERICAN REPUBLIC.

1782—1794.

THE war in the United States was virtually closed by the battle of Yorktown. But the hostilities between Great Britain and the allies of the United States continued. Spain and Holland had been drawn into the quarrel, and their paths over the seas were no longer safe. The fleets and cruisers of the allied nations were to be found throughout the Atlantic. The vessels bringing home sugar and other West India products had to be guarded by ships of war; and the settlements themselves were in danger, in spite of the great victories won by Admiral Rodney. The Spaniards took back the peninsula of Florida, which had not joined the thirteen colonies. The French had taken St. Vincent, St. Lucie, and Tobago, and several of the lesser islands. Demerara was first taken by the Dutch, and then retaken by the English.

Count De Grasse, with his fleet, after the great success in Chesapeake Bay, sailed to the south, meaning to make a grand descent on the two chief English islands, Jamaica and Barbadoes, but Admirals Rodney and Hood were there to watch him. They could not save St. Kitts from being taken, but on the 5th of April, 1782, they fought a tremendous battle, which did immense damage to the French fleet. Captain Cornwallis had the satisfaction of avenging his brother's disasters by taking the *Ville de Paris*, De Grasse's flagship, with the Count himself on board, and thirty-six chests of treasure, intended to pay the French troops which were to have taken Jamaica. The French lost nine ships, the English none; the French lost nearly three thousand men, the English not two hundred and fifty. Thus England could finish the war with a victory, and peace was made.

The rights of England to the United States were given up, and their boundary traced where they touched on Canada and Nova Scotia. In the West Indies the islands seized on either side were given up, except that the French kept Tobago. The Dutch and English likewise exchanged conquests, but the Spaniards kept Florida. The French were at that time attempting much in Guiana, or Cayenne, as they called it, and settlements of intelligent people were

made there. The wonderful natural history of the
place began to excite interest in Europe, and so far as
so unhealthy a region could prosper, it flourished greatly.

Sir Guy Carleton had been sent out to America in
1782 to supersede Sir Henry Clinton, and he bore the
olive branch. Congress declined to treat except in
conjunction with France, and in Paris; but Sir Guy's
conciliatory manners, and his putting a stop to the
border cruelties of "rangers" and Indians, had a great
and salutary effect. Peace already existed when, on
November 30th, 1782, the provisional treaty between
Great Britain and the United States was signed in
Paris. The final treaty, which awaited the negotia-
tions between England and the continental powers,
was not signed till nearly a year later. But the provisional or preliminary treaty was accepted as conclu-
sive. Early in April official intelligence was received
of the signing of the treaty, and on the 19th of that
month George Washington, in general orders, announced the cessation of hostilities. He directed the
chaplains with the several brigades to render thanks,
and he did not forget to remind the army that the day
was the anniversary of the battle of Lexington. "On
such a happy day, which is the harbinger of peace,
a day which completes the eighth year of the war, it
would be ingratitude not to rejoice."

In November the British army left New York, a city of which they had held possession ever since, seven years before, Washington had retreated before them. The embarkation was leisurely made, permitting Americans who still adhered to the crown to take with them their effects. On the 25th an American force marched in and took formal possession. " Evacuation Day " is still kept as a holiday. But bitterness against the " Tories "—as British loyalists were called —wore away. A stipulation of the treaty was that the loyalists should not be harassed with confiscation. The laws against them were generally repealed. Many returned to their homes ; and this lenity prevented the embarrassment of the new nation by a disaffected faction.

The United States had hitherto continued under the " Articles of Confederation " adopted during the war ; but it was soon discovered that a confederation without a head, and a legislature without an executive, would not serve. In 1787 a convention was called, under the sanction of Congress, but independent of it, to revise the articles. The convention met in Philadelphia, and Washington was elected its presiding officer. Eleven States sent delegates. After four months' consultation a Constitution was put forth, to be in force when nine States should have ratified

it.   By the month of July, 1788, ten States had
accepted, and the others presently came in.   At the
first session of the new Congress of the United States,
ten amendments of the Constitution were proposed and
afterward adopted by the States.   Two more were
added at intervals of several years.   The thirteenth,
fourteenth, and fifteenth, relating to the altered condition of the slaves, and the adjustment of the country
after the war of the rebellion, were adopted in 1865
and 1870.

Each State has a separate government of its own,
but for the management of national matters there are
a national Legislature, or Congress, and a national
Executive.   The choice of a President is made by
electors chosen by the people.   The term of office is
four years, but the incumbent may be re-elected.
Congress consists of two Houses—representatives
elected by voters in their districts, and a Senate chosen
by the Legislatures of the States.   The representative's term is two years, the senator's six.   Each State
has two senators, and one is elected every three years,
making the Senate a perpetual body, over which the
Vice-President of the United States presides.   The
Vice-President, chosen at the same time as the President, must be taken from a different State.   To
prevent jealousy it was decided that the President

should live and Congress sit in a place belonging to no State, and a tract of country was ceded by Maryland and Virginia. It is called the district of Columbia, and includes the cities of Washington, Georgetown, and Alexandria, the former being the seat of government. It was laid out by Washington himself in 1791, as the "Federal City." In 1800, after the death of Washington, Congress held its first session there, and the city took the name which it now bears. The district has now nearly two hundred thousand inhabitants, exclusive of Government officials. The inhabitants proper have no vote in national affairs, and the office-holders who retain their State citizenship must go home to vote.

All men are pronounced in the Declaration of Independence " free and equal," but did this mean black men as well as white ? The Constitution left the question to the several States. But the words slave and slavery are not used in the original instrument. In the north, Negroes had been inherited from the old English and Dutch settlers, and their masters were rather ashamed of possessing them. In Massachusetts, a black woman named Elizabeth Freeman, commonly called Mum Bet, had, as early as 1766, appealed to the courts of law, and with Theodore Sedgwick as her advocate, obtained her freedom and

compensation for twenty-one years' service. She spent
the rest of her life as a hired servant in the Sedgwick
family. Many Negroes followed her example and were
declared free. In 1777 a vessel from Jamaica, with
several slaves on board, was brought into Boston as
a prize. Her cargo was advertised, including the
Negroes, but the authorities interfered, and the Negroes
were released. In 1783 a master was found guilty of
assault for whipping a slave. The Bill of Rights,
adopted in the State Constitution in 1780, was
appealed to on the trial, and the decision of the court
put an end to slavery in Massachusetts. In 1787 one
of the last acts of the Congress of the Confederation
was to pass an ordinance by which slavery was forbidden in the territory north-west of the Ohio River.
In 1820 the degree of latitude 36° 30′ was established as
the line north of which slavery could not be established.
Massachusetts was the only State, at the close of the
Revolutionary war, in which slavery was illegal. Six
more of the northern States immediately or gradually
abolished slavery, but the six southern States clung to
the system.

Washington was the first President of the United
States. He was chosen in 1789, receiving the votes
of all the electors, and he lived in considerable state.
" His Excellency " was tacitly adopted as the title of

the President ; but Congress refused to authorize any other title than " President of the United States," which has always been the official designation. Washington was inaugurated President on the 30th of April, in New York, which was then the seat of government. His journey from Mount Vernon to New York was a continued triumphal progress. He landed amid salvos of artillery, and the hearty cheers of thousands. A carriage was prepared for him, but he preferred to walk to his lodgings. The streets through which he passed, attended by a long civil and military train, were decorated with flowers, banners, and all other possible tokens of welcome. On the day of the inauguration he was drawn by a single pair of horses, in a chariot prepared for the ceremony, on the panels of which were emblazoned the arms of the United States. Washington Irving, his biographer, refers to four and six horses with servants and outriders in rich liveries, with which the first President of the Republic sometimes appeared in New York. Such style was not unusual in the colonies before the Revolution. Washington was passionately fond of that noble animal man's best brute friend, the horse. The Revolutionary war, in the hands of its leaders, was not the destructive work of a mob, and old society customs were maintained. At Washington's levees, to which every one came in full dress, he wore a black velvet coat, with a white satin waistcoat, silver buckles at his knees, and his hair powdered and gathered into a bag.

During Washington's administration, three more States were added to the Union. Vermont, the Green Mountain State, was separated from New York. Kentucky (the Indian word for the Long River), the wild western part of Virginia, grew to a population large enough to become a State, though there was so much fighting with the Indians that it was called "the dark and bloody ground." Among its oldest towns is Lexington. The settlers were laying out the place in 1775, when the news of the battle of Lexington reached them in the wilderness, and they took the name for their new town. Tennessee was cut off from Carolina ; and thus one free State and two slave States were begun.

All forms of religion were free; none had any help from the State, none any advantage over the other. In the procession at Philadelphia, in honour of the new Constitution, the Hebrew Rabbi walked between two ministers of different Christian denominations. But the Episcopal Church was at a great disadvantage; nearly all its places of worship had been closed during the war. Many of its ministers and missionaries, especially those who were English born, felt compelled by their

ordination vows to adhere to the crown. Most of
them retired quietly. But the Rev. Mr. Boucher, of
Annapolis, in Maryland, preached obedience to the
utmost. He was told that he would be punished if he
went on reading the prayer for the King. His answer
was from his pulpit, on which he had laid a brace of
pistols. He took for his text Nehemiah's defiance of
his enemies (vi. 10, 11), and his sermon ended with:
"As long as I live will I, with Zadok the priest, and
Nathan the prophet, proclaim, 'God save the King!'"
His property was confiscated, and he was driven back
to England. The Episcopal Church shared in the
enmity against England. Even in Virginia, where it
had been supported by the State, that protection had
been withdrawn. Yet George Washington was a
Churchman, and William White, an Episcopalian, was
the first Chaplain of the Continental Congress in 1777.
After the war the Episcopal Church could no longer
look to England for clergymen, and there were no
Bishops in America to ordain them. Under existing
laws no English Bishop could consecrate unless the
candidate would take the oath of supremacy. The
Scottish bishops, not being thus bound, consecrated
Samuel Seabury, the first American Bishop, at Aber-
deen, on the 14th of November, 1784. On the 4th of
February, 1787, Parliament having passed a per-

missory Act, Bishop White, of Pennsylvania, and
Provoost, of New York, were consecrated in Lambeth
Chapel, the two Archbishops of England, and three
others, uniting in the office of consecration. Bishop
Madison, of Virginia, was consecrated at the same
place, on September 19, 1790. In September, 1792,
the first consecration of a Bishop in the United States
took place; that of Bishop Claggett, for Maryland. In
1789, a Prayer-book, much resembling the English one,
was set forth, and thus began the " Protestant Episcopal Church in the United States of America." Each
diocese elects its own Bishop, subject to the approval of
the others; and each enacts its own canons, in a convention of its clergy and elected laity ; and each parish
chooses its own rector. The diocesan canons must be
in harmony with the canons of the General Convention.
That body meets triennially, and is composed of clerical
and lay deputies chosen by the several dioceses, with
the bishops who, holding their seats *ex officio*, are a
perpetual body. The House of Bishops is presided
over by their senior, and sits with closed doors ; while
the debates in the House of Delegates are open. It
may be noted that in the Act of Parliament authorising
the consecration of American bishops, there was a
proviso that no clergyman of the American Church
should officiate in England. This restriction was

removed in 1840. Whether it had been enforced before, or not, Bishop Doane, of New Jersey, was the first American Bishop to officiate in England. He preached at the consecration of the parish church in Leeds, in 1841.

In Virginia, and the Carolinas, and Georgia, were the most Episcopalians; and in the Carolinas there was a considerable Huguenot element. Pennsylvania was still Quaker, modified by Presbyterians and Episcopalians. In New York the Dutch Church had been firmly planted, but the Episcopal Church had many and influential adherents, as it had also in New Jersey. New England was Congregational, or Independent, with an abiding leaven of Puritanism ; the Baptists being in church organization Congregational. The Presbyterians were influential, wherever they took hold; and the Methodists were a rising body, their ministers having found adherents almost as soon in America as in England. Louisiana remained Roman Catholic. Maryland, though settled under the auspices of a Roman Catholic proprietary, gave Protestants equal rights, for her charter required it. There were all sorts and varieties of sects ; and the recoil from the free-thinking of France introduced in America the modern "revival of religion"—a revival of zeal without persecution—a religious and salutary contagion.

CHAP. XXXI.—THE REVOLUTION IN HAITI.

1791—1803.

THE French had been very prosperous in the West India isles, especially in their half of the large and fertile one of Hispaniola, or St. Domingo. There, as in all the other Indian isles, the population consisted of whites, who, if born there, were called Creoles; of black slaves; and of a coloured race, the offspring of the other two, who were called Mulattoes. Mahogany, satinwood, and other valuable timber, grew in the forests; cotton, coffee, and sugar in the plantations; and the Creoles, both there and in Martinique, were very rich and prosperous, and, in general, were not bad masters to their slaves.

In Europe, however, the French revolution had begun. The success of the American revolution, and the sympathy with republicanism which the aid of France in the War of Independence had created, had set the ideas of liberty at work. In the National Assembly the affairs of the colonies were taken up. In 1790 it was decreed that each colony, by its assemblies freely elected, should express its wishes in regard to a national constitution. This opened the fearful war of races. The Mulattoes, though not slaves, were not recognized as citizens. The Creoles claimed the exclusive right to vote, the Mulattoes insisted that they had an equal right to the suffrage and to representation. In 1791 the French Assembly issued a decree in favour of the Mulattoes, conferring equality on all free persons of colour. The Creoles, utterly shocked at this decision, had organized an Assembly of their own, and trodden the tricoloured cockade under foot.

While the Creoles and Mulattoes were contending, a fearful catastrophe impended over them. The Negro slaves were not considered in the matter, and were regarded as too ignorant to enter into the question. But soon reports came that the slaves were everywhere rising in arms; and white people came hurrying into Cape Town, having scarcely escaped being murdered by their servants. All the women and children whom the ships could carry away were put on board, and all the Creoles took up arms to defend themselves. In the meantime the slaves moved about in the open country, gathering in numbers wherever they went,

burning and plundering the places where they had
worked, and massacring whole families of the French.
There were striking exceptions. The slaves of Count
Lopinot rallied round him in a body, and at last came
away with him to the British island of Trinidad, where
he obtained a grant of waste land, and made a new
home with them. Another Negro saved his master's
two little ones, of five and three years old, took them
to Carolina, and there toiled hard himself to maintain
them, and give them a good education. In spite of
such instances of attachment, in two months' time two
thousand whites were slain, one hundred and eighty
sugar plantations, and nine hundred of coffee and indigo
were ruined, and one thousand families were brought
to poverty. The whites were everywhere driven into
the cities, and there besieged. No less than ten
thousand blacks perished in these attacks, but they
still remained in force in the plains.

In 1791, commissioners arrived at Cape Town from
France to endeavour to re-establish order. A general
amnesty was proclaimed. The basis of the adjustment proposed to leave the internal affairs of the
colony to its own Legislature. This was in effect revoking the former decrees. But the planters absolutely refused any concessions whatever, even to the
Mulattoes, and demanded the unconditional submission

of the slaves. Of course this made the coloured people desperate. The Mulattoes now sided with the Negroes, and the war became more horrible than ever, the whites treating the blacks like wild beasts, and the Negroes retaliating with the most horrid barbarities. The blacks had now an organized force of forty thousand men, under François Dominique Toussaint, who was surnamed L'Ouverture. He was a truly great man, able as a general, competent as an organizer, and humane as a soldier, repressing the violence of his followers. He was a born slave, but did not join the insurgents till he had secured the escape of the agent of the estate and his family, from whom he had received kind treatment.

In Europe things scarcely less barbarous were happening. The National Convention had succeeded the Assembly, and the frightful guillotine was in action. The Republic had been proclaimed, and Louis XVI. had been executed, January 21, 1793. The Jacobins classed the hapless planters of Haiti with the enemies of the Republic; and, irritated at them for not having submitted to the measures proposed, the Convention sent out a new commission after revoking the powers which had been conferred on the Legislature of the island. A quarrel arose between the sailors of the French fleet at Cape Town and the Mulatto population;

French politics entered into the disturbance, royalists and Jacobins, whites and Mulattoes made the streets run with blood, and the Negroes from outside the town rushed in; and in slaughter and desolation Cape Town was reduced to ashes. Immediately upon this event the French commissioners published a decree proclaiming freedom to all blacks who should enrol themselves under the banner of the French Republic. Toussaint with his troops passed into the service of the French, and Negro slavery was abolished for ever.

And now appeared the British upon the scene. England and the French Republic were at war, and Sir John Jervis, having captured Guadaloupe, Martinique, and most of the other French islands, arrived at Port au Prince, and espoused the cause of the planters against the Negroes. He occupied Port au Prince, and commenced a systematic warfare for the reduction of the island. Toussaint, however, at the head of the French troops and the Negro forces, aided by the yellow fever, the worst enemy of the English, pressed the invaders back, and they were forced to leave the island and its deadly fever to the management of Toussaint.

A frightful war now broke out between the Mulattoes and Negroes, which ended in the defeat of the former, their murder by thousands, and their expulsion from Haiti. The Spanish end had been ceded to France by Spain, and Toussaint, who held his appointment still as an officer of the French Republic, was acknowledged in the Spanish colony; and in 1800 his authority was admitted through the whole island. He sent an envoy to Napoleon, now First Consul, who returned with a decree from Napoleon, confirming Toussaint in his command as General-in-chief, and taking Haiti under the shield of the last French constitution. In a proclamation the First Consul called on the "brave blacks to remember that France alone had recognized their freedom." The leading chiefs of the island met and drew up a constitution. They conferred on Toussaint unlimited power, under the title of President and Governor for life, with the right to name his successor. This constitution was sent to Paris, with a letter to Napoleon beginning with the words, " The First of the Blacks to the First of the Whites."

The " First of the Whites " did not quite like this. Peace was made in 1801 between England and France. The French islands were restored to France. The first use Napoleon made of the peace with England was to send out a great fleet and army under his brother-in-law, General Le Clerc, to reduce Guadaloupe and Haiti. In Guadaloupe the same scenes had been enacted as in Haiti. The Mulattoes had risen against the Creoles, and the Negroes against both, and while the factions were at war the French arrived. The Mulattoes, in terror of the Negroes, joined the French, and the old state of things, including slavery, was restored. Warned by these things, Toussaint prepared to resist, and with Henri Christophe, his able lieutenant, kept up a guerilla warfare. Both sides grew wearied of the contest, and the French succeeded in detaching, by a separate treaty, Toussaint's principal officers, who accepted rank and pay in the French service; but Toussaint himself disdained the bribe, and retired to his farm on the faith of a treaty. The yellow fever now broke out among the French, and Le Clerc, anxious to complete his secret instructions to seize and transport the black leaders, betrayed Toussaint by an invitation to a personal interview. The black First Consul fell into the trap, was seized and sent in chains to France, where he was taken to the Temple Prison. He appealed to Napoleon, but he was pitiless; and, more cruelly than if he had caused him to be shot, he sent this child of the tropics to the castle of Joux, in the coldest part of the Jura. He was shut in a damp cell, with only straw for his bed, and scanty food; and there, in the winter of 1803, he was found dead in the straw.

Maddened by the restoration of slavery in Guadaloupe, the insurgents rose again in Haiti. The black chiefs who had gone over to the French revolted again. On the renewal of the war between England and France in 1803, the blacks were supplied with arms by the British cruisers. The yellow fever was the terrible ally of the blacks (whom it never attacks), and General Le Clerc was one of its victims. The remains of the French troops made their escape. The English cruisers made havoc of their fleet, which was almost completely destroyed, and of a force of thirty-five thousand men sent out under Le Clerc, scarce seven returned to France. Dessalines, one of Toussaint's generals, was crowned emperor in 1804, and attacked and killed by Christophe in 1806. Christophe was proclaimed as Henry I. of Haiti in the same year, and thus was the old Indian name resumed. Christophe, in his turn, was conquered by a Mulatto chief named Boyer, and killed himself rather than be made prisoner. Boyer united the whole island under one government in 1821; but in 1843 the Negroes rose in insurrection and forced him to flee the island. After a struggle, a Negro named Soulouque had himself proclaimed emperor, and was chiefly distinguished for a fearful massacre of the Mulattoes. In 1858 he was forced to abdicate. The island was divided into two republics, by no means friendly, and so remains. Santo Domingo, largest in area, is least in population. The prevailing religion is Roman Catholic; but Haiti has also a Protestant Bishop, coloured, a missionary of the Episcopal Church in the United States.

Thus upon the first place in America where slavery was introduced, and at a time when its sordid results were most profitable, first fell the disastrous consequences. Except in Haiti and Guadaloupe, the Negroes did not rise; and the French kept Cayenne as a place to which the proscribed who escaped the guillotine in Paris could be transported to die in the swamps. Among the historical personages connected with these events was Josephine Rose Tascher de la Pagerie. She was born in Martinique, and was early taken to France to marry the Viscount Beauharnais. She returned to Martinique to attend her sick mother, but when these troubles took place, she made her escape to France. There, in 1794, her husband was guillotined, and Josephine herself was among the proscribed. She barely escaped, to become the wife of Napoleon Bonaparte. The sharp, quick suffering of the guillotine might have been less than the lengthened torture of the repudiated wife.

CHAP. XXXII.—SPANISH AMERICA.

1806—1808.

FOR two hundred years Spain had quietly possessed her American colonies, which reached
from California on the north, down to Paraguay in the
south, embracing in name all the southern continent
west of the famous papal line of demarcation.

These colonies were managed by a Board at home
called the Council of the Indies, at which the king was
supposed to preside. The Council appointed Viceroys to Mexico and Peru. All the northern provinces
were under Mexico, the southern under Peru; and
the viceroys were like kings, living in very great
splendour, and with a nobility sometimes descended
from the old Aztecs and Peruvians, with whom the
Spaniards had intermarried. Everything was in the
power of the Council of the Indies. Even the Pope
could only act on the American Church through this
Council, and it appointed the archbishops and bishops.

All notion had been lost in Spain of ruling her
dependencies for their good.   All that was thought of
was how to get as much out of them as possible.
The gold, silver, and quicksilver mines belonged to the
crown, and were wrought for the king's benefit.   Tobacco was grown and sold only by Government in
Cuba and the other islands.   Licenses had to be bought
for growing sugar, coffee, cocoa, and indigo.   Flax and
hemp might not be grown at all, because the colonists
were to buy their clothes from the mother country.
No trade with any foreign country was allowed ; no
foreign vessels could find shelter in the ports ; and such
articles as Spain could not supply were only permitted to be brought in by merchants after paying a
huge price for a license.   Even in Spain, no ports but
Seville and Cadiz might trade with the New World,
and there were very heavy taxes for this privilege.

All this was bad enough in itself, but it was made
worse by the Council's habit of selling every office to
the highest bidder.   Out of fifty Mexican viceroys
only one had been born in the country, and all offices
were so entirely given to the Spaniards that it was
hardly possible for the Creoles to obtain justice on any
suit ; while in common life, they were violently and
hardly treated by these officials and the soldiers.

The Church was in a dreadful state.   It had been

richly endowed, and the people accepted whatever was
taught them. The bishops, however, being appointed,
as we have seen, by the Council for money, were
seldom faithful. They let the parish clergy be ignorant, careless, and vicious ; and of course the people
were worse, and added thereto horrible murderous
ferocity, especially where, as in Mexico and La Plata,
the Spanish blood had been mixed with the native,
and preserved the bad qualities of both. There was
superstition enough in Spain, but in America it was
grosser still. Shrines of images said to work miracles
were set up, and the worship paid to them could be
called nothing but idolatry. The Council of the
Indies bought Indulgences from Rome wholesale,
and sold them in America at their own price. Such
a state of things could only be kept up by ignorance
on the part of the people, and the Inquisition was in
full force, prohibiting all learning more modern than
the Reformation, and seizing all books that could open
people's minds. There was scarcely any occupation
for those who were not forced by slavery to work,
except gambling in various forms, especially on
fighting cocks and horse-races. There were perpetual
quarrels, which the knife or the pistol was generally
used to settle.

Never had a trust been more misused than that

which the Spanish kings sincerely believed had been committed to them by the dispensation of Heaven. Could it be without effect that the English colonies, on provocation that was a mere trifle compared with such oppression, had broken from the mother country? The very few who were aware of the fact began to be stirred. First of all awoke Francisco de Miranda, a youth of good family in Caraccas, a seaport town in Venezuela, and an officer in the army at that place. When only twenty years old he had set out on a journey on foot through the whole of Spanish South America. In 1783 he visited the United States, and contrived to get into correspondence with Washington and Lafayette, whom he made his models. Thence he went to Europe, and began again his travels on foot, and visited most of the countries in Europe, especially Spain, which he found in such a rotten state of decay that he was the more determined to break from it. On his return to South America he talked so much of the wrongs his country had suffered, that he was accused of revolutionary intentions, and to avoid being arrested he escaped to the West Indian Islands, and thence to England. He visited Russia, where the Empress Catherine wanted him to enter her service, but he preferred joining his friend Lafayette in France, which was in the midst of the Revolution.

A command in the French army was given him, but
he was unsuccessful, and was twice before the Revolutionary tribunal. Escaping with his life he repaired
to England, and tried to interest Mr. Pitt in the
freedom of South America. Spain and Portugal had
been forced to ally themselves with France, and thus
were reckoned the enemies of England. This cut
their colonies off from much intercourse with home,
for no fleet could stand against the British, and almost
all the islands had been seized by the British navy.

In 1806 Admiral Sir Home Popham and General
Beresford, without orders from home, crossed from the
Cape of Good Hope, and seized Buenos Ayres, on the
Rio de la Plata. Thence they sent home a million of
dollars, and announced that the land of gold was
found. But the Guachos, a fierce race of half-savage
herdsmen, who drove the cattle of the plains in desperate rides on their wild horses, rallied under Liniers,
a French officer, crossed the river in a fog, and
attacked Beresford in Buenos Ayres. There was a
terrible battle from house to house, ending in all the
English in the town being made prisoners, though
Admiral Popham continued to blockade the river.
Reinforcements were sent out to him, but the Spanish
colonists defeated them, and recovered their city.
This affair is regarded as important, since it showed

the colonists that they could contend with a European force ; and planted the germs of courage for the future revolution.

Miranda, finding that Mr. Pitt would not help him, came to the United States in 1806. The relations between the States and Spain were by no means friendly. The purchase of Louisiana from the French had caused disputes about the boundary of Florida. President Jefferson's government was no doubt in sympathy with Miranda, and so was popular opinion, but no open government aid or recognition was given him. He made preparations, with a show of secrecy, for an expedition to Caraccas ; and, while the expedition was fitting out in New York, resided some time in Washington. He bought, or chartered, a ship called the *Leander*, with the aid of numerous ardent young men who called themselves "sympathizers," and enlisted as volunteers two or three hundred men. With these he sailed for St. Domingo, where he obtained two smaller vessels as transports. The Spanish governor had notice, and sent out a ship of war, which captured the transports, with some sixty men on board. The *Leander* escaped to Trinidad, and the English captains there undertook to protect Miranda's landing in Venezuela. He took possession of two or three towns on the coast. But it was yet in vain ; the

Spanish force was too strong, and the indolent minds of the Creoles were not yet sufficiently stirred to make them rise to join Miranda, so that he was forced to return to Trinidad, and the expedition was broken up. Meanwhile, the promoters of the enterprise were prosecuted in the United States, to avoid compromising the government with Spain. They were, however, acquitted.

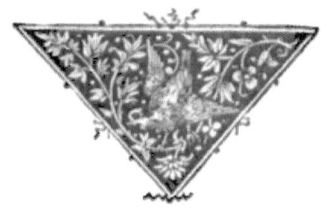

CHAP. XXXIII.—THE REVOLT IN SPANISH AMERICA.

1807—1813.

NAPOLEON had entirely cowed the King of Spain, Charles IV., who made no objection when, in 1807, a proposal was made to him to divide Portugal with Spain. The reigning Queen of Portugal, Maria I., was insane, and her son João (John VI.), who ruled in her name, made no resistance to the invaders, but shipped his mother and all his family off for Brazil, and set up a court at Rio Janeiro.

Next, on pretence of settling a family quarrel, Napoleon invited the King of Spain and his son to Bayonne, and kept them there, in captivity, while he gave their throne to his brother Joseph. Neither the Spaniards nor Portuguese would submit to this monstrous injustice; and the English, coming to their aid, carried on the Peninsular War against the French; while a junta, or committee, at Seville represented the Spanish Government.

The battle of Trafalgar had so crippled the French fleet that Napoleon's whole power was on land. Thus the English mastered all the islands belonging to France or its allies. In Cuba a Cortes, or council, swore to preserve the colony for the true Spanish king, Charles IV. In Martinique the Negroes tried to make a rising, like that in Haiti; but French and English joined to prevent such horrors, and it, with the other French islands, was held by England. So also were the Dutch isles, together with French and Dutch Guiana, Holland having been by this time absorbed by France.

The Spanish-American colonies acted in diverse manners. None would have any concern with Bonaparte, but in each of them there was one party, chiefly of Spanish officials, who held by the old country, and another of Creoles, who thought this the time for breaking loose. Only in Peru, as early as in 1806, an officer tried to raise the people; but no one would attend to him, and he was put to death at Cuzco, declaring that no one who was not in office knew the wickedness of the Spanish Government towards those under it, and that a reckoning must follow.

In Mexico the national party called on the governor, Don Jose Ituregarry, to call an Assembly; but the Spanish officials prevented this by throwing him into prison, under charge of wanting to become a king. They carried on the government against the increasing disaffection for two years, but there was a bitter hatred growing up against the name of Spaniard, and a fellow feeling between the Indians, Mulattoes, and Creoles was growing stronger.

The outbreak came at last, in 1810, begun by the Curate of Dolores, Miguel Hidalgo—a little, thin white-haired man. He and his people surprised the Spanish officials, and burned their houses, and the villagers around began to join them. They took several small towns, and wherever they found a Spanish house they plundered and destroyed it, often murdering the family. They gathered numbers as they went on, till sixty thousand had come together, and marched upon the city of Mexico.

The viceroy, Don Francisco Venegas, sent for a famous image of the Blessed Virgin called *Nuestra Señora de los Ramedios*, and having had it placed in the cathedral, went thither in full uniform, placed his staff in Our Lady's lap, and besought her to take command of the city. The tidings had such an effect on the devoutly superstitious insurgents that they turned aside to their hills without firing a shot. The troops followed, and twice defeated them. Hidalgo was captured while trying to go to procure supplies from the

United States, and was shot July 27th, 1811 ; but the wild peasantry continued to keep up an outlaw warfare from their refuge in the forests.

Miranda, in that same year, 1810, landed again in Venezuela, hoping to stir the people. He gained an important assistant in Don Simon Bolivar, a man of good birth at Caraccas, who had been educated in Madrid, and had travelled through Europe. There he married a Spanish lady, who died of yellow fever immediately upon her arrival at his native home. He visited the United States after the death of his wife, and was so struck with their institutions that he joined Miranda with heart and soul. A Junta, or committee of government, was summoned, in which all the provinces under the Spanish Captain-General were represented. This Junta began issuing its decrees in the name of the King of Spain, who was held captive by Napoleon ; but the Spanish colonial officials, declining to join in what was a revolutionary movement, were thrown into prison. An appeal was made by Bolivar to England ; but England had enough to do in aiding Spain to get clear of the Bonapartes, and declined to interfere, especially as Spain, represented by her juntas, was the ally of England. Blanco White, an able man, half Spanish, half English, published in London a Spanish journal, in which he pleaded the example of

the American revolution to show that it was vain to
suppose the old severe yoke could ever be reimposed.
But the Cortes in Spain were furious, and it was determined to force the old system on the settlements.

Upon this, on the 15th of July, 1811, Venezuela
declared itself independent, and the war began with the
Spaniards who held by the mother country, commanded
by General Monteverde. In the midst, on the 26th
of March, 1812, Maundy Thursday, there was a
most frightful earthquake, which almost destroyed the
town of Caraccas, and killed twenty thousand people,
besides those who died of hunger and misery afterwards. The people took this as a token of the wrath
of heaven, and lost heart. Bolivar was in command
of the citadel of Puerto Cabello. The fortress was
given up by treachery, and he had to surrender.
Miranda also was forced to yield, and contrary to
promise was treated as a prisoner, and sent to Spain,
where he died in the dungeons of the Inquisition.
Bolivar would have had the same fate, but he had
timely warning and fled to Curaçoa.

In the south, Prince John of Portugal had laid claim
to Buenos Ayres, but in vain. The Viceroy Cistieros
kept him out, but could not maintain the Spanish
power. His secretary, Mariano Moreno, became the
leading spirit of a Junta, which, in May, 1810, made a

declaration of independence. Monte Video would not join it, and the whole country fell into a dire state of utter confusion and lawlessness.

Things went on in the same fashion in Chili on the west coast. There were no nobles there, but there had been much less mixture of the Spaniards and Indians. The colonists were chiefly Biscayan mountaineers, and as the climate is temperate, they had not lost their vigour and energy. The Indians were civilized and intelligent, and the Spanish system never was felt so severely on the west as on the east coast ; so that but for the fall of the kingdom at home, there might have been no revolt. In April, 1811, however, independence was declared, a Junta appointed at Santiago, and a young man named Juan Jose Carrera made General.

But Peru had never revolted, and troops came from thence, who though twice defeated by Carrera, reduced Chili to obedience in 1813. Thus, it may be convenient to remember, that in 1810–11, there were four declarations of independence—in Mexico, Caraccas, Buenos Ayres, and Santiago, the chief cities of all the Spanish possessions except Cuba and Peru ; and that, in two years, all the republicans had been defeated and reduced, except those in the city of Buenos Ayres, and wanderers everywhere in the hills and plains.

CHAP. XXXIV.—THE LAKE WAR.

1812—1814.

THE two great men to whom the United States owed most, lived to see the nation prosperous. Franklin lived to be eighty-four, and died in 1790. The French revolutionary leader said of him that "he was the sage whom two worlds claim as their own." He died while Washington was President. After his second election, having served eight years, the good general refused to be elected a third time. He retired to Mount Vernon, where he died, full of years and honours, in 1799. As Congress declared, he was "first in war, first in peace, and first in the hearts of his countrymen." The centennial of his birthday, February 22, 1832, was duly honoured by the nation, and the day is still observed as a holiday. To him John Adams and Thomas Jefferson succeeded; and it is worthy of note that these two great men died on the 4th of July, 1826, within a few hours of each other.

Both were members of the committee which reported the Declaration of Independence, fifty years before.

Two chief inventions secured the power of America. Eli Whitney, a Massachusetts schoolmaster in Georgia, seeing the trouble and loss of time in separating the cotton seeds from the wool, invented a machine called a gin, which made the process so cheap and easy, that Carolina and Georgia could send out cotton to all the world. But this made the slaves who cultivated it so valuable, that there was less chance than ever of their being set free in the South.

In 1807, too, Robert Fulton, of Pennsylvania, launched his first steamboat on the Hudson, and although for a long time steam was only used for short distances, it did much to make the large country of distant States communicate more readily within itself.

During the great struggle that England had made with France, each of the two powers had forbidden neutral nations to trade with the other, and though the United States did not get concerned in the quarrel, their ships were seized by the English if they traded with the French, and by the French if they traded with the English. Moreover, the English men of war claimed the right of searching all American vessels, and pressing into their own service any Englishman whom they found sailing under another flag. As it was not always easy to tell an Englishman from an American, and the captains were not particular, it was said that full a thousand Americans had been forced to fight in the British navy. Quarrels could not but arise, and at last, in 1812, when James Madison was President, war was declared between the mother and the daughter countries.

The Americans went from Detroit, in Michigan, to attack Malden in Canada, accomplished nothing and returned. They were followed by the English General Brock, and the American commander surrendered. The English then occupied the post of Detroit, and indeed the whole territory. This was in July, 1812. In October of the same year, a force of a thousand men crossed from New York, to attack Kingston in Canada. This battle is known in history as that of Lundy's Lane. After hard fighting the victory fell into the hands of the English. In this affair General Brock was killed, and the loss on both sides was terrible.

In the month of August, 1812, occurred the first important success of the American navy. The frigate *Constitution* captured the *Guerrière* after an action so sharp, though short, that the prize was burned. But the most remarkable fight was in 1813, between the English *Shannon*, a thirty-eight gun ship, and the *Chesapeake*, an American with the same number of guns, but much better "found" as sailors say with the newest improvements. The *Chesapeake* had an old quarrel with England. Vessels of war, as well as military regiments, have their traditions. As long before as 1807 an English ship, the *Leopard*, had claimed the right to search the *Chesapeake* for deserters, and on a refusal had fired, killing four men and wounding sixteen. The *Chesapeake* was unprepared. The commander indignantly hauled down his colours, and offered his vessel a prize to the English. But the English commander refused to accept a surrender which would have been the opening of war. He boarded the *Chesapeake* and took from her crew four men. Three of them proved to be Americans, the fourth was hanged. The British Government disavowed the admiral's orders, under which the *Leopard* had acted, recalled the admiral, and returned two of the three Americans, the other having died. But the affair added to the irritation; and the relations of the two countries grew more and more unpleasant, while the war party in America grew in strength from the popular excitement, until hostilities resulted. When the *Shannon*, which had taken and destroyed twenty-five prizes, came and lay off Boston Harbour, waiting for a ship to come out, and Captain Broke sent in a written challenge to the American fleet, Captain Lawrence, in the *Chesapeake*, sailed out to fight a sort of sea duel. It was a fierce and desperate engagement. Lawrence fell mortally wounded, crying out " Don't give up the ship ! " The ship was taken, though Broke was severely wounded. Captain Lawrence died five days after the battle, and was buried by his captors with military honours.

The dying words of Lawrence became a naval motto. A brig built by the Americans on Lake Erie was called after him, and on her signal flag were embroidered the words of the dying captain. The *Lawrence* was the flagship of Lieutenant Perry, who commanded a squadron of nine vessels, carrying from twenty guns to one only. Opposed to him was the English squadron of six vessels, and it is hard to compare the relative strength ; but it is safe to say that the men on each side behaved gallantly. Perry's ship was shattered, and he was forced to go to another in an open boat. But he won the victory, and he had the honour of being the only man to whom an entire British squadron ever surrendered.

Following the engagement on Lake Erie came, in October, the " Battle of the Thames." The Thames is a river of Canada, nearly opposite Detroit in Michigan. General William Henry Harrison, Governor of Michigan, and afterward President of the United

States, seeking to recover his territory, invaded Canada. With the aid of Perry's fleet, as transports, he landed his troops, met General Proctor, and defeated him. In this battle Tecumseh was slain. Previously to the breaking out of the hostilities between England and America, this famous chieftain was making war upon the United States upon his own account, and was defeated by General Harrison at Tippecanoe. He joined the British cause, and it is supposed that it was by the hand of Colonel R. M. Johnson that the brave Indian fell. The remote consequence of this battle was that Colonel Johnson became Vice-President of the United States in 1837, and Harrison President in 1841. Harrison died in one month after his inauguration. The rallying cry in the election of Johnson and of Harrison included their military services. Detroit was evacuated by the British upon the approach of Harrison. An expedition of the Americans against Montreal, in this same year, was a humiliating failure.

Admiral Cochrane, with an English fleet, having on board General Ross and four thousand men, entered the Chesapeake in August, 1814. They landed, unopposed, at a point about fifty miles from Washington, and met their first repulse at Bladensburg, on the Potomac, where an American force of about one thousand regulars and five thousand militia awaited them, hoping to save the city of Washington. It was a hard fight, and there was much loss on both sides ; but at last the Americans were forced back, and were obliged to leave Washington to its fate. General Ross burned the President's house and the Capitol, with many valuable papers and records. It was an ungenerous deed, but the English had not yet got over their bitterness of feeling, and still viewed the Americans as successful rebels. The English troops, on the night of the day after their entry into Washington, silently evacuated the city, leaving their camp-fires burning, and, reaching the point where they had landed, re-embarked. Their severely wounded were left in Washington.

On the 13th of September the British forces landed at North Point, on the Patapsco River, about fourteen miles from Baltimore. In a skirmish General Ross was killed. The Americans retreated, but formed again. A second and sharper encounter took place, but as Baltimore was approached the siege of the city seemed impossible, and was given up. The fort guarding the approach to Baltimore by water was bombarded by the fleet, without making any serious impression upon it, though the fire was kept up for twenty-four hours. Francis Scott Key, an American

lawyer and poet, who had gone on board one of the
English vessels, was detained through the bombard-
ment, and composed during the night the famous
American lyric, " The Star Spangled Banner." An
attempt was made during the night of the 14th to
land troops from barges, but it was beaten off. The
commander received a mortal wound, and in the
desolate retreat slowly bled to death, as he was borne
away. The attack on Baltimore was abandoned, and
the English fleet withdrew from the Chesapeake.

On the lakes the struggle still continued, whence
this is sometimes called the Lake War. There was a
battle on Lake Champlain, in which the Americans
gained a complete victory, and this prevented Sir
George Prevost from invading the States. The war
on the Atlantic coast continued, and many seaports,
north and south, were attacked or laid under contri-
bution. In Florida the English took possession of
Pensacola, which was still Spanish, and made it a
military and naval station. Thence they attacked
Fort Boyer, in Alabama, but were driven off. General
Andrew Jackson marched upon Pensacola, for this
breach of neutrality, and entered the place without
difficulty. The English blew up the forts they had
occupied, and sailed away.

Then the English made an attempt against New

Orleans, in the hope that the half-French inhabitants might like the American Republic no better than the Canadians did. But the Louisianians disliked the English name; and the volunteers and militia from Tennessee, Kentucky, aided them in resistance. General Andrew Jackson, in command of the American forces, was vigilant and active. There were several days of sharp fighting on the banks of the Mississippi. On the 8th of January, 1815, the decisive battle took place. General Packenham, the leader of the English forces, was killed in an attack upon Jackson's entrenchment, and the English army retreated with immense loss. New Orleans was saved, and the 8th of January became a national holiday. The title of Hero of New Orleans was made the rallying cry for Jackson, and in 1829 he took his seat as President of the United States.

In these days of telegraphs it is hard to realize that this battle was fought fifteen days after a treaty of peace was signed at Ghent. Of the numbers engaged in the battle there are contradictory accounts. The invading force is stated at seven thousand. The Americans are said to have numbered twelve thousand. But many of them were without arms, and employed in digging trenches and throwing up fortifications, and the actual number engaged was but a fraction of the force. They had the advantage of position, and the comparative loss of the two armies —two thousand on the side of the English, and about four hundred on the American—shows how great this advantage was. War has never been renewed between England and America, though controversies have occurred. The two nations were taught mutual respect.

CHAP. XXXV.—INDEPENDENCE OF LA PLATA AND VENEZUELA.

1812—1820.

BY 1812 almost all the revolted colonies of Spain had been reduced; but in another year they were up in arms again. On the Rio de la Plata, Monte Video held out for Spain, Buenos Ayres for independence, till, near the end of 1812, the former place was taken. Five or six thousand loyalists gave up their arms, and the countries on the river were free to carry on their quarrels and their lawless habits after their own fashion. As La Plata means silver, they took the name of the Argentine Republic, consisting of thirteen provinces; and they succeeded in defeating all Spanish attempts to reconquer them, so as to get their independence acknowledged in 1817.

Bolivar had come back to Venezuela in 1812. The insurrection in that quarter had never been quite extinguished, but was maintained in New Granada by a youth of twenty-two, Jose Antonio Paez. When seventeen, he had been sent by his uncle, the parish priest of Azanac, to carry a large sum of money to another curate. He was mounted on a mule, and armed with an old sword and pistol. The lad was foolish enough to tell his business at the inn where he dined, and was in consequence pursued by two robbers, who demanded his money or his life. He shot one man, and a pistol bursting wounded the other in the face, then rushing on them with his sword, he put them to flight. But justice was so uncertain that he feared revenge, and durst not return home. So he betook himself to the Llanos, or huge flat plains, where the country is one vast tract of grass, roamed over by large herds of wild horses. The only occupation of the inhabitants is herding them, catching and branding, and sometimes selling them. Paez hired himself out at one of these horse farms, under a Negro overseer, who made him do the most dangerous tasks, undergo terrible hardships in the heat of the plains, and end the day in such servile work as bringing water and washing his Negro master's feet.

In 1810 Paez became a soldier in the patriot army, but was made prisoner. Once he escaped being shot, by the mere chance of having borrowed a hat which caused him to be mistaken for an officer, and remanded. A night or two after, a sudden alarm made the Spanish army break up their camp, and leave their prisoners, so that Paez escaped. The story rose that he had been delivered by an army of the ghosts of his friends, who frightened away the Spaniards.

After this, Paez, with a small body of horsemen, resolved to try to win the Llanos, thinking that if he could prevent the Spaniards from getting horses from thence, the cause would be gained. He was just the man to gain the affections of the Llaneros, having lived their life, and grown perfect in training the wildest horse, hunting down the fiercest bull, and killing the crocodile in his own river. After gaining a victory over General Don Rafael Lopez, he succeeded in driving him out, and the wild Llaneros gladly flocked to fight under such a leader. He had the pleasure of having the old Negro foreman brought to him as a prisoner, and treated him kindly, only now and then teasing him by calling out in his voice : "Josè Antonio ! bring water for my feet !" on which the old man would reply, " Boy, boy, you have not forgotten your tricks !"

Mercy, however, was not common. The Spanish general, Monteverde, barbarously punished the rebels ; and Bolivar put forth a proclamation of " War to the Death !" after which all prisoners were killed on both sides. Beginning with only five hundred men, Bolivar drove Monteverde out of city after city in Venezuela, increasing his army at every step ; defeated Monteverde at Lasto-guanes, and took Caraccas, where, in 1814, a convention of officers proclaimed Simon Bolivar Dictator of their new republic.

But the royalists rallied against him, and as, in the year 1814, Napoleon was overthrown, and Ferdinand VII. returned to the throne of Spain, troops were sent to recover the colonies. General Morillo, with an immense army, and quantities of artillery, arrived to reduce Venezuela to obedience. Bolivar was obliged to flee to Jamaica once more, and Morillo began to exercise cruel vengeance on Venezuela and New Granada.

Numerous families fled to the Llanos, and were received by Paez. Their hardships were terrible. There was nothing to eat but the flesh of the wild cattle, nothing to wear but their hides, no shoes, no hats, no shelter, continual rains, and rivers overflowing. The refugees said they courted danger, to escape their miserable life. However, having caught and tamed enough wild horses to mount everybody, Paez chose one thousand of his best men, and two thousand white horses, because these were said to be the best swimmers ; and, each rider leading a spare horse, he crossed the River Apure in time of flood, fell on the city of Barenas when no enemy was dreamt of, drove out the Spaniards, and brought back the horses, laden with all that his camp of wanderers required. Afterwards he gained the city of Achaguas, and, in a battle on the River Apure, defeated and killed General Lopez, and established himself in that province.

General Morillo, who had come out from Spain, was an able captain, but he fancied the insurgents a mere band of semi-savages. He defeated Bolivar at Ocumare in 1816, and another patriot shortly after; and, in January, 1817, marched upon Paez. The battle of Las Margaritas had convinced Morillo, as he wrote, that these men were not "a small gang of cowards." Fourteen times did Paez charge the infantry of Morillo with his wild horsemen, setting the dry grass of the Llanos on fire, so that if the Spaniards had not reached a spot previously burnt, they would have had no standing ground. At last they retreated, and Bolivar soon after returning, the insurgents began harassing the royalists in all the country of the Orinoco.

Defeats befel the patriots again, and nothing but the perseverance of Bolivar could have carried them through. The two generals joined forces on the Apure, where Morillo had a large flotilla of gunboats; and the wonderful cavalry of Paez did what probably never happened before in the history of the world—

captured these boats. Fifty mounted lancers, without saddles, dashed into the river, and swam up to them, assisted by their good horses, and captured them all. Morillo then retreated, and the next spring, 1819, lost another battle at Angostura.

A Congress was there held, and Venezuela and New Granada agreed to unite in a republic to be called Columbia. They had one more great battle to fight with General Torre, who had succeeded in the command, Morillo having returned to Spain. The place was Carabobo. Bolivar commanded the foot, Paez the horse, and they were assisted by fifteen hundred British volunteers. The Spaniards had nine thousand men, but were totally routed. The battle took place in June, 1820. Two months later Bolivar entered Caraccas in triumph, and a constitution was formed for Columbia on the model of that of the United States, Bolivar becoming President, and Santander, who had fought under him, Vice-president.

In Brazil, João VI. had become actual King of Portugal, by his mother's death in 1816. But he remained in Brazil until 1820, when a great disturbance broke out at Lisbon, and he was forced to return to Spain, leaving his son Pedro in America, as Viceroy.

CHAP. XXXVI.—INSURRECTION IN MEXICO.

1812—1820.

THE insurrection in Mexico had not been extinguished by Hidalgo's death. In fact, a land like this, full of mountain passes, was very hard to conquer, and the inhabitants were ready, all over the country, to live a bandit life. General Rayon, who took the command on Hidalgo's death, called a Junta, which offered to acknowledge Ferdinand VII., if he would come out and reign in Mexico, as the Portuguese sovereigns were doing in Brazil. But Ferdinand was too fast in the clutches of Napoleon, even if the proposal had been made in earnest.

Another priest, Don Josè Maria Morelos, had distinguished himself by taking Acapulco with a very small, ill-armed force. In the beginning of 1812 he was at the gates of Mexico, and so highly was he esteemed, that on the news of his approach Don Josè

Maria Fernandez Guadalupe de Victoria, a rich young lawyer, twenty-two years old, at once went out to join him. The Viceroy, Venegas, sent for the Spanish general, Calleja, to defend the capital, and received him as if he had been a great conqueror. Indeed, he did come through terrible difficulties across a country where there were no roads, and his men had to cut their way through such a forest, that once they took twenty-four hours in going three miles. He was a hard, vindictive man, and whenever an insurgent place fell into his hands, he burned everything in it except the churches and convents. He and Venegas could not agree, and he soon marched from the city of Mexico to take Cuautla. His cruelty made the Mexicans resolute to resist his assault. Every one fought with the utmost bravery, Morelos repulsing the assailants, and the Indians on the roofs of the houses keeping up such a shower of stones that they could not form again. Then Calleja established a regular siege, sending for artillery from Mexico. Still Morelos held out, but as he had never expected a regular siege he had laid in no stores of victuals, and there was a dreadful famine. Bats, lizards, rats, and mice were sold at large prices, and when an ox strayed near the walls there was a sharp fight to secure it. When Morelos attacked a battery and drove out the enemy, there was no keeping his soldiers from throwing themselves on the salt meat and cigars, and they lost so much time that they were driven out again. So Morelos did not venture to attack the camp, being sure that he could not keep his hungry men in order when once they saw food. But when he could hold the city no longer, he came out at midnight, and marched his men in dead silence right through the besieger's lines. At last they came to a hollow ravine, over which they had to lay hurdles, carried by the Indians. A sentry heard them, and fired his musket. The Spaniards woke, but Morelos gave the word for his men to disperse, each man shifting for himself, to meet again at Trucar. The Spaniards, in the confusion, began firing at each other, and killed many men before they found out the mistake; but they avenged themselves by most horrid cruelties on the unhappy city of Cuautla.

Morelos himself was hurt by a fall from his horse, but his army met again with very little loss, except of the gallant Leonardo Bravo, who was taken prisoner. His son, Don Nicolas, soon after gained a success, in which three hundred prisoners were taken, and Morelos made him a free gift of them, that he might offer them in exchange for his father's life. But the Viceroy would not listen to the offer, and caused Don Leonardo to be immediately put to death. On this, young Bravo at once released all the three hundred, "to put them out of his power," he said, "lest, in his grief, he should be tempted to massacre them in revenge for his father." However, Morelos soon gathered troops in such numbers, that, after defeating three Spanish divisions, he attacked the large city of Oaxarca. Here Captain Victoria swam across the moat sword in hand, and cut the ropes of the drawbridge in the face of the enemy, who were so amazed that he did not receive a single wound. The troops rushed in and took the place. Acapulco was soon after taken, and then Morelos collected a Congress, and an Act of Independence was put forth on the 13th of November, 1813. This was the great wish of the heart of Morelos, but from this time a series of disasters set in upon him. He tried to take the city of Valladolid, but was there defeated by General Llano and Colonel Iturbide. One of his best chiefs, Matamoras, was taken, and though a large number of Spanish soldiers were offered in exchange, the captive chief was shot by order of Calleja, who had been made Viceroy instead of Venegas. Thenceforth the insurgents shot all their prisoners.

Iturbide gained further successes, and Morelos was obliged to escort the Congress from Oaxarca to Puebla for safety. On his way he was surprised by two bodies of the enemy. He commanded Don Nicolas Bravo to escort the Congress with all the men except fifty, with whom he would do his best to stop the Spaniards. Most deserted him as soon as the firing became hot, but he still stood his ground so undauntedly, that the royalists durst not come near him till only one man was left by his side. Still unhurt, he was disarmed, made prisoner, and conducted, in chains, to General Concha. By him the patriot leader was treated with respect and carried to Mexico, where the whole people flocked out to gaze at him. He showed great calmness and dignity, and said that, in establishing the Congress, he had done the work he cared for in his life, and was willing to die. As a priest, he was given up to the Inquisition, and was by that tribunal degraded, having all clerical insignia taken from him one by one in the face of the whole people ; and this was the only thing that seemed to grieve him. Afterwards he was given back to "the secular arm." He dined with Concha, whom he embraced and thanked for his kindness. He was allowed to receive the sacraments, and then was led out to die. He knelt and prayed aloud: "Lord, if I have done well Thou knowest it; if ill, to Thy infinite mercy I commend my soul." Then he bound a handkerchief round his eyes, and gave the signal to fire. He seems to have been a really good man, driven into rebellion by the cruelty and injustice of the Spaniards. He had given his life to save the Congress, but his officers cared little for that body; and there were quarrels between Congress and the military, until, as the royalists pushed them harder, the contest between the civil and military leaders resulted in rupture. General Teran, the soldier in command in the province of Puebla, dispersed Congress by force, and the leaders fought each for himself without any plan, so that one by one they were put down.

Nicolas Bravo held out on the mountain of Coparo till he was at last forced to yield, and kept in prison. Guadalupe Victoria, in the province of Vera Cruz, lived a wild outlaw life, and seized all that did not travel with a strong escort between the port and the capital; but at last his band was broken up, and he wandered alone with nothing but his sword in the mountain forests. There he lived for three years; in the summer on fruits, in the winter in such hunger that he sometimes had to gnaw the bones of dead animals which he found.

In 1817 Don Xavier Mina, a Spaniard who had been baffled in trying to get a freer government in Spain, made an attempt to revive the cause of freedom in Mexico. He landed with a body of enthusiasts of different nations, some of whom were English. But he came just as the insurgents had been crushed, and the only leader in power was a priest named Torres, in the province of the Baxio, a ferocious, cruel man, who robbed and burned villages and towns under the pretence of cutting off the enemy's supplies. After a year of fighting, during which Mina grew disgusted with his cause, he was taken and shot in his 28th year. Torres was shortly after killed, and in July, 1819, the Viceroy wrote to Madrid that the insurrection was over, and that he wanted no more soldiers from Spain.

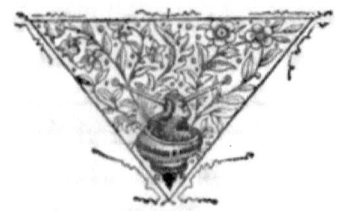

CHAP. XXXVII.—THE INDEPENDENCE OF MEXICO.

1820—1853.

THE Viceroy, Apodaca, had written to Spain that the rebellion was entirely put down, but he was mistaken. The battle had chiefly been fought by men of Creole birth, commanded by officers in the royal army; and in times of need, large promises of favour had been made them. As soldiers in the royal pay, they had fought against the patriots as bandits, and the cruelties on either side had made them bitter against one another; but when the rebellion was put down, they began to think that, after all, it had been the cause of their own country against which they had been fighting, and that Spain was a hard mistress, who made her colonies her slaves.

Spain was in an unsettled state, and Ferdinand VII. had been forced, in 1819, into accepting a constitution or rule, by which the King was checked by the Cortes or Parliament, and the Inquisition was abolished. Of the Spaniards in Mexico, some held with the old rule, some with the new, which of course they had been obliged to accept. The Viceroy, Apodaca, thought the constitution would overthrow religion, and everything good, and he resolved to proclaim a return to loyalty, to the *King,* not to the King and Cortes. He trusted for help to Don Augustin de Iturbide, a Creole who had risen to high command for his valour against the insurgents, and who had been terribly cruel. There is a letter of his still existing, dated Good Friday, 1814, in which he said that *in honour of the day,* he had commanded three hundred excommunicated wretches to be shot. The Spanish authorities fulminated the decrees of the Inquisition against rebel prisoners as heretics.

Apodaca, in 1820, gave Iturbide the command of a body of troops, who were intended to restore the power of the King. Instead of this, Iturbide proposed to them to maintain the Independence of Mexico, the Catholic Faith, and union among themselves. As they guaranteed these three points, they called themselves the Army of the Three Guarantees. The Spaniards in Mexico deposed Apodaca in their fright, and Iturbide continued to make progress. When Guadalupe Victoria had disappeared in the forests, at the dispersion and defeat of the insurgents, he told two Indians who were the last to quit him, that on a certain rugged mountain perhaps they would find his bones. As soon as the Mexicans were again in arms for their country, these Indians went to the spot, and spent six weeks in searching the woods in vain, till just as they were going to give up the quest, one of them saw prints of feet which must have worn shoes. He waited two days in case Victoria should return thither, and then being obliged to go home and get food, he hung on a tree the last meal he had, four little maize cakes. Two days later Victoria came to the spot and found the cakes, when he had been four days without food, and two years without tasting bread. He hid himself and waited, and in due time he saw his Indian friend appear, and sprung out to meet him. The Indian, seeing a spectre-like figure, covered with hair, and no clothing but an old cotton wrapper, and sword in hand, ran away in terror; and only on hearing himself called by name, did he turn back and recognize his old master. He took him to his home, and no sooner was it known that Guadalupe Victoria was found, than all the old patriots of the province rallied round him, and marched with him to join Iturbide, who was on his way to besiege the city of Mexico. However, a new Viceroy, Don Juan O'Donuju, had been sent out by the liberal party in Spain, and, finding Iturbide too strong for him, he recognized the independence of Mexico, in the name of King Ferdinand, and gave up the city of Mexico to the army of the three guarantees, on the 24th of August, 1821, all the old Spanish party being allowed to take refuge in Cuba.

A Junta was appointed, and Iturbide made President-General ; but the old patriot party soon found that he was not to be trusted, and Victoria took to the woods again. A Congress was called together, and there were hot disputes. Some wanted to offer Mexico as an empire to the brother of the King of Spain, others to have a republic, and those who feared Iturbide's ambition wanted to reduce the army, of which he was General-in-chief. Thereupon, he took his measures secretly, and on the 18th of May, 1822, the sergeants, common soldiers, and beggars, assembled before his house, and proclaimed him Emperor Augustin I. of Mexico, with loud shouts of *Viva !* and firing of guns. He filled the galleries of the hall of Congress with his soldiers, and thus forced the deputies to accept him, upon which Bravo and the other old patriots withdrew, as Victoria had done.

The new emperor made demands upon the Congress which were quite unsuitable to any notions of freedom ; and when these were not granted, he first arrested fourteen of the deputies ; afterward, when the rest would not bend to his will, he followed the example of Cromwell and Bonaparte, by sending his soldiers to turn the whole assembly out of its hall, and locking the door.

His whole dependence was on his army; but before he had reigned a year, he had quarrelled with one of his chief officers, General Santa Anna, Governor of Vera Cruz, who with his garrison declared that Iturbide had broken his oath by dissolving the Congress, and pledged himself to get it assembled again. The officer who was sent against Santa Anna at once turned against Iturbide. Guadalupe Victoria once more appearing, the chief command was given to him ; and most of the army, and all the country besides, were unanimously against Augustin I. He called together all the members of the old Congress then in Mexico, and offered to abdicate. But they said that to accept his abdication would be to allow that he ever had any rights, which they denied that he had ; but that he and his family should be allowed to depart, and should receive an income of £5,000 a year. He chose General Bravo for his escort, and was sent off in a ship to Italy. However, he could not rest there, and returned to Mexico in 1824, but was almost immediately taken and shot, lest he should begin a fresh disturbance.

Victoria, Bravo, and Negrete managed affairs while a fresh Congress was being elected to decide on the new form of government. It was to be a federal republic, after the fashion of the United States. There were thirteen provinces, reaching from the Isthmus of Darien up to the River Colorado, Texas being the most northerly ; and five more thinly settled territories, Tlascala, New Mexico, Colima, and Old and New California, these last lying westward of the United States. There was a Congress, divided into a House of Deputies and a Senate ; a President and a Vice-president, each to hold office for four years, and, unlike the American President, never to be re-elected for the next term of office. The President and all officers of government were always to be Mexicans, but the clergy of all degrees might come from any country. The Mexican Congress declared that no form of religion but the Roman Catholic should be tolerated, and did not interfere with the property of the Church, but abolished the Inquisition. The Mexicans were, however, put into great difficulties by the Pope, who viewed them all as rebels, and refused to sanction their appointments to bishoprics. Thus the Mexican Church has been left to itself, and as the

people were terribly ignorant, though devout, superstition has grown worse on one side, and misbelief or
infidelity on the other. This division of the people
introduced the matter of religion into the feuds and
dissensions of the republic. Though several of the
priests before the revolution were distinguished as
patriots and even as soldiers, the great body of the
clergy remained conservative, and with them were
joined a large portion of the better class of people.
On the other side were those of no religion, and those
who, still adhering nominally to their superstition,
hated the priesthood for its exactions, and who discovered how little morality, and how little sincerity,
many of the priests possessed. In a word, the popular
party, mixing religion and politics, understanding
neither, and debasing both, became a party of de-
structives. Brigandage prevailed ; sometimes dignified
with the name of patriotism, often robbery pure and
simple. While the country districts were unsafe, the
cities harboured gamblers, thieves, and idlers. Even
the better and more prominent men were not free
from the first of these vices. Public buildings, roads,
churches, and monasteries were destroyed, and the
proof of manliness was to strike at anything good
which had been Spanish, and was still preserved by
the conservative party. Nothing was repaired, the

cities had no police, and there was really no government. The Spaniards, in their two centuries of rule, had more than restored the damage they had done in their conquest ; but independent Mexico relapsed into a far worse condition than she was in under Aztec dominion.

In 1853, Santa Anna, then an exile, was recalled by the Mexicans and made Dictator. The history of this man is truly remarkable. He was a distinguished soldier in the war of the Mexican revolution, and was the first to proclaim the Mexican Republic in 1822. All his life he was appearing, disappearing, and reappearing in Mexican affairs ; now dictator, now in exile, now at the head of the army, and then in prison. In the time he had been upon the stage, some thirty changes of government had succeeded each other; during which Mexico had lost the Central American provinces and Texas and California. His recall was followed of course by his expulsion. He was unquestionably the most able man that Mexico had produced, though in his nature he shared in the cruel ferocity which seemed inseparable from the character of Mexican leaders.

CHAP. XXXVIII.—THE EMPEROR
MAXIMILIAN.

1858-1882.

MEANTIME out of the chaos in Mexico rose in 1858, Benito Juarez, "*le petit Indien*," as the French styled him, from his parentage. He seized Vera Cruz, where he could command the customs, revenues, and confiscated Church property to replenish his coffers. He even knocked down Church buildings, and sold their sites. It is said that a Belgian was the purchaser of one church for £19 10s. All this made him the idol of the anti-clerical party. He was elected President of the Republic, and executed the decrees against the Church with great severity. The foreign commercial residents in Mexico, thinking they had found at last a powerful strong-handed man who could settle the government, made him large loans for that purpose, to repay which the revenues of the customs were pledged by Juarez. But payment was evaded or refused, and after Juarez decreed suspension, for two years, of the pledge of the customs and the payment of foreign debts, his course brought the combined demand of England, France, and Spain for indemnity and reparation. A fleet, composed of vessels of the three nations, appeared in the Gulf of Mexico. Vera Cruz was occupied, and the threat made to advance upon the capital. An armistice was held, to the terms of which Louis Napoleon refused his assent ; and England and Spain, suspecting his ulterior designs, withdrew. The French troops still remained. In 1862, the French finally declared war against Juarez, and were joined by adherents of the clerical party. France had indeed entered into the civil war in Mexico, under the old rule "divide and conquer." The other European nations held aloof, the United States exercised diplomatic pressure against France; but her troops pressed on, took the city of Puebla by siege, and on the 10th of June occupied the city of Mexico. Juarez fled from the capital, and transferred his seat of government to San Luis Potosi.

A provisional government was established, of course in the anti-Juarez interest. An "Assembly of Notables" was summoned, representing the clerical party, with some others, perhaps, who were ready to follow any road out of anarchy. The Notables decided on a limited hereditary monarchy, with a Catholic prince for sovereign. The crown was offered to Maximilian, Archduke of Austria, and younger brother of the Emperor, and accepted by him. With his newly married wife, Charlotte, daughter of Leopold, King of Belgium, he sailed for Mexico, and was warmly welcomed, June, 1864, by the clerical party. He was a fine, high-spirited young prince of thirty-four, full of eagerness to do good. But Juarez was still in the field, and the larger part of the nation were determined to accept no foreign government. The Emperor and Empress were excellent people, who longed to bring the restless nation into good order. But they were not as clever as they were good, and were too German to suit those tropical people, the Mexicans, who hated their simple earnest activity and honesty. The national pride of the Mexicans chafed besides at having French soldiers everywhere.

The young Emperor had fallen into the hands of bad advisers. His Mexican counsellors tempted him into Mexican practices. He issued a proclamation in 1865 declaring the republic extinct in law and in fact, by the close of the term of Juarez and the vacancy of the Presidency. Juarez replied that he was President till another could be elected. In the same proclamation Maximilian threatened death to persons taken in armed resistance against his government. Under this edict many estimable and popular officers were put to death, and the army of Juarez gained strength in volunteers and recruits. Furthermore, Maximilian lost respect by consenting to the restoration of slavery, and other abuses, which in his heart he condemned. More trouble awaited him. The United States had, all the time, recognized the Republic of Mexico, and refused recognition of the prince, who, they said, had thrust himself where nobody wanted him. The United States having conquered its own difficulty, strong representations were made to the French Government against the presence of French soldiers in Mexico. Denied at the outset support from England and Spain, finding moral support nowhere, and pressed by the great expense of the army in Mexico, Napoleon withdrew his troops in 1866, and the Empress went to Europe to beg assistance. It was in vain. Maximilian was entreated to abdicate when the French departed, but felt bound in honour to remain. The nation rose against him. He made a brave defence, but on the night of May 14, 1867, was betrayed into the hands of his enemies by one of his officers, who is said to have received 3,000 golden ounces for his treachery. With two of his generals the emperor was tried by court martial and shot. The European ministers protested in vain against this breach of the laws of war. But it was no departure from Mexican precedent. The charges against him were based on his unfortunate decree, under which the officers of Juarez had been shot, and the two Mexicans who were executed with him were implicated in that unhappy measure. "Poor Charlotte!" he was heard to murmur, as he dropped the handkerchief as a signal to his executioners. Well might he say so ; for, shocked at his misfortunes, she became hopelessly insane.

The Mexican comment on these transactions was the election of Juarez as President, in the autumn of the same year. Re-elected in 1871, he died in office in 1872. The character of "le petit Indien" is open to many charges, but his ability and patriotism are unquestioned. Mexico still remains a republic, though it cannot forget its old propensity to rebellion and civil war. Its prospects just now seem to brighten. There has been no rebellion for six years, and the present President, Gonzales, was quietly chosen in 1880. The Panama railway, since it immensely shortens England's communication with her Australian colonies, makes peace very important. Though not traversing Mexican territory, it has its influence over her through her neighbours. In Mexico proper there are more than five hundred miles of railway, the latest in construction connecting the republic with the United States. Security for trade is promoted, and the condition of Mexico is now better than ever before.

One truly hopeful sign of light appears. Some of the devout and better educated of the Mexican clergy, aided by the missionaries, money, and sympathy of members of the Protestant Episcopal Church in the United States, are founding a new church organization, which promises to give vitality to the old stock ; rejecting errors and superstitions, but retaining its historical continuity. The name chosen is " The Church of Jesus."

CHAP. XXXIX.—INDEPENDENCE OF CHILI, PERU, AND BRAZIL.

1817—1882.

THE Chilian revolt had been put down by Spain in 1813; but by 1817 the patriots were up in arms again. The Argentine Republic, on the opposite side of the continent, sent them help, and they defeated the Spaniards at Chacabuco.

Thereupon they proclaimed a republic with General San Martin at its head; but in the midst of their arrangements the royalists gave them a severe beating. However, success made the Spaniards careless, and the Chilians won another great victory on the plain of Maypu. But what was worth much more to them was the volunteered aid of Thomas Alexander, Lord Cochrane, afterwards Earl of Dundonald. He had fought bravely under the British flag; but, on a false accusation about money matters, had been dismissed. He came to his title and estates in 1831, and was restored to his rank in the navy, and as Knight of the Bath.   Meanwhile he sailed about the world, tendering his sword wherever love of adventure or of freedom led him.   He came with his family to Valparaiso, entered the service of Chili, and with numerous English sailors and officers set himself as resolutely as Drake or Hawkins of old to drive the Spanish flag from the Pacific, not only from the Chilian, but from the Peruvian harbours.   Sailing for the great harbour of Callao with seven vessels, two fire-ships, and four hundred soldiers, he sent a flag to challenge the Viceroy of Peru to fight him, ship for ship.   The challenge was declined, and he resolved instead to attack Valdivia ; because it was deemed so impossible of capture that the enemy would not be on their guard. He could take with him upon this enterprise but three ships, and his own was so badly strained that he could only keep it afloat by pumping continually ; and to encourage his men he took his spell at the pumps with his own hands.

Valdivia was very strong, and defended by nine forts ; but they were far apart, and he made a dash at them one by one.   His boldness so dismayed the Spaniards that they surrendered the whole city to him on the 5th of February, 1820.   He went on sailing up and down the coast, seizing Spanish ships ; and on one of these voyages was dismayed to see his little boy of five years old perched on an officer's back, waving his cap and shouting *Viva la Patria !* having run away from home and got on board.

One night a Spaniard broke into Cochrane's house, which was a little way out of Valparaiso, and threatened his wife with death, unless she would reveal the secret orders with which her husband had sailed. She refused, and the man had actually once stabbed her with a stiletto when her servants came in and saved her.

Cochrane made a descent on the rocky islet of San Lorenzo, near Callao, with a fort upon it, in which he found thirty-seven Chilian prisoners, working in manacles, and chained at night by the leg to an iron bar. He made it a manufactory of rockets and munitions for fire-ships ; and sailed about capturing Spanish treasure ships. He sent parties to seize the trains of mules laden with treasure coming down from the mines in the Andes. On the 3rd of November, 1820, he sailed with a fifty-gun frigate through the narrow passage between San Lorenzo and the mainland, entering the harbour of Callao by a way in which it was thought no large ships could come. That same day tidings were brought that the city of Guayaquil had proclaimed its independence, and sent off its Spanish governor, without shedding a drop of blood.

There was only one large ship of war in Callao Harbour, but there were four lesser ones, and fifteen gun-boats, protected by the batteries on shore.   On the night of the 5th, Cochrane, with two hundred and fifty men in boats, stole up to the huge Spanish ship, the *Esmeralda*. Springing up the side of the ship, Cochrane shot the sentry, and shouted to his men : " Up, my lads, she's ours ! "   There was much hard fighting before she was won, and Cochrane was slightly wounded.   But he captured the ship with three hundred and twenty men in her, and thus did the greatest exploit in the war.

Peru had remained quiet under colonial rule, but the republics of Columbia on the north, and Chili on the south, felt it needful to root out the power of Spain. While Cochrane was attacking Callao, which is the seaport of Lima, General San Martin with a Chilian army beseiged Lima, and on its yielding, the independence of Peru was proclaimed, in 1821.   The royalists were strong however ; they regained possession of the city, and there was a good deal more fighting.   General Bolivar led an army from Columbia in 1822, gained a great victory at Pichincha, and took Quito.   He then marched upon Lima, which the royalists evacuated at his approach ; but their forces, under General Rodil, threw themselves into the forts of Callao.   At last, in 1824, the battle of Ayacucho finally broke the strength

of the Spaniards, though Callao held out with true
Spanish constancy, through eighteen months of
blockade, and only surrendered in 1826. General
San Martin was declared Protector of Peru in 1821,
but in 1822 summoned a Congress, into whose hands
he resigned all his authority, quitting the service of
Peru in disgust. He refused all money grants, but
accepted the public recognition of his valour and integrity. He retired to Chili, and thence to Europe. The
Peruvian Congress conferred upon him the honorary
title of Generalissimo and Founder of the Liberty of
Peru, and gave Cochrane public thanks for his services.

Upper Peru, namely the southern part, which con-
tains the higher Andes and the mines of Potosi,
refused to belong to Buenos Ayres, but requested
Bolivar to form a constitution for it as a separate State,
and called itself after his name, Bolivia. He gave it
a President for life, who was to have power to name
his successor. Bolivar was accused of intending to
join this new State with Peru and Columbia, and make
himself perpetual Dictator. However, he was so really
honest that the Columbians soon felt him to be their
only safe head, and he was elected President in 1828.
He kept the chief power in Columbia till his resigna-
tion in 1830. His death occurred in the same year.
Peru, which had elected him perpetual Dictator, had

meanwhile cast him off, and proclaimed a President. But he was a truly great man. He had spent almost all his fortune in the cause of South American liberty; and though he had much public money in his hands, he died poor. He had done great good in improving law and justice, and bringing in education; but he found it a weary and disappointing task, and was followed by constant suspicion and dislike. In truth, these men of Spanish and half-caste or mestizo birth were unfit for free institutions; and the fifty years that have passed since their emancipation have been full of disturbances and revolutions. Shortly before his death, Bolivar issued a farewell address vindicating his character; and his countrymen have done him the tardy justice which death procures for great men. In 1842 his remains were removed from their first humble place of sepulture, and interred at Caraccas, where a triumphal arch was erected to his memory.

The South American republics are Ecuador or Equator—containing the seaport of Guayaquil — Columbia, Peru, Bolivia, Paraguay, Uruguay, the Argentine Republic, and Chili. Patagonia remains unsettled and in the possession of the natives. England, France, and Holland retain their possessions in Guiana. Brazil remained nominally united to Portugal till 1826. When John VI., or João, with the

royal family of Portugal, fled to Brazil in 1807, Dom
Pedro, the heir to the Portuguese throne, was taken
with him. In 1821, John VI. returned to Portugal, and
left Dom Pedro as Prince Regent in Brazil. When
in 1822 the Brazilians made their demonstration for
independence, they took a middle course and elected
the Regent Emperor of Brazil, with the title of Pedro
I. The republicans in some districts refused submission ; and Cochrane, who had left Chili, gave his
services to Dom Pedro. The malcontents were suppressed, and the area of Brazil widened, and Cochrane
was created by the Emperor Marquis of Maranham.
In 1825 Dom Pedro I. was recognized by the Portuguese Cortes ; and in 1826, his father having died, he
claimed the crown of Portugal, but resigned in favour
of his daughter, Maria de Gloria. His Brazilian
subjects grew discontented, and demanded a constitution like that of England. Dom Pedro I. could not
make up his mind to grant this, and abdicated in 1831
in favour of his son Pedro, then about five years old,
now reigning in Brazil as Dom Pedro II. Leaving
his son to be educated by his ministry, Pedro I.
returned to Europe, and replaced his daughter on the
throne of Portugal, which had been usurped by her
uncle Miguel. The double abdicator, Dom Pedro I.,
died in 1834.

CHAP. XL. — THE EMANCIPATION OF NEGROES IN THE ENGLISH ISLES.

1772–1838.

ALL this time a great question affecting America was being fought out in England. It was the question whether it was right towards God or towards man, that one human being might be seized and made the property of another, like a sheep or an ox.

Good men took it up, and tried to argue it out. They said slavery was allowed by the Bible, and even in Christian times, and that Negroes were too dull to think for themselves ; and that though strong to work in hot climates they were so lazy that they must be made to work, and that it was better for them to be slaves than savages.   On the other hand, it was argued that, in the state of society under the Old Testament, if prisoners of war had not been enslaved they must have been slaughtered, and, likewise, that the Law guarded slaves carefully from cruelty.   The

Gospel had so worked on men's hearts that gradually freedom had come to all slaves in Christian lands, and that it had been really going back to heathen ways to enslave Negroes. Moreover, though a good man might train his slaves well, many only used them like tools, left them in gross vice and ignorance, and worked them harder, and used them far more barbarously, than the Law of Moses had ever permitted.

The first step to a better state of things was made by Mr. Granville Sharp in 1772, when he took up the cause of a Negro named Somerset, whom his master had brought from the West Indies, and claimed as his property to take back. The judges decided that no one is a slave in Britain, and that a slave thus becomes free from the moment he touches the soil of the British Isles.

Then Thomas Clarkson and William Wilberforce set themselves to stop the slave trade, namely, the actual stealing of men and women from the coast of Guinea, and selling them in America. It was a twenty years' struggle. Wilberforce began in 1787, and went on every year bringing his bill before the House of Commons; but it was not till 1807 that his perseverance at last succeeded in getting a bill passed which made it unlawful for Englishmen or English ships to be men-stealers.

But this was of little use while other nations went on with the horrid traffic, so the rest were asked to pass the same law. The United States did so at once ; and so did the republics of Chili, Venezuela, and Buenos Ayres; and Sweden and Denmark, Holland and France, when the great peace of 1814 was made.

But Spain and Portugal wanted to be paid for the loss, and even then Portugal only abolished the slave-trade north of the equator, and promised to put an end to it in eight years ; and Spain made the same promise, but did not keep it. Indeed the laws were of little use when there was no one to put them in force, and high prices could be had for blacks all over the hotter parts of America. So by further laws, agreed upon by the nations, it was ruled that slave-trading ships should be dealt with as pirates, and a right of search was granted. British ships were kept cruising in the Atlantic to search any vessel suspected of being a slaver, and seize it if any slaves were found on board. It was seldom possible to return the poor Negroes to their homes, since they had generally been captured by some fierce tribe, and therefore the British settlement of Sierra Leone, in Africa, which had been already begun for liberated slaves, was made into an abode for them to be trained in civilization and Christianity.

High prices still tempted the lawless men of all nations to run all the risks of carrying on the slave trade ; and the miseries of the wretched captives were increased as the vessels were made as small, light, and swift as possible. The slaves were hidden between decks in a fearfully crowded state, jammed together standing, and with so little air, water, or food, that numbers died, and the horrors and sufferings were unspeakable. Nothing could cure this while slaves could still be bought and sold, and Thomas Fowell Buxton and Henry Brougham (both at that date untitled) were working to do away entirely with slavery in English possessions. If coffee, sugar, and cotton could not be grown without slave labour, it was better, many thought, to do without them altogether. There were difficulties in the way, for it was unjust to ruin the West India planters, and the Negroes needed to be trained for freedom. Reports that their liberty had been decreed came to Jamaica in 1831, and they rose upon their masters, committed sundry murders, and they burned plantations, so that it was feared that the Haitian horrors would come over again. However, they were put down by force of arms, and in 1833 a grant of twenty millions was made to compensate the owners, and on the 1st of January, 1834, eight hundred thousand slaves were set free. They were to serve as apprentices to their masters for six years, but this was found not to answer. The Negroes could not understand their semi-freedom, and by 1838 this apprenticeship was given up, and there was not a slave in the British dominions.

The loss was heavy. The Negroes just released would not work when they were not obliged. In the West Indian climate the very smallest labour suffices to produce plenty of food, and the Negroes did not care for anything more. In the sugar and rum manufactures, and all else that had made the isles rich and prosperous, there was a falling off to the extent of three-fourths or more, and in some plantations production was entirely given up, and many families were ruined. Yet the evils of slavery are so great that even at this cost its abolition was well gained. There were cases, more frequent than otherwise, in which the master was good, and felt the responsibility of his charges ; but the misfortune was that there was no effectual legal mode to prevent power from being so used as to be cruel to the slave, and ruinous to the character of the master. Public opinion and, what is better than that, conscience, did not affect those who most needed control.

The liberation of the West Indian slaves, and the injury to the plantations, enhanced the value of slaves where slavery still existed. Other causes operated to raise the value of slave products. In the southernmost of the United States, especially in the rice swamps, and on the sugar plantations where it was thought only Negroes could possibly labour, their work was harder ; and the price of an able-bodied man or woman, and even of children, was raised to an extravagant sum. Slavery was chiefly profitable in a new soil, and in raising peculiar staples. In Virginia, where the soil was worked out by tobacco and farm crops, and in other middle State districts, people used to sell their superfluous slaves to the South, taking children from their parents, and entirely disregarding the tie of marriage. The child of a slave-mother was always the slave of her master, whoever the child's father might be. In a free land, an objectionable servant can be discharged, or a useless one dismissed. Under the slave system the only way to reduce the expense, or get rid of a bad servant, was to sell.

Yet the more the Abolitionists tried to make the Northern States ashamed of the institution with which they were politically associated, the more the Southern States prided themselves upon it. There always had been a jealousy between the two divisions, and it grew worse and worse. The free and slave States were equal in number, for whenever a free State was admitted at the North, another slave State was made at

the South. Of the eight Presidents elected previous to
1838, five were from the South, and the necessity of
courting the Southern vote kept that region most
powerful, though the North was strong in thoughtful
and influential men. Attempts were made to give
religious teaching and education to the slaves, their
own mistresses often acting as teachers. But this was
dreaded by the masters, whose apprehensions never
were realized, though many of the more intelligent
Negroes became restless, and ran away to the Florida
forests and to the swamps, and not a few made
their escape to the North, and thence to Canada. Yet
the history of slavery in the United States records
very few instances of violence or attempts at rising.
For whatever difficulty the Southerners had or feared,
the Northern abolitionists were held to blame ; and the
life of a man known to be on that side of the question
was hardly safe in some districts of the South, and his
presence was tolerated nowhere. Strangely enough,
all this time people in the North loathed and shrank
from Negroes, and would not let a coloured person eat
with them, or sit in the same seat at church, or in the
same public carriage. The condition of Haiti was a
bad precedent for the Negroes ; and the experiment
in Jamaica was pressed also against their emancipation.

Yet in Jamaica the result vindicates the laws of right

and justice. The coloured people are law-abiding and inoffensive. Extreme poverty is not known among them ; and while they produce enough for their own needs, they raise even something for exportation. The old plantations once deserted are being taken up by Cubans and others. Labour is supplied by "Coolies," or East Indians, who are brought under a system of indenture to this and other tropical regions, to take the place of the Negroes. Liable to abuse, and full of difficulties, the subject has been so guarded by legislation, that the strong objections made to it as a new system of slavery are being removed. There was a difficulty in Jamaica in 1865—a Negro rising—which was suppressed in a summary manner. Since then the island has gone on improving. There is little doubt that it will recover its former commercial prosperity. And there is no doubt that freedom is better than slavery.

It is to the credit of the Spanish American republics, with all their faults, that their constitutions prohibited slavery. The European nations followed the example of England as to their colonies. Only in "ever faithful Cuba," still a dependency of Spain, does slavery exist in the western world. However nominally faithful to Spain Cuba may be, the ruling party, the native Spaniards in the island, disregarded the edicts of the

Spanish Government against the slave trade ; and hold still with an iron grip the Negroes whose gradual emancipation the home authorities have decreed.   The importation of slaves has ceased ; Coolies and Chinese are introduced to take their place, and are treated with rigour.   For three years, from 1868, a rebellion was in active progress, during which over forty thousand prisoners were put to death.   The aim of the insurgents is the independence of the island and the abolition of slavery.   The native Spaniards, against whom the insurrections is aimed, form scarcely more than one-tenth of the population.   Against them are opposed Creoles, free Negroes, and slaves ; the same discordant elements which existed in Haiti.   The end of slavery must come—and let us hope without more horror and bloodshed.

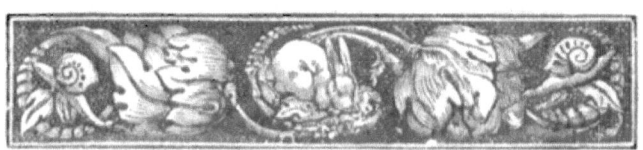

CHAP. XLI.—BOUNDARY QUESTIONS.

1838—1848.

ALL this time England's possessions to the north had been becoming more thickly peopled. A company for trading in furs, which had been formed in 1670 by Prince Rupert, and called the Hudson's Bay Company, had stations and forts for dealing with the Indian hunters all over the cold regions of Labrador and Rupert's Land. The operations of the company eventually extended across the continent to the Pacific Ocean, and round their stations a certain amount of population began to spring up.

Nova Scotia was chiefly peopled by descendants of the royalists who had left the States on their independence. Newfoundland harboured among her fogs colonies of fisher-folk ; and into Upper Canada there had long been a continual stream of settlers, many of them officers of the navy and army, who, being no longer needed after the great war, had obtained, on easy terms, grants of land in the backwoods.

Upper Canada was almost all British, Lower Canada chiefly French. There were jealousies between the two provinces ; and a feeling of discontent against the British Government was shown in a struggle of the Legislatures against the governors who were appointed in England. This opposition was most marked in Lower Canada, and resulted in actual rebellion in 1837. It was soon put down by the loyal militia, under Sir John Colborne, a tried old Peninsular general. Meanwhile, discontents were rife in the upper province, where the loyalists proved able to take care of themselves. There were many "sympathizers," as they were called, in the United States, and the rebels who escaped from Canada derived aid from them. A "Provisional Government" was formed by the insurgents in Upper Canada, which existed chiefly on paper, and made liberal offers for volunteers. This "Government" took possession of Navy Island in the British shore of the Channel of Niagara, and made it a rendezvous for volunteers, and a depôt of arms stolen from American arsenals. An old steamer called the *Caroline* plied between Navy Island and the United States side. In the night of December 29, 1837, while moored at her American landing, this vessel was seized by a party of Canadian loyalists. One man of her crew was killed in the struggle, and the captors set fire to the vessel, and sent her drifting down over the cataract, but without a living soul on board. Navy Island was abandoned, and the arms were restored. The rebellion in Canada had already been subdued before this affair. There was much soreness and some diplomatic correspondence on the subject, but this matter, with others, was adjusted by the Treaty of Washington in 1842. By that treaty the boundary between Maine and the British possessions was determined by mutual concessions being made ; and five years later the line between the United States and British territory on the Pacific coast was settled on the forty-ninth parallel.

An incident growing out of the Canadian rebellion was the arrest and trial of a man named McLeod. He boasted in the city of Buffalo of his share in the destruction of the *Caroline.* He was arrested and put on trial in a court of the State of New York, charged with the murder of the one man who was killed. Each country watched the case with much anxiety, but the prisoner was acquitted in default of evidence. Serious questions of national importance would otherwise have been involved.

In 1867 Upper and Lower Canada were united so

as to have one Legislature; and Nova Scotia and the other provinces, together with the immense tracts held by the Hudson's Bay Company, have been joined with them in one great government, called the Dominion of Canada. It is larger than Europe, but has fewer inhabitants than Scotland. The chief city is Ottawa. Almost all the population is British, except the Lower Canadians, and the Indians who still live at the west in large tribes. Government protects them, and they are not ill-treated; but it is impossible to hinder traders from selling them liquor, which ruins them. Some are settled round missionaries, who keep them in good order, and teach them to till the land; but their constitution seems best fitted for a wandering life, and they dwindle and die out, even when taken care of.

On the western outskirts of the United States frequent wars have taken place, of more or less consequence. It is the old, old story over and over again, and the Red men have had to fall back, step by step. Reservations of tracts are made for them, annuities are paid them, good men try to teach and Christianize them, and the laws forbid selling them " fire-water," as they call it. But greedy traders let them have arms, quarrels break out with the settlers, revenge begins, the Indians do some horrid deed of cruelty, and punishment follows. But the worst features of Indian warfare have been softened since the days when desperate scattered colonists fought for their lives. The Indians now feel the power they cannot resist. Still they are being swept away, though on the reservations missionaries labour for them, and large sums are raised by religious bodies to support the work. Many youths, male and female, are brought to establishments in the old States for instruction, and so far, with excellent results ; chieftains voluntarily offering their children to learn white men's ways.

Meantime difficulties arose about Texas, a large Mexican province, very scantily inhabited till settlers from the United States began obtaining grants. The Constitution of Mexico was like the United States, federal, and the settlers organized their State. In 1836 General Santa Anna overthrew the Federal Constitution. The Texans revolted, Santa Anna invaded Texas, and the Texans, under General Samuel Houston, conquered the invaders, and made Santa Anna prisoner. Texas became an independent republic, and so remained until 1845, and was recognized by the United States and the European powers. In that year it was admitted as a slave-holding State, into the United States under President Polk, though not without resolute opposition. Aside from the question of slavery, it was said the annexation would lead to war. And war followed. Though Mexico had recognized the independence of Texas, there was a disputed boundary. The quarrel of Texas became that of the United States. General Zachary Taylor (afterward, and in consequence of his military successes, President of the United States) was ordered to occupy the disputed territory. He was attacked by the Mexicans, and in the battles of Palo Alto and Resaca de da Palma defeated and drove them out of the territory in dispute. The Congress of the United States declared that war existed by the act of Mexico. Volunteers were called for, Taylor was reinforced and ordered to invade Mexico. He besieged and took Monterey in September, 1846, and then at Buena Vista defeated Santa Anna with about six thousand troops, against the Mexican force of about twenty thousand.

In March, 1847, General Winfield Scott, a veteran of sixty, Commander-in-Chief of the United States army, landed with twelve thousand men at Vera Cruz. That city surrendered on the 26th, and General Scott took his line of march upon Mexico, which city he entered as conqueror on September 14th. On his way he had fought and won six battles with the Mexicans, who, though superior in numbers, were signally defeated. One of the causes of his success was that his army had mainly subsisted by purchase, not by forage. The city of Mexico was not now on an island in a lake, but in a valley, and contained one hundred and forty thousand inhabitants. The provinces of New Mexico and Chihuahua were invaded, but the signal event of the war was the acquisition of California. Colonel John C. Fremont, who was there as a surveyor and explorer, rallied the settlers from the United States, and with the aid of a naval force which had appeared on the coast, took possession of the country. The Mexicans, with their capital taken, were forced to make peace, giving up New Mexico and California, and admitting the Texan boundary about which the war began. For this surrender of territory they received a large compensation, as the institutions of the United States are against acquisition of territory by conquest.

All this had been much disapproved of by many. The war was expensive, and *Texas* was said only to mean *Taxes*, spelt in another way, and annexation to be a mere fine name for robbery. There was something, however, to be said for the provinces themselves, which might well wish to join a well-governed and prosperous Union like the United States, rather than belong to such a country of misrule and anarchy as Mexico. And California was found to be a much greater prize than had been supposed. In February,

1848, out of the sands of the Sacramento River were picked particles of gold, and the soil was found to be full of small lumps, which only needed to be sifted and washed out. On the news, thousands upon thousands came from all countries to make their fortunes. In two years the city of San Francisco alone had fifteen thousand inhabitants, and the gold region nearly a hundred thousand, against about forty thousand before the gold discovery.

The slave-holding interest had gained a great point in the admission of Texas. California was now the great point of dispute. Here free labour and slave labour were brought face to face. The hardy miners —and mining meant labour—would not work side by side with slaves, and while the politicians were discussing the matter, the Californians met in convention, and in September, 1849, formed a constitution excluding slavery, and were admitted to the Union the following year.

In 1867 the United States purchased from Russia the territory of Alaska, the north-western corner of the North American continent, separated from Asia by Behrings Straits, and bounded on the north by the Polar Sea, and on the south by the Pacific Ocean.

MONTGOMERY STREET, SAN FRANCISCO.

CHAP. XLII.—DEVELOPMENT OF THE REPUBLICS.

BRAZIL had quietly slipped, as we have seen, out of colonial bondage, and gradually modified her institutions to suit her new condition. She escaped the fearful warfare with the parent country, by which the other colonies were desolated. Her internal disputes have been few, and not ferocious. From the interference of neighbouring States, trying to promote insurrection, she has had some trouble; and one long war with Paraguay grew out of that fruitful source of dissension—disputed territory. Her progress, though not rapid, has been satisfactory; and during late years increasing. She has now an improving trade, about fifteen thousand miles of railway open for traffic, and more under construction, and about four thousand miles of telegraph. The Roman Catholic is the established religion, but all others are tolerated.

The Emperor, Dom Pedro II., left at five years of age under tutors and governors, was, at the age of sixteen, crowned Emperor, and at eighteen married. In 1853 the importation of slaves from Africa was forbidden. In 1871 an act for the gradual manumission of slaves was passed, and under that act, by government aid and private generosity, the gift of freedom has been rapid rather than gradual. Dom Pedro II. is judicious and practical, patient to observe, and anxious to learn, welcoming emigrants, and encouraging the arts of peace. In 1876-7 he visited the United States and the continent of Europe, extending his tour to Egypt and Syria.

Following the history of Chili and Peru down to the present time is no agreeable repetition of the old story of wars and violence. For centuries before the Spaniards landed in Peru, the natives had used a peculiar substance called "guano" as a fertiliser, and the use of it in South America has never ceased. It was not till 1841 that it was introduced into England. Since that time the annual importation into England alone has risen from about three thousand to three hundred thousand tons. It has been a source of great wealth to Peru, and of great misery to the "coolies" inveigled to the Chincha Islands and other places to dig and load it.

In 1863 there was a quarrel on a Peruvian estate between some Spanish emigrants and native labourers. The next year a Spanish fleet came out, demanding indemnity for injury to Spanish subjects, and seized the Chincha Islands. Ineffectual attempts were made to settle the matter by treaty. Peru was excited, Chili sided with Peru, and in 1866 another Spanish fleet came out. Valparaiso, in Chili, was shelled, and great mischief was done. The fleet then moved on to Callao, and the commander warned the inhabitants to retire to Lima, as he intended to burn their town. But the ships and batteries of Callao gave him a thorough beating, and in five hours he and his ships were driven off. The 2nd of May, on which this happened, has since been kept as a holiday by the Peruvians in Callao.

The history of Peru has been one continued series of revolutions. In 1872, just as a National Exhibition had been arranged, there was a terrible one. Tomas Guttierez, the Minister of War in President Balta's Cabinet, set on foot an insurrection, and the President was shot in his bed by a file of soldiers. Guttierez proclaimed himself Dictator, and for four days murder and terror reigned. His two brothers were with him in the plot. One of them in command of a fort was shot, and the garrison then sided with the infuriated people. Another brother was killed by them, and the Dictator

of a day was himself hunted to his house and found
hiding in a bath. Shots and blows were showered
upon him till long after he was dead. Two of the dead
bodies were hung for a time from the cathedral tower,
and on the next day the remains of the three brothers
were burned together. Such ferocity leaves only the
hope that the British and other Europeans and the
North Americans, who are drawn to these countries by
their mineral and other wealth, may create a better
spirit. Indeed, such a change has already begun.
Foreigners are protected by their respective govern-
ments. Foreign capital and enterprise furnish employment, and the building of railroads and other
improvements is teaching people to work. Unfortunately, for obvious reasons, the upper classes are
alienated from the Church, and have lost the restraint
of religion. The ladies, without the advantages of
good education, though devout up to their knowledge,
are too inert to exert themselves. They are beautiful
and lively when young, but sink into dulness and
apathy in their hot climate.

Of the Republic of Chili there was, until recently,
less to tell than of some others. The people have
been fairly steady to their own government, though
aggressive against their neighbours. The chief
domestic events, other than those of a pleasant

character, have been earthquakes and a fearful casualty at Santiago. On the 8th of December, 1863, the eve of the Feast of the Immaculate Conception, when the Jesuits' church was perfectly full, chiefly of women, some of the decorations took fire. The flames spread, the frightened women crowded up the doors, and no less than two thousand were killed, being either burned or trampled to death.

The Chilians are terrible enemies. Probably their very loyalty to their own government makes them formidable to others. They have more energy than the residents nearer the Equator. There were of course territorial disputes, and out of these grew a war with Bolivia. A secret treaty between Bolivia and Peru brought the latter into the quarrel. War was waged by sea and land. The Chilians invaded Bolivia in the beginning of 1880, pressed on to Peru, and, in January 1881, occupied the Peruvian capital, Lima; and, indeed, the whole country. There they are still (1882) demanding terms of peace so severe that Peru could not comply if she would, and remains helpless at the mercy of her conqueror. The Chilians were resisted step by step. Fierce battles on both sides were lost and won, towns sacked, and the country desolated. The government of the United States has tried in vain to act as umpire.

CHAP. XLIII.—ARGENTINE CONFEDERATION. WAR WITH PARAGUAY.

1835—1870.

IN the Argentine Confederation, Buenos Ayres is naturally the leading State. It comprises, in the first place, the city from which it takes its name, and a few other cities, centres of population. Beyond these is an immense plain, one hundred and eighty miles in breadth, which is for one half of the year covered with clover, and the other half with enormous thistles. These grow up in the summer, and in the autumn all die, and their hard, dry stems rattle one against another till they are broken down and carried away by hurricanes. Beyond is another great plain, full of salt lakes, with the plants that love salt ; and then the Andes begin to rise. Tribes of Indians dwell in the far interior, and the Guachos, or people of mixed blood, are scattered about at intervals in the Pampas, or plains of thistle and clover. Huge herds of wild cattle and of horses roam on these plains, and the lives of the Guachos are spent in catching them. Enclosures, called corrals, are arranged, into which the Guachos, who are desperate riders, chase the animals, riding along beside them at full speed. Then with a lasso, or long cord with a sliding noose, they contrive to entangle one at a time, and to throw it down without injury. If the creature be young and not immediately wanted, this is done for the purpose of branding with the owner's initials, and it is let go again. If a horse, it is kept to be broken in, used, or exported. The cattle are killed and boiled down for the sake of the tallow, which, with the hides, furnishes the chief article of export. Much of the meat is wasted, and fences are made of bullock's bones. Nobody could be wilder and more ignorant than the Guacho. Though baptized, he has little of the Christian about him, and places superstitious trust in some favourite image of a saint, or in a relic worn like a charm.

Lawless and brave men like these are sure to be ready for any disturbance, and thus Buenos Ayres became embroiled with Brazil. There were attempts made to spread republican feeling in the contiguous Brazilian province of Rio Grande, and this led to a war in which the Brazilian fleet blockaded Buenos Ayres for a year and a half. Then the English

Government interfered, and peace was made in 1828; but this only left the Argentine provinces free to make war upon each other.

At last a successful general, named Juan Manuel Ortiz de Rosas, became governor or dictator of his native province, Buenos Ayres, and in 1835, President of the Argentine Confederation. His was a reign of terror, which is still recollected with horror and dismay. He had a band of Guachos in his service, whom he sent forth to stab or shoot any who were obnoxious to him or to his favourites, or else to bring them before him, when, after a pretence at trial by court martial, he had them shot. No one dared to disobey his orders, as, for instance, when he decreed that all houses should be coloured red, and every one wear the same colour as a token of loyalty to the republic. The effect of the glare of the hot sunshine is said to have been to increase the violence and ferocity of natures already too cruel.

Rosas made war with the two States of Paraguay and Uruguay to compel them to join the Argentine Confederation. This involved war with Brazil, and England and France joined to repress him. While the fleet of Rosas was besieging Monte Video, it was captured by the allies, and the navigation of the River Parana thrown open to all nations.

After this the English and French fleets returned home in 1848-49. But Brazil continued the war, while Rosas resisted fiercely, and kept down all opposition at home by his savage band of assassins. But in 1851 he was totally defeated by General Juste Josè Urquiza, commanding the troops of Brazil, Paraguay, and Uruguay at the battle of Monte Caseros ; and being hard pushed, he was obliged to flee to England, where he spent the rest of his life as a refugee.

Urquiza became Dictator of the Argentine Confederation. But in 1852, General Bartolemé Mitre came forward as a leader in a movement of Buenos Ayres against Urquiza, which resulted in the separation of Buenos Ayres from the confederation ; though Urquiza continued to wage war against the revolted province. General Mitre was chosen Governor of Buenos Ayres when, in 1860, that State returned to the confederacy ; and in 1862, when the Confederation was first called a Republic, he was elected President. Mitre was an educated, sensible, and enlightened ruler. He did all in his power to improve the republic by opening schools, finding new employments, beginning railways, and encouraging English and Germans to settle in the country, and bring industry with them. Trade and commerce increased. Sheep were introduced into the Pampas, and some efforts made to bring those vast plains under cultivation.

The Republic of Paraguay had prospered under its Dictator, Dr. José Gaspar Rodriguez Francia, who died in 1840, over eighty years of age. For nearly thirty years he had been absolute Dictator. His policy was complete isolation, and it was next to impossible for a foreigner to get into Paraguay, or out if once in. Travellers published books calling Francia's rule a " Reign of Terror," but under it Paraguay flourished. Dr. Francia was succeeded by his two nephews as consuls, one of whom, in 1844, was made Dictator. Dying in 1862, he was succeeded by his son, Don Francisco Solano Lopez, who managed to become embroiled with three of his neighbours at once.

In the little State of Uruguay party dissensions broke out into civil war. Unfortunately the son of President Florez was identified with the faction opposed to his father. He held a command in the army. Visiting his father in the palace, he had an altercation with him, and, following hard words, the son struck his father in the face, ran from the palace to the barracks, led out his regiment, and marched his command through the streets, making seditious shouts. A Monte Video paper, commenting on this transaction, called it, " his son striking him out of an excess of filial love." The seditious movement was almost instantly suppressed. But President Florez was a few days later murdered in the streets by a band of masked assassins. Indeed, such was the frequency of murder in those lands, that there is a monument in Buenos Ayres to a man who, the epitaph says, was " assassinated by his friends."

Brazil intervened in the quarrel in Uruguay. Lopez, Dictator of Paraguay, demanded that Dom Pedro should withdraw his troops from that republic. Brazil refused, and Lopez proceeded to settle disputed boundaries by armed occupation, and to seize Brazilian provinces. In his aggressions on Brazil he crossed Argentine territory. The Argentines protested, and Lopez made war upon them. The first intelligence of the war at Buenos Ayres was the news of the capture by Lopez of two Argentine vessels. The people of Buenos Ayres paraded the streets in great excitement, with cries of " Down with Paraguay ! " President Mitre took advantage of the popular fury ; the Argentine Republic joined with Brazil, and Uruguay came also into the alliance. Paraguay was invaded in 1866, and for four years made desperate resistance. The Guaranis, among the soldiers of Lopez, were distinguished for wild courage. Volunteers were accepted, and conscripts

drawn of all ages between twelve and seventy. Even
women, it is said, bore arms, disguised as men. It is
computed that nine-tenths of the Paraguayans lost
their lives in the struggle. The war ended with the
life of Solano Lopez, who was defeated at the battle
of Aquidaban, in March, 1870. He was shot while
attempting to swim the river, and the remains of his
army surrendered. His last words were, " I die for
my country." His love of country is undisputed; but
his idea of patriotism was unhappily controlled by his
grasping personal ambition. His rule was despotic.
Over his own people he was arbitrary and cruel; he
imprisoned members of Foreign Legations; and only
the timely arrival of war vessels from the United
States saved some members of the mission from that
country. They were accused, together with other
foreigners and certain leading Paraguayans, of conspiracy. The latter suffered torture and death.

Brave little Paraguay, exhausted by external foes
and internal suffering, gave way when she had no
more a leader. The rivers which her dictators had so
jealously guarded were opened. A large portion of
her area was surrendered, and for several years
Brazilian troops occupied portions of her territory.
She is now nominally independent, though really
under Brazilian control.

Disputed possessions have been the fruitful cause of wars in South America. The regions at the extreme south, inhabited by about thirty thousand Patagonians, still free and unsubdued, long an open question between Chili and the Argentine Republic, have been ceded to the latter. Practically the wild lands of Patagonia and the Tierra del Fuego islands have been left to their natives, except for the brave and self-devoted attempt of Allen Gardiner, an English naval officer, who endeavoured to begin a mission for their instruction in the Christian faith. He was to have supplies sent to him, but these failed him, and he and his companions all perished from cold and hunger. Allen Gardiner's body was found in an open boat at Picton Island, in the Straits of Magellan, with a diary by his side, full to the very last of expressions of faith, hope, love, and even joy.

CHAP. XLIV.—NORTH AND SOUTH.

1848—1859.

THE slavery question was becoming more and more an anxious matter in the United States. At one time the Northerners, though unwilling to be slave owners themselves, had been willing to defend the institution; or, at least, to argue that its disposition was reserved to the States in which it existed, secure from interference by the terms of the Union. But a feeling in favour of abolition was spreading more and more; and statesmen could not but see that the preponderance of either—the party of freedom or the upholders of slavery—could not satisfy the minority. The question became a political one. In the moral aspects of the subject, also, the nation was being instructed. Lectures were delivered, sermons preached, and books written, showing up the evils of slavery in the strongest light, and winning over numbers to an active course, who had hitherto preserved an attitude

of silent disapproval. Among the books written was
"Uncle Tom's Cabin," by Mrs. Harriet Beecher
Stowe. It had, and still has, a world-wide circulation,
and has been translated into several languages. In
the heat of controversy and the zeal of partisanship,
it was impossible that special instances of cruelty
and hardship should not have been represented as
types of the general condition of things. Had the
slaves, as a class, seen their own case in the light that
the free men of the north regarded it in, there would
have been, when war opened, such an uprising of the
bondmen as would have given the masters enough to
do at home, without warring against the North. No
such uprising took place. The slaves, as a body, remained apathetic. No outrage or violence is laid to
their charge. If this was in part due to their ignorance, more is due to their docile and affectionate
nature. Slaves, during the war, carried on the plantations, and ministered to the families of masters who
were in the field fighting to retain the institution. If
there is in this something due to the honour of the
slaves, so is there to the masters. Slavery in the
United States has now been for twenty years a thing
of the past ; and the dispassionate observer has had
time to admit that in the American Union it did not
exist in its worst form, undisputed as were its evils.

Slaves who could escape found friends in the North who assisted them to fly from the miseries of being returned. The usual fate of captured fugitives was to be sold into labour the most severe, in tracts from which escape was impossible, and into a condition where the amenities of mutual confidence could not exist. The slave "catchers" had no pity on those who stole themselves, hunted them down with bloodhounds, shot them in the chase, and would nearly as soon shoot an abolitionist as a mad dog. Of course such extreme measures as these could only be practised in the swamps and deserts of the slave States. In the free border States the runaways were often "kidnapped," their pursuers finding aid from mean and mercenary fellows of the baser sort. These abettors of the kidnappers were held in huge contempt at the North; and it is only justice to say that at the South the professional slave-catchers were despised, even by those whom they served, though the preservation of the system compelled their employment.

The constitution of the United States provides that no person held to service or labour in one State, escaping into another, shall be discharged, but must be delivered up on claim of the party to whom such service is due. The legal construction of this article compelled the courts at the North to decide that

A SLAVE GANG.

a slave owner might pursue his property even into a free State. The abolitionists arranged what was called the Underground Railway, namely, the designation of families, at intervals, from the slave line to the Canadian frontier, who would shelter, hide, and pass on the runaways till they were safe on British ground. In 1820, the American Colonization Society founded a colony in Africa, called Liberia. The members of the society comprise Southern as well as Northern men. To this colony such slaves were transported as were manumitted by their masters, or released by purchase; the emigration being voluntary. The emigration still continues, so far as the liberality of the friends of the colony will admit. These Liberians have so far prospered, the colonists being among the best of their race. The present population of Liberia is about twenty thousand of the colonial stock, and over seven hundred thousand aborigines. It is now an independent republic, and so acknowledged; and though the colony has exercised no perceptible effect in diminishing the blacks in America, it promises great good to the Negroes on their own ground.

In the discussion of the question of slavery there were many good men at the South who honestly held that it would be cruel to turn so many dull and helpless creatures loose to provide for themselves, without having trained them. And there were wise men in the North, who wished to devise some plan by which the slaves might gradually be enabled to deserve and earn their liberty, as each became able to attain it. But unfortunately there were such party questions and sectional jealousies mixed up with the subject that neither North nor South could think or work it out clearly, and every wrong done on either side inflamed people's minds.

The far West, in the mean time, was being settled. The admission of California, without slavery, met with earnest opposition from the Southern interest. Other perplexing questions arose, and a solution of all was attempted by the great statesman often called "The Great Compromiser," Henry Clay. He introduced in the Senate a series of measures, popularly called "The Omnibus Bill," which, after exciting debate, was substantially adopted. The most important provisions were: California was admitted as a free State; Utah and New Mexico were erected into territories, admitting slavery or not, as they chose; the slave markets were abolished in the district of Columbia, in which Washington is situated; and a law was passed providing under-officers—and by commissioners appointed by the United States—for the recovery and return of fugitive slaves. This last matter had hitherto been left to the State authorities. As a compromise, this was better than most compromises. Utah, New Mexico, and much of California (under the arrangement by which the State of Missouri was admitted in 1821), were slave territory, in which, the South claimed, slavery already existed without special enactment. This claim was surrendered. The slave marts in the city of Washington had made the capital of the nation a man-market. These were closed. The fugitive slave law was all that the North was called on to concede. But while it created violent opposition on moral grounds, it made matters no worse for the fugitives. Northern men were moreover indignant that they were required under the provisions of this law to aid the officers when called on to assist in the capture of slaves. Practically this amounted to nothing, since no one heeded it except such as were ready to aid the slave-catchers before.

At Utah, near the Great Salt Lake, a strange colony settled in 1847, having been driven out of Illinois. They had aimed to go beyond the territory of the United States, but were included by the cession from Mexico as part of California. In 1816, an invalid preacher, named Solomon Spalding, died in Pennsylvania. He left the manuscript of a romance, in which he professed to describe the fortunes, in

America, of the lost tribes of Israel. The book was written in chapters and verses, like the Bible. One Joseph Smith adapted and corrupted this, and in 1830 began, on this foundation, the Mormon delusion. Smith was killed while under arrest in Illinois. Brigham Young, who succeeded Smith as prophet, introduced the plurality of wives into the system. As this could not be permitted in any Christian country, Young carried the people he had deluded into what was then a desolate wilderness; but he showed such ability in irrigating and cultivating it, that the spot became exceedingly beautiful and fertile. For a time so many persons among the ignorant and easily-deluded in Europe and America were ready to follow his emissaries, that he seemed to be going to set up a power like Mahometanism. But after a few years the infection ceased, as it became known that there was a cruel tyranny in Utah against all who presumed to differ from the prophet. Now that the great Pacific Railway crosses the territory, which is on the highway to California, there are over seven hundred miles of railways in Utah; Salt Lake City is the terminus of three. The " Gentiles," as the Mormons call the rest of the world, are crowding the " Latter Day Saints," as they term themselves; five or more Christian denominations have missions and churches in the very citadel of Mormonism; the United States Government is employing repressive measures; emigrant parties of the deluded are becoming few and far between, and many children of Mormons are receiving Christian instruction. Since Young died, in 1877, his followers seem to be diminishing. Polygamist delegates are excluded from Congress, but though the delusion perish, and the seat of the high priest of polygamy remain vacant, the beautiful Salt Lake City of Utah will remain as its memorial, when the name "Deseret," as the Mormons call their country, is forgotten.

In 1853, the peace which had been made by Clay's "Omnibus Bill" was broken. The "Kansas Nebraska" Bill was passed, by which two Territories north of the slave line were created, with permission to have slavery or not, as they chose. The North said this was a violation of the Missouri compact. The South said that the compact was broken already by free California. Kansas became the battle-ground. The question of slavery was to be decided by the majority of the settlers. So each side struggled hard to get the most in, and keep the others out. Kansas borders on Missouri, and the slave interest was made odious by a set of fierce men, who earned the title of Missouri Ruffians. They invaded Kansas by violence to keep out or intimidate free settlers, using freely their revolvers and bowie-knives, and making the direct way to Kansas, through the State of Missouri, impassable. There were two hostile camps in Kansas, actually fighting, and "Bleeding Kansas" was a familiar cry. John Brown, of Ossawotamie, of pilgrim Puritan descent, was, with his four sons, among the foremost on the free side. Once, with sixteen men, he beat off several hundred Missouri marauders, who had burned villages newly settled by Northerners. Settlements being broken up, each side lived by plundering the other, and used to talk of a pro-slavery horse, or an anti-slavery cow. The two rival parties, free and slave, each held a convention and prepared a constitution. Neither went into operation, and Kansas did not enter the Union as a Free State till 1861, after the Secessionists had withdrawn from Congress and war had begun. It is not surprising that Kansas contributed a larger proportion of her population to the Union army than any other State. Nebraska was admitted in 1867.

Two events increased the excitement, and aided to precipitate the crisis. A Negro in Missouri, named Dred Scott, brought a suit in 1857 for his freedom, on the ground that, having resided in a free State with his master, he could not be remanded to slavery. This plea was in accordance with all practice and precedent;

the Constitution requiring that fugitives should be delivered up, not that the free States should defend the claims of masters over slaves whom they themselves carried into places where slavery was illegal. If "Dred" had refused to return, he could not have been compelled. The Supreme Court of the United States dismissed the case for want of jurisdiction. Dred remained a slave. The Chief Justice, Taney, added opinions which, as he had dismissed the case, sound lawyers pronounced *extra judicial*—namely, that, as inferior beings, Negroes have no rights "which a white man is bound to respect," and that the Missouri compromise was unconstitutional. Whether the judge's opinion had official weight or not, it had immense influence on the adverse side of the slavery issue, and added to the growing excitement.

Another cause of anger at the South and perplexity at the North was the misdirected zeal of the famous Kansas partisan, John Brown. While the troubles in that territory were still rife, he undertook to raise the standard of insurrection in Virginia, and to lead the slaves against their masters. With a handful of men he seized the United States Arsenal at Harper's Ferry, whence he meant to supply arms for the slaves; but there was no sign of an insurrection, and within twenty-four hours Brown and his party of twenty-two were virtually prisoners in the arsenal. Fifteen hundred militiamen and a detachment of United States troops soon arrived in the village, and the party fought desperately against such fearful odds. Nearly every one was killed or wounded. Among the former was a son of Brown's, and among the latter John Brown himself and another son. He was tried by the Virginia authorities, condemned, and executed December 29, 1859; and six of his companions were hung at a later day. With the knowledge from the history of Haiti, and other instances, of what a servile insurrection may mean, there were few who could dispute the legality of these sentences. John Brown was a man of superior mind, of high courage, and no doubt intended to prevent violence and cruelty; but he tried what was impossible. His captors and judges testified to his courage, fortitude, simple ingenuousness, integrity, and truth; and a witness of his execution, himself a slaveholder, said, "When I meet death, I hope it will be with the composure and fortitude of John Brown." Still, as in the case of many other martyrs to their convictions, it must be said that he was a fanatic, who pursued his purpose regardless of the evil of his methods. On his way to the gallows he displayed a personal characteristic by kissing a Negro child, held up to him by the slave mother.

CHAP. XLV.—SECESSION.

1860—1861.

IN the seventy-two years from the adoption of the Constitution in 1788 to 1860, there had been fifteen Presidents of the United States—Washington, John Adams, Jefferson, Madison, Monroe, John Quincy Adams, Jackson, Van Buren, Harrison—who, dying in his term, was succeeded by Vice-President Tyler—Polk, Taylor—whose death gave place to Fillmore—Pierce, and Buchanan. The election, in 1860, of a successor to Buchanan, was made in a time when party spirit was running very high. From the time of the adoption of the Constitution, the question underlying all others was the question of "State Rights"—that is to say, how far the sovereignty of the single State in the Union is affected by the Federal compact. South Carolina, in 1832, asserted the right of a single State to "nullify" the Acts of Congress. From this extreme position she was forced to recede; but State Rights became more and more a Southern idea, since the subject of slavery was affected by it.   In the North, the Federal, or Union sentiment was the stronger ; in the South, loyalty to the State in which a citizen resided.   The Northern Democrats acted with the South.   The party afterward known as Republicans came into power, as against the Democrats, on this issue.

But the positions assumed by the Southerners created a division of opinion among the Democrats themselves. The Missouri Compromise of 1820 forbade slavery beyond a certain line.   The Compromise broken, the Northern Democrats maintained that slavery might be established, in new territories, by the choice of the settlers.   The Southern Democrats maintained that slavery *did exist*, as a natural and political law, until abolished by legislation.   The Northern Democrats apologised for slavery, and even defended it, to preserve State Rights *in* the Union.   The Southern defended slavery for itself, and sought to break up the Union, to perpetuate it, and to maintain ultra views of State sovereignty.

Thus, the Democrats were divided, while the Republicans held together, and elected as President Abraham Lincoln, of Illinois, an able, sensible, honest man, who had worked himself up in the world from very small beginnings.   He had been a boatman, a

rail-splitter, or fence-maker, a shopkeeper, and a surveyor. During all the time of these occupations he
was a student, and settled at last upon the profession
of the law, and was admitted to the Bar. Like many
country lawyers in the United States, he figured as a
political orator; and the republication of his speeches,
after his nomination as President, greatly helped his
election. He had held a seat in the Legislature of
his own State, and in Congress. He was known to
disapprove of slavery, but to see the difficulties of
emancipation, and to think that, though the slave
States could not, under the Constitution, be disturbed,
Congress ought to forbid the bringing of slavery into
the territories. In the hot feelings of the Southerners,
they reckoned him as the enemy of their interests.
They knew he would uphold the power of the Central
Government as opposed to that of individual States;
and, as nothing but self-interest could make slavery
seem right, that they would be the losers, unless they
legislated for themselves. The planters in South
Carolina were sure that the other slave-holding States
would back them in any opposition to the North, and
decided on their course.

Lincoln's election took place in November, 1860,
and in December the South Carolina Convention met
at Charleston, and repealed its acceptance of the United

States Constitution, declaring the secession of the State from the Union amid public rejoicings. The same thing was done in the States of Mississippi, Florida, Alabama, Georgia, Louisiana, and Texas, and the seceding States agreed to join in a Southern Confederacy, and to elect a President and Vice-President of their own. Jefferson Davis, of Mississippi, was chosen President, and Alexander H. Stephens, of Georgia, Vice-President ; and slavery was boldly declared by him to be the corner-stone of the new Confederation, since it was said to be a divine decree that the lower races of men should be in bondage to the higher.

Though the election had taken place, President Buchanan would not go out of office till March, 1861, and he ought to have taken vigorous measures, but the Secretary of War, Floyd, a Virginian, who had practically the command of the army, had liberally distributed the national military stores to the Southern arsenals, leaving the Northern unprovided. These, with the ships at Southern Navy Yards, were seized by the Secessionists. Major Robert Anderson, of the United States army, in command of Fort Sumter, in Charleston Harbour, asked for reinforcements, and was refused.

When President Lincoln entered upon his office in

March, he declared that he had no wish to meddle with slavery; but he also said that secession was rebellion, and this, together with a refusal of the Secretary of State to recognize the official position of the Southern Confederacy, was the signal for war. On the 11th of April, Major Anderson was summoned by General Beauregard, at the head of a large force of volunteers, to give up Fort Sumter. On his refusal, he was fired upon. He held out two days, but he had only eighty men, and his powder was almost gone; so he was forced to surrender, marching out with the honours of war, and spending his last powder in a salute to the Stripes and Stars. Not a man had been hurt on either side; but the cannon that had been fired showed that each party was in earnest, and that the country must now prepare itself for the miseries of a civil war. The central States had to choose sides. The Virginians, who were proud of Washington's work, were loth to upset it. But they had slaves, and likewise cared for State Rights; so they joined the Secession, as did Arkansas, North Carolina, and Tennessee, though in all these States there were some persons unwilling to break up the Union. Richmond, in Virginia, was made the seat of the Southern, or Confederate, Government. Washington was, of course, coveted by both parties, but the Federals, or men of the North, were able to garrison it, and it was defended by earthworks and a large body of troops.

Nobody was really prepared for war. The United States had always kept a small standing army, with officers carefully trained at the Military School at West Point. These officers had gained experience in the Mexican war, and were now pretty equally divided between the North and South, according to their homes, and their political opinions. Under them were the Volunteers and Militia, called from their ordinary work, needing drill to be made into soldiers. There was plenty of stout courage and high spirit, and each side had the fullest confidence in its right, but neither had any training ; and, on the whole, the Southerners at the outset were the fiercer and the stronger men. But it was a great disadvantage to them that they had not much power of manufacturing, and still less of ship-building ; while the Northern navy, though only at first consisting of four available ships at home, was soon increased enough to blockade their seaports. Moreover, the labouring classes at the South were all slaves, with interests contrary to their masters, while the North could draw on its whole population for soldiers. The only wonder was that the Southern slaves did not add to the horrors of the war by cruelties to the helpless families of their masters, but retained their submissive habits, and in many cases showed all the best points of the Negro nature, in kindliness or faithfulness. On the whole, European sympathy went largely to the South ; for the Federals were accused of making the slavery question a cover for their desire to crush " State Right ; " and their scornful loathing of the Negro was cast up against them as a sign that they could not be sincere.

CHAP. XLVI.—THE WAR OF SECESSION.

1861—1862.

THE boundary between the Confederate States and those which adhered to the Union was formed by the Northern State lines of Virginia, Tennessee, Arkansas, and Texas. The great object of the Federals was to cross this boundary, overrun the country, and reduce it to submission. In Western Virginia, where there were many Union men, General George B. McClellan succeeded in driving out the Confederates, and the district was afterwards separated from the old State, and admitted, under the name of Western Virginia, as a free State into the Union. Next an attempt was made to advance upon Richmond, the capital both of the State of Virginia and of the New Confederation. This led to the first serious battle of the war, that of Bull Run, July 21, 1861. The forces engaged were estimated at thirty thousand on each side. It was in this fight that one of the Southern leaders, pointing to another officer's division, called out, " There's Jackson, standing like a stone wall ;" and as the name Jackson was not uncommon, this dashing, daring officer was always after distinguished as "Stonewall Jackson." At three o'clock the South was in great danger ; but the Northerners were exhausted, and a fresh body of their enemies coming up totally routed them. Nor was the Confederate army in a condition to follow up its success. The Union soldiers, who had no training, could not retreat in order, but fell back on Washington, like a disorderly mob. " Don't stop me, sir, I'm quite demoralized," cried a man in newspaper language to his officer.

Three months after Bull Run, the Unionists met a sad blow at Ball's Bluff, on the Potomac. A detachment of the Union army, crossing the river at that point, was routed and driven back with a loss of eight hundred men. These events showed the North that the South was a terrible enemy, and there was a great muster of men from every quarter and occupation. The women arranged excellent plans for nursing and feeding the wounded, and sending supplies of warm clothing and extra rations of food to the camps. Even the little girls at school made "comfort bags," holding a few things that each man might be glad to have, such as warm cuffs, a handkerchief, a few needles and

some thread, a little book, or card, with scripture text.
A national Sanitary Commission was created, and
with the Young Men's Christian Commission systema-
tized and directed the efforts of individuals. Volunteer
nurses of both sexes went to the camps and visited the
hospitals. Soldiers on their march to the scene of war
were hospitably entertained in the cities, and returning
men on furlough or sick leave were cared for. Indeed,
there never was a war marked by so much effort to
lessen its horrors, and by so little wanton cruelty ; for
however confident each side might be in its cause,
there was hardly a man who had not friends in the
opposite party. It was felt that the contention was
between brethren.

There were in 1862 fearful battles for the possession
of Richmond. General McClellan, after his successes
in Western Virginia, had been appointed to the command of the Army of the Potomac. His advanced
guard approached within six miles of the capital of the
Confederacy in May. It was attacked and driven back,
but being reinforced, pushed the Confederates into
Richmond. After two months' inactivity, McClellan
undertook to change his base, and approach Richmond in another direction. Then at the end of June
followed the engagements known as the "Seven Days'
Battles of the Peninsula," in which, it is said, a hun-

dred thousand men were engaged on each side, and the loss of each was fifteen thousand men. In the last of these battles, that of Malvern Hill, July 1, the Confederates were defeated.

General Robert E. Lee, a Virginian by birth, a graduate of West Point, an officer in the United States service, a hero of the Mexican war, who held the confidence of General Scott, and was summoned to Washington at the commencement of the difficulty for consultation, resigned at the critical moment, and went over to the rebellion. His devotion to his State mastered other considerations. He proved to be a dashing soldier yet a good strategist, with more enterprise than McClellan, who was sometimes hesitating and always cautious, but to whom, for the drilling and discipline of the Army of the Potomac, the Union owed much.

General McClellan was relieved of a portion of his command, and General John Pope appointed commander of what was termed the Army of Virginia, occupying the northern part of the State. General Lee threw the chief of his force against Pope, and on the 19th and 20th of August the Union army suffered a disastrous defeat at Manasses, or Bull Run, where the first great battle occurred. General Pope retired within the lines of defence near Washington, and was transferred, at his own request, to another command. He had been very successful in Western engagements, but the fortune of war was against him in Virginia. General Lee, early in September, crossed over into Maryland. General McClellan, who had been re-instated in his former command, followed him. Closely pressed by the Union forces, and failing to find the sympathy in Maryland for which he hoped, and to which he appealed, General Lee made a stand at South Mountain. After a hard fought engagement he was defeated, and fell back to the Potomac. Here took place one of the great battles of the war, called the Battle of Antietam, from the name of a creek which enters the Potomac. After two days of skirmishing, on the 17th of September the bloody but indecisive battle was fought. The Union army kept possession of the field, but General Lee with his army crossed the Potomac, into Virginia. One hundred and fifty thousand men on both sides were engaged, and the loss, including that at South Mountain, was more than fourteen thousand on the Union and twelve on the Confederate side. The troops engaged in the Union army far outnumbered their enemies, and much dissatisfaction was expressed at Lee's escape. But the Battle of Antietam was so far a success that President Lincoln took a step which he had delayed until a propitious time, when it would not be considered an indication of despair. On September 22nd, as a war measure, by virtue of his position as Commander-in-Chief of the Army and Navy of the United States, he issued a warning proclamation that all slaves should be declared free in the States in rebellion, on January 1, 1863.

On the 7th of November General McClellan was superseded by General Ambrose E. Burnside. A new advance on Richmond was attempted. General Burnside on December 13th, attacked Fredericksburg, but was repulsed with heavy loss by General Lee. It was a desperate battle, in which the Union army lost over twelve thousand men in killed, wounded, and missing. At a previous period in the war, Burnside, serving under McClellan, had occupied Fredericksburg, and been compelled to retreat, and the two events are sometimes confounded. The Union army, after the serious battle of Fredericksburg, fell back to the vicinity of Washington. So closed, for 1862, active warfare in the East.

Four of the slave-holding States never joined the secession movement, though many of their citizens were in sympathy with it. Missouri, one of these States, was the scene of furious partisan warfare. Kentucky claimed to be neutral, but neither party would consent to this. A military post in the south-

western corner of the State was occupied but abandoned, and the wave of battle rolled on into Tennessee.
Western successes somewhat relieved the disasters at
the East, though there was an immense slaughter of
men and waste of property in more battles and encounters than there is space here to recite. General
Ulysses S. Grant, who had risen rapidly in command
by previous brave and skilful conduct, captured Fort
Donelson on the Tennessee river, with about thirteen
hundred prisoners. The fort surrendered February
16th, and as the only stipulation to which Grant would
assent was "unconditional surrender," the initials of his
name suggested Unconditional Surrender as the popular
name for the General who had gained the first brilliant
and decisive success of the Federal arms. The battle
of Shiloh, or Pittsburg Landing, took place on the 6th
and 7th of April. It has been aptly called the "harvest
of death." On the first day the Confederate general,
Albert Sidney Johnston, was mortally wounded, and
the loss of each side in the two days is estimated at
near twelve thousand men. Beauregard succeeded
Johnston in command. Victory on the first day was
with the Confederates, who were the attacking party,
but on the next, General Grant having reformed his
lines and received heavy reinforcements, Beauregard
was forced to retreat.

The Navy of the United States, increased by building and buying vessels, was by this time so powerful that the blockade of the southern parts was established so far as so vast a line of sea-coast could be. Many points on the coast were taken and occupied by the Union forces. The harbour of Charleston, South Carolina, was blocked up by a great bar of sunken ships. England, France, Spain, and Portugal had recognized the seceding States as having the rights of belligerents; and swift ships, which were called "blockade runners," slipped past the Federal ships to bring into the Southern ports goods which sold at a very large price to make up for the risk. In April Admiral D. G. Farragut, commander of the Gulf blockading squadron, passed up the Mississippi, and, despite of forts, batteries, gun-boats, and fire-rafts, reached New Orleans on the 24th, and the city surrendered. On his way he sunk or disabled six rebel steamers. It was a daring exploit. General B. F. Butler was put in command of the city. It was a centre of slave-holding interests; the inhabitants were very violent, and insulted their victors. General Butler was forced to keep up the strictest and sharpest rule. He at once executed a man who cut down the United States flag, and his manner was so blunt and harsh that he was exceedingly hated and abused. But he said, probably with truth, that if he had not been so severe in silencing the people of New Orleans and protecting his soldiers from insult, his army would have been provoked into acts of revenge, and cruelty would have really begun.

Farragut steamed up the Mississippi and bombarded Vicksburg, the last stronghold of the Confederates on that river. For the want of co-operation by land forces the siege was for a time given up.

CHAP. XLVII.—THE WAR OF SECESSION.

1863—1864.

ON New Year's day, 1863, President Lincoln
issued his second proclamation confirming the
former one, and declaring all slaves in rebel states
free. Early in the war General Butler in Virginia
had declined to return escaped slaves to their masters.
If they were men, he could not give up fugitives or
deserters on demand of the enemy. If they were
property, they were "contraband of war." Contraband became through the war the designation of the
Southern Negroes. Those who were employed in the
Union camps were declared free, and this declaration
finally extended to all fugitive slaves. After this
coloured soldiers began to be regularly enlisted. It
was time. General Butler had found in New Orleans
some free coloured troops preparing for the Confederate service, and took them into the service of the
Union. Up to the time of the first proclamation

(September 22, 1862), the formation of coloured regiments had not been much in favour. After that the enlistment proceeded, and the coloured troops fought well and were excellent in discipline.

The spring of 1863 was opened with what must be classed among the most notable events of the war, introducing into real work the terrible modern inventions for making naval warfare more effective. At the beginning of the contest, the United States forces had been compelled to withdraw from the Norfolk Navy Yard, destroying the ships and vessels as far as they could. A blockading squadron was kept by the United States in Hampton Roads. On the 8th of March there came steaming out of the James River a nondescript craft, which was said to look like a whale boat, bottom up. It was an old war steamship, called the *Merrimac.* Over her deck was a canopy fore and aft of timber and railroad iron, and her bow was furnished with a steel ram. She made sad havoc of the blockading squadron, whose shot glanced from her armour, while she was furnished with heavier guns than had ever before been used on shipboard. She sunk one vessel, burned another, and drove a third aground, and then retired up the James River to refit. That same evening there came into Hampton Roads another nondescript, which looked "like a cheese-box on a raft." It was the *Monitor*, an armour-clad turret-ship, invented by John Ericson, an engineer and naval architect, a citizen of the United States, of Swedish birth. The *Monitor* was commanded by Captain John L. Worder of the United States Navy. When the *Merrimac* came out for a second day's work she found an unexpected antagonist. The two vessels fired at each other at short range for two hours without much effect, till a shell thrown through a porthole of the *Merrimac* forced her to retire, with many of her crew killed or disabled.

In 1863 the campaign opened with a most disastrous defeat of the Union troops. General John Hooker, who had succeeded Burnside, advanced into Virginia, taking a strong position at Chancellorsville. Here he was attacked by "Stonewall" Jackson in May, and on the 3rd a disastrous defeat compelled him to fall back. The Union loss in this advance and retreat was about seventeen thousand, including five thousand prisoners ; the Confederate about twelve thousand, of whom two thousand were prisoners. But the heaviest loss to the Southerners was that of "Stonewall" Jackson, who was shot on the night of the 2nd by his own men in mistake.

Both sides were getting depressed and weary. Volunteers in the North were used up by the terrible slaughter of the battles, and men had to be drafted, which occasioned great dissatisfaction, culminating in the city of New York in a fearful riot. General Lee thought it was a good time for another rush into the North. He crossed the Potomac and advanced into Pennsylvania, with all his available force, and on June 27th had massed his army near Chambersburg. The Union army moved north and concentrated at Gettysburg, a few miles distant. General George G. Meade, who had succeeded Hooker in the command of the army of the Potomac, having learned by an intercepted letter that Lee could expect no reinforcements, offered him battle and chose the ground. A frightful battle it was, lasting the first three days of July, and covering the field with forty thousand dead and wounded men. Lee retreated, and the battle of Gettysburg was the turning point of the war.

At the very time that this battle was being fought, Vicksburg, the great Confederate stronghold on the Mississippi, was being surrendered to General Grant, Farragut co-operating with his fleet. After nearly six months' operations against the post, with fearful loss of life, ending in a close siege, Vicksburg capitulated on the 4th of July, and Grant received the parole of twenty thousand prisoners. Other posts were captured, and after two years of battle, blockade, and siege, the

Mississippi River was open to the Gulf, and all Confederate supplies from the west of the river were cut off.

Now President Lincoln began to say that peace did not seem so far off; but war had to be pushed all the more to secure it. The Confederate cause was desperate, but the Southerners still were resolved to "fight it out till they had," as they said, "played their last man." In September they attacked and defeated a large Federal force which had occupied Chattanooga, near the border line of Tennessee and Georgia. From this point, as a base, it was intended to invade Georgia. But at Chickamanga the advancing Federals were met, defeated, driven back to Chattanooga, and besieged there almost to the point of starvation. The siege works included batteries on hills overlooking the town. In November Grant came to its relief, and on the 24th the battle of Chattanooga was fought, pronounced one of the most remarkable in history. The Federal troops made their preliminary movements with such order and precision that the Confederates thought they were only holding a review, so complete had their discipline become. They charged the Confederates in their works, fighting uphill, and the encounter of one of the attacking divisions, commanded by General Hooker, familiarly called "Fighting Joe," is spoken of as the "battle above the clouds." The besiegers were dislodged and routed, the Confederate army was shortly driven out of Tennessee. Congress voted thanks to the General and his army, and a gold medal to General Grant. The office of " Lieutenant-General," first held by Washington, then vacant until the time of General Scott, vacant again upon his retirement, was revived by special act of Congress, and the appointment conferred upon General Grant. The Lieutenant-General, the President of the United States being General in chief, has actual command of all the armies of the Government. The loss in these two battles was over twenty thousand men on each side.

Grant issued his first general order as Commander-in-chief in March, 1864, and announced that his head-quarters would be with the Army of the Potomac in the field. General W. T. Sherman was left in command of the department of the Mississippi. Grant, on the morning of the 4th of May, crossed the Rapidan River with a force of one hundred thousand men. The country into which they marched was dotted with forests, having an almost impassable under-growth. Here commenced, May 6th, a series of the most fierce and sanguinary battles of the war. Generals Grant and Meade, with Richmond as their object, were kept at bay, and fought successively six battles, the Battle of the Wilderness being first; and there were several minor affairs and skirmishes. After each engagement Grant pushed farther south. Had he moved towards Washington, such movements would have been called retreats. On the 12th of June he crossed the James River above Richmond, having lost in these battles sixty thousand men, in killed, wounded, and prisoners. The Confederate loss was about one-third as many. The scene of the struggle was transferred to the southern side of the James River. The main body of the army of the Potomac was, by the middle of July, before Petersburg, twenty-three miles south of Richmond. Repeated attacks upon the Confederate works cost the Union army over ten thousand men. The slower process of a regular siege was adopted, and such a siege, by the courage and skill of its defenders, the Confederate force, with the army of Lee behind it, sustained for nearly ten months.

General B. F. Butler had in May, while the fierce battles of the wilderness were going on, advanced up the James River. Deceiving the Confederates by a feint against Richmond, his troops were on the night of the 4th of May embarked in transports, on York River, and in twenty-four hours were landed within fifteen miles of Richmond, at Bermuda Hundred, at the confluence of the James and Appomatox, with entrenchments in their front, and gun-boats on both flanks on the rivers. Thus the James River was kept open for the supply of recruits for the sadly depleted Union army. General Butler's force of thirty-five thousand men included a brigade of coloured troops. Though the first position at Bermuda Hundred was secured without any loss, there was fierce fighting afterward. The Negroes, invaluable as labourers, in entrenching and mining, exhibited in battle and in storming entrenchments a fierce courage and contempt of danger unexceeded by any soldiers in the army. Colonel Robert B. Shaw, who commanded the first Massachusetts coloured regiment, fell with a large part of his troops in an assault on Fort Wagner, near Charleston, and was buried by the Confederates in a common grave with his dark soldiers. In the West Confederate commanders had given the warning, "No quarter will be shown to Negro troops whatever." Fort Pillow, on the Mississippi, was taken by a Confederate force in April, 1864, and three hundred of its garrison massacred, both coloured and white; the latter as traitors to their southern birthplaces. It is just to say that this atrocious act was without its parallel during the war.

CHAP. XLVIII.—DEFEAT OF THE SOUTH.

1864—1865.

WHILE the Union operations against Petersburg and Richmond were in progress, July, 1864, Lee aimed to relieve Richmond by a demonstration again Washington. An expedition under General Jubal Early invaded Pennsylvania and Maryland, and put Washington and Baltimore in peril. Washington was reinforced, and Early, after several sharp encounters with Union troops, and firing Chambersburg, fell back into Virginia. In the Shenandoah Valley General Philip H. Sheridan and General Early were brilliant commanders, well matched. Early was defeated in the battles of Winchester and Fisher's Hill. The Union army then was posted at Cedar Creek, a position so strong that General Sheridan, leaving another officer in command, went to the city of Washington on official business. General Early, on the morning of October 19th, surprised, defeated, and

compelled the Union troops to retreat. A part of
their artillery was captured and turned upon them.
General Sheridan, who had reached Winchester on his
return, unsuspicious of any disaster, was alarmed by
certain indications, and hurried forward to the rescue.
This incident is known as "Sheridan's Ride." He
met and rallied the fugitives, led them back, recovered
the camps and the abandoned cannon, and routed in
their turn the late victors.

The vessels belonging to the United States mer-
cantile marine had by this time nearly disappeared
from the ocean. They had been sold to foreign
merchants, or taken by Confederate privateers. Of
these cruisers there were six afloat in 1864, which
captured over two hundred American vessels, burning
or destroying four-fifths of their prizes. But in June,
1864, a check was given to these piratical exploits.
The *Alabama*, a Confederate cruiser built in England,
with the best modern appliances, met her fate, after
having captured sixty-seven American vessels, forty-
five of which she destroyed. The *Alabama* was lying
in the French port of Cherbourg, when the U. S.
steam frigate *Kearsarge*, Captain John A. Winslow,
appeared off the harbour. The commander of the
Confederate ship, Raphael Semmes, sent a challenge
to the *Kearsarge*, and on the 19th, Sunday, steamed

out for the "sea duel," which was witnessed by thousands on the French shore. An English yacht followed. The battle lasted a little over an hour, the two vessels steaming round and round delivering broadsides, till the *Alabama* was found to be in a sinking condition and shortly after went down. Sixty-five of her crew were picked up by the *Kearsarge*. Semmes, his officers, and some men were saved by the yacht and landed in England. In this memorable sea-fight, one of the most remarkable incidents of the great Secession War, not the least marvel was that on both sides only ten men were killed and twenty-three wounded. Of the latter, two were drowned. The loss of the *Kearsarge* was only one killed and two wounded. The *Shenandoah*, another Confederate cruiser, was meanwhile operating in the Indian Ocean. She captured some twenty vessels on her cruise, and then, treacherously flying the U. S. flag, made her appearance in the Arctic seas and "lighted up the ice floes with incendiary fires," [1] capturing ten whale ships and burning eight of them in a group. This was in June, 1865, after the war closed, and after the pirate knew it. But he did not regard the newspapers as "official."

---

[1] Lossing.

The blockade of the southern ports was now so far effective that only two remained accessible to the runners, Mobile in Alabama and Wilmington in North Carolina. Mobile was taken in August by Admiral Farragut, with the co-operation of a land force. Both places were defended by strong fortifications, and at each was a formidable ram modelled after the famous *Merrimac.* Farragut's squadron passed the forts, but the vessel in advance, the ironclad *Tecumseh,* struck a torpedo, and sunk, carrying down her commander and nearly all his officers and crew. Only seventeen escaped. Farragut in his flag-ship took the lead, directing the movements of his fleet from the maintop of his vessel, where he was fastened with a rope. The gun-boats and the ram were next encountered, and the day ended with the capture of one of the enemy's boats and the withdrawal of the others to the inner harbour. The next morning the formidable ram came rushing down, but was pounded by the Union fleet till she struck. In this engagement the Federal fleet was far superior in the number of vessels. But the Confederates had the co-operation of the forts, which were not taken until several days after their fleet was destroyed ; and they had also the hidden terror of torpedoes, one only of which exploded. Mobile was closed to the blockade runners. So, soon after, was Wilmington, after a desperate resistance. Her "ram" was sunk by a torpedo boat, managed by a young lieutenant, William B. Cushing. Meanwhile raiding parties had cut off the roads to Richmond, leaving the Confederate army there only the hope that the troops from the South would come to their relief.

President Lincoln had, in November, 1864, been re-elected by a vast majority over McClellan, who was the opposing candidate. While the South now hoped, the North waited. But all doubt was soon removed. The Union troops at the south-west kept the Confederates busy in a series of fierce battles. In December President Lincoln received a despatch from Sherman, presenting as a Christmas present the city of Savannah. Close upon this tidings the Congress of the United States took up and passed the "Thirteenth Amendment" abolishing slavery, on the President's earnest recommendation, and thus, the States afterward assenting, the "War Measure" became a constitutional provision for peace in the future.

On the 16th of November General Sherman, with sixty-five thousand men, had commenced from Atlanta, Georgia, his "march to the sea." The army moved in two columns, subsisting on the country. Previously to his departure Sherman fired and destroyed the

business portion of the town, which had been a chief
source of supply of war material to the Confederates.
He renounced all idea of a "base," occupied no posts,
kept no line of communication, sent advance detachments to secure the roads and fords before him, and
destroyed bridges and roads behind him, as he pressed
forward. He cut the wires and shut himself from
telegraphic communication with friend and foe. In a
month he reached Savannah, whence, as we have
seen, he was "heard from." Here he was put in
communication with the United States blockading
fleet. He summoned General Hardee to surrender,
and was refused. While Sherman was making ready
for an assault, Hardee escaped in the night of the
20th December, and marched with fifteen thousand
men for Charleston. The Union army occupied
Savannah unopposed, and here, for the first time in
his march of two hundred and fifty miles, Sherman
left a garrison. On the march he lost only five
hundred and seventy men. Sherman's army next
took Columbia, the capital of the State, February 15th.
The beautiful town was burned, the disaster resulting
from the attempt of the Confederates to burn bales of
cotton which would else have been captured. Charleston, which had endured a siege and blockade for
months, was abandoned by the Confederates, General

Hardee leaving with his troops, after effecting as much destruction as possible, making, as he did from Savannah, his movement in the night. The next day the Federal forces moved in, and set to work extinguishing the flames which had been lighted by the retreating Confederates. During the conflagration five hundred persons were killed by the explosion of magazines. Sherman still pursued his way to the North, and after two battles and much skirmishing reached Goldsborough, North Carolina, on March 23rd, where he was joined by the Union troops under General Schofield.

The campaign opened near Richmond in March, 1865, with various movements at first directed to the cutting off the connections of that city with its sources of supply, and then to the capture of the Confederate capital and army. On Saturday, April 1st, the Confederates were defeated at the battle of the Five Forks; and on the evening of the same day a cannonade was opened on the whole Confederate line round Petersburg. It was continued till four o'clock on Sunday morning, and then with furious fighting an assault was made, and Lee's army was driven within its interior lines. Reinforcements arrived, and Lee ordered a sortie against the besiegers. It was the last charge, though made with desperate courage.

The Confederate party fell back, and Lee telegraphed to Jefferson Davis in Richmond that the capital of the confederacy must be evacuated.

Davis received the telegram in church. His face and manner indicated sad tidings as he hastened out. The information was not communicated to the public; but the religious services were closed, the congregation dismissed, and rumours distracted the city. When by the removal of boxes from the public offices the whole truth was discovered, the rush of those who wished to get away was made in wild confusion. Huge sums were paid for horses and waggons. The gold in the banks was sent off. Jefferson Davis and all his government left the city, its sole representative remaining behind being an officer in the War Department. It was a pity he had not gone too. With nightfall came terror and dismay. The city council ordered the destruction of all spirituous liquors. The gutters ran with whisky, and parties of the intoxicated soldiers, joined by mobs, sacked the shops and set fire to many buildings. The warehouses containing cotton and tobacco were fired by order of the representative of the government, and the official torch once applied, incendiary fires increased. Ships were burned, not only government but private property; and the explosions of magazines and war vessels added horror to the night's alarms. As the last of the retreating soldiers crossed the James River, they destroyed the bridges behind them. It was said that over seven hundred buildings were destroyed.

At eight o'clock on Monday morning the Federal troops marched in, a brigade of coloured soldiers heading the column. Their first work was the extinguishing the fire which had destroyed one-third of the city. The place was put under martial law, the flag of the Union floated over the Virginia State House, order was established, and not a few of the citizens rejoiced at their deliverance. The blacks were jubilant, but, true to their character, were guilty of no violence. Over the North flew the tidings, and it was a day of such rejoicing as found expression not only in hilarious gatherings but in devout religious services.

On the next Sunday, April 9th, Lee surrendered to Grant at Appomatox Court House. The terms, highly honourable to the victors, were release of the vanquished on their simple word of honour and the usual surrender of arms ; and rations were at once issued to the famished Confederate soldiers from the United States stores. Private cavalry men, who owned their own horses, were even permitted to ride home upon them. The week had been a wearisome one. General Lee had made bold attempts to get away with the remnant of his army, but was foiled. His men had dropped step by step from sheer hunger ; and many had thrown down their muskets, too faint to carry them.

And yet there remained another crushing disaster for the South. On the 14th of April, 1861, General Robert Anderson surrendered Fort Sumter to the Confederates. On the 14th of April, 1865, he hoisted over Sumter the same old tattered ensign, which he had saved for years, in the faith of its restoration. On the evening of the same day, Abraham Lincoln was murdered by an assassin while seated with his wife and friends in a theatre in Washington. It was the crowning defeat of the South. The feeling of compromise, which had begun to show itself among many persons at the North, disappeared. The North stood up in the fury of what at first appeared a righteous anger ; and the South, humiliated, disclaimed the act of the miscreant, who had followed his crime by ranting on the stage the motto of Virginia, "*Sic semper tyrannis.*"

CHAP. XLIX.—CONCLUSION.

DISMAY and grief went through the land with the tidings of the murder. Men looked at each other with questioning fear whether the distracted country which had borne so terrible a strain in open warfare could yet contend with a dark conspiracy. The assassin escaped from the scene of his crime, finding a horse ready saddled, and no one could say who or how many were leagued with him in guilt ; no one could tell how far the foes of the Republic had spread the mine, the explosion of which was to hurl back into anarchy the peace which had been won by brave conquerors over a foe as brave. Indignation was re-awakened in the North against such persons as were known as open advocates of the Southern cause, or suspected as sympathizers. A multitude of excited men had gathered in the city of New York, ready at a word to move on the work of destruction. Suddenly there appeared upon a balcony above them a man whose mien betokened a leader of men. He waved the flag of his country, as bespeaking attention, and the crowd hushed to listen. They thought, perhaps, that here was the man for whom they waited. Among the first words he spake were: "The Lord God Omnipotent reigneth!" They asked, "Who is this? and what does he mean?" It was James A. Garfield, as a soldier, brave; as a statesman, wise; as an orator, eloquent; and as a man, not ashamed to confess and to worship "Him who sitteth between the Cherubim, be the earth never so unquiet." He reasoned the turbulent multitude into forbearance, and inspired them with his own hope and courage. New York was saved from deeds of violence, which might by the example have set the whole land in a blaze.

If the murder of Abraham Lincoln was the crowning defeat of the South, the proudest victory of the North was in the generous course which was taken by the nation with those who lately sought to destroy it. Probably, had Lincoln not been murdered, there would have been greater leniency still. The serpent of slavery might have been "scotched, not killed." A brief time restored the national confidence. The Vice-President, Andrew Johnson, assumed office as the constitution provides, and the functions of government, not stopped for a day, went on. Within six hours after the death of the

President his successor took the oath of office. Investigation narrowed down the conspiracy to nine persons ; and diligent search failed to implicate any more. Of these, the murderer, John Wilkes Booth, was shot and mortally wounded while resisting his captors ; eight were tried by court-martial, of whom four were hanged and four sentenced to imprisonment. The charge against them included a murderous assault, made at the time when Lincoln was murdered, upon the Secretary of State, William H. Seward, who survived his wounds still to serve his country.

After Johnson came General Grant, who served eight years, and after Grant, Rutherford B. Hayes, who served one term. After Hayes came the broken term of Garfield. Under these successive Presidents the work of " reconstruction " went on, and the States late in rebellion came back under prescribed conditions. It were tedious to tell the political difficulties which this work involved, nor has it been possible to note all the men who have figured in the stirring events of the Great Civil War. Many of those events, each of itself a history, have been passed over.

The freedmen have been quiet, and though thousands of them are not yet competent to exercise the right of suffrage, they are eager to learn. Of the articles which it has been the fashion to say could only be raised by slave labour, the annual returns are, on the whole, as large as ever. In some there is as yet a falling off, but the later cotton crops are among the greatest ever raised. No coolies have been needed to produce this result ; for the coloured people number over six millions and a half of the fifty millions of people in the United States : about two millions more than in 1870. Of Asiatics, chiefly Chinese, of whose "invasion" so much has been said, there are only about one hundred and six thousand, and they are not increasing. Some excitement was produced a few years ago by the "exodus" of freedmen from their former slave homes. It is the privilege of freemen to go where they list, and this evidence of freedom no doubt had its effect. But a curious fact appears from the census tables of 1880. The relative proportion of coloured people to white has largely increased in nine of the former slave States, and especially in those from which the exodus took place.

A leading American Gazetteer, with pardonable complacency, remarks that a stranger visiting the United States would scarcely realize that so great an internecine war had raged so recently. If the hand of time has in a brief period covered the traces of ruin and desolation, the memory of the bitterness of the past and its causes can also be charitably buried. There was terrible suffering in prisons and prison camps ; and there have been acts of violence and intimidation against the freedmen, now become by the gift of suffrage the political rulers of their former owners. On these we need not dwell. The truth that " life, liberty, and the pursuit of happiness " are the heritage of all men is asserted before all the world, on the continent which has tested so many vital questions. No one who believes in a controlling Providence can doubt the issue.

The Americans claim that the union of their States is stronger than ever. It would seem that all nations conceded that claim when their co-operation gave to the United States Centennial Exposition of 1876 a splendour never achieved before, and when the youngest nation in the world received the elder nation with the hospitality, if also with the confident poise and easy self-assurance, of an heir just come into his estate, despite all other claimants.

Honour was farther rendered when General Grant, successful leader in the closing triumphs of the contest which the nation made under Abraham Lincoln, laid down his military and his civil authority, and travelled round the world, the private citizen of the great Republic. Such personal tribute no untitled man, with no power in his hands or benefits in his gift, ever received before. But the nation stood behind the man, and the honour given, while his own just due, was paid also to the people he represented, and to the cause of the Right which he, with his patriotic countrymen, had vindicated.

Again upon the United States the eyes of the world were turned. A second time the chief magistrate was stricken down by the hand of an assassin. The wretched murderer in this case had no associates, and his act had no public significance. Scarce had the newly elected President, in 1881, entered upon his duties, when he fell. James A. Garfield, with his living voice for the right, had held a nation in check, when roused to fury by a foul deed like that by which he now was sacrificed. For many sad weeks, and weary with sorrow, the world waited for his dying breath. From all lands came the expression of deep sympathy. Shot down on July 2nd, 1881, he died on the 19th of September, meeting the "last enemy" like a hero and a Christian. The Queen of England laid her offering upon his bier, and forgetting the Empress in the woman, spake comfort to his widow.

Marcus Ward & Co., Limited, Royal Ulster Works, Belfast.

www.ingramcontent.com/pod-product-compliance
Lightning Source LLC
Chambersburg PA
CBHW021323110726
47900CB00005B/1325